Prairie Sunset
Of Love and Magic

A Novel by

Eric Wilder

Other books by Eric Wilder

Ghost of a Chance
Murder Etouffee
Name of the Game
A Gathering of Diamonds
Over the Rainbow
Big Easy
Just East of Eden
Lily's Little Cajun Cookbook
Morning Mist of Blood

ISBN: 978-0-9791165-4-4
Gondwana Press LLC
Edmond, OK 73013

Prairie Sunset – Of Love and Magic is dedicated to all the unheralded heroes of World War II, including my father Jack (Army), my Aunt Carmol Tackaberry (Marines), and my friends George Massad (Army), Gilbert LaPiere (Army Air Force), Bill Cleary (Navy), every veteran of every war, and also to my mother Mavis, myself, and everyone else that has lost a loved one long before their time.

For Anne

Foreword

How old is too old to fall in love? The question haunted me when I read a newspaper article in the Oklahoman about an old man that had disappeared from his son's house during a late spring snowstorm.

The numerous casinos now prevalent all over Oklahoma weren't in existence when I wrote this book. There was, however, Indian bingo. I drove through Red Rock, Oklahoma—site of a huge bingo gaming facility—the very day I read the article about the old man. It was springtime, flowers blooming and trees just beginning to bud. Like the flowers and trees, the story sprang forth in my mind, not letting me rest until I'd committed it to paper.

The Battle of the Bulge tale that John tells is true, at least as far as I know, recounted to me by my own father, a code clerk during World War II. Growing up, he was always my hero. His era produced many heroes, mostly unsung, their stories never told.

When is it too late to fall in love? Read John's story and discover the answer.

Prairie Sunset
Of Love and Magic

A novel by
Eric Wilder

Chapter 1

—Tulsa Oklahoma, 1994—

A blue afternoon in Oklahoma, snow had begun falling before sunset. Cynthia Warren didn't notice as she sorted through rows of expensive clothes draped together in her walk-in closet. Young and attractive, she was also a klutz, bumping into a stool after selecting a pale blue gown.

"Dammit!" she said.

After rubbing her leg, she hurried to her dressing table, colliding with her husband and knocking the drink from his hand. Dan Warren, tall and thin with dark wavy hair, daubed at the wet spot on his tuxedo pants, barely noticing as he continued reading the newspaper in his hand.

"Will you hurry?" Cynthia said. "The sitter will be here any minute."

Getting no reaction, she glanced at her husband in the mirror.

"Jake Thompson died last night," he said.

Slipping the dress over her head, she sat on the edge of the bed to straighten her hose.

"Who's that?"

"Dad's best friend," he said, smoothing thick brown hair with his long fingers. "War buddies."

"Have you told him?"

He shook his head, his expression revealing momentary pain just behind his pale blue eyes.

"I can't talk to him anymore. He just vegetates in his room in that old chair, staring out the window."

"Don't be so hard on him," she said. "He's just lonely."

"Senile's more like it. I may as well tell him about Jake, and break the news about Crestview."

Standing in front of the bathroom mirror, Cynthia frantically brushed her hair.

"I'm still not sure we're doing the right thing. Can't it wait till tomorrow?"

Dan fixed another drink from the Scotch bottle on the dresser before starting upstairs to his father's room.

"I've already put this off long enough."

Cynthia stopped brushing her hair and stared at her husband as he went upstairs, a look of resolve on his face. Rapping on the old man's door and not expecting an answer, he entered without waiting for one. Sitting in an Afghan-draped rocking chair, staring listlessly out the window, was his father. Pale skin on the old man's neck seemed to coalesce with the faded orange Afghan.

"Dad, let's have a talk." When the older man didn't answer, or even bother turning around, Dan continued anyway. "Mom died three years ago. The girls start school next year and Cyn's doing more charity work. My case load with the firm has increased, and I'm in line for partnership this year. Do you understand what I'm trying to tell you?"

The older man answered in a low, almost inaudible voice. "Son, I'm proud of you. If your mother were still alive, I know she'd also be proud."

Dan tried breathing deeply, almost choking on his frustration. Instead, he lowered his head, clenched his teeth and toyed with a strand of errant hair. When the book in the old man's hand dropped to the floor, neither father nor son seemed to notice the dull thud it made when it struck the carpet. Dan opened his eyes and continued speaking with measured words.

"That's not what I'm talking about."

As if in a trance, the older man seemed to pay no attention to the severity of his son's tone and continued staring out the window at slow-falling snow. It was more than Dan could take. Grabbing the chair, he wheeled it violently around.

"Damn it! Look at me when I'm talking to you."

Pressing even further against the Afghan, the old man thought for a moment his angry son might strike him.

His voice cracked when he said, "I'm sorry, Son."

Dan let go of the chair. Again he tried breathing deeply. His efforts only prevented veins of erupting redness from deserting his face. Pacing to the opposite wall, he banged his hand against it and tossed the newspaper, wadded like a club, to the floor. This time a paperback Western, on the nightstand beside the bed, tumbled to the carpet. Dan kicked it under the bed.

"Cynthia and I want you to be with people your own age. You've vegetated in this room since you broke your hip. You don't talk. You don't come downstairs to eat, and frankly I'm fed up to here with your bullshit." Touching his throat to show just how fed up he was, he added, "Come Monday, like it or not, we're taking you to Crestview."

"Son . . ."

"No! That's it. Damn it to hell! I'm so mad right now I can't see straight. You're going Monday and that's that."

Dan Warren, tumbling yet a third book to the floor as he abandoned his father, backed out the door and slammed it behind him.

When he returned to the bedroom, Cynthia said, "Is he all right?"

"Yeah," he mumbled, still frowning as he buttoned his shirt.

"Is who all right, Mama?"

Trish and Emily, identical twins, entered the room, already dressed for bed. As beautiful as their mother, both little girls also had blue eyes and raven hair. Unlike their mother's close-cropped, sophisticated cut, long dark braids tied with bright red bows framed their pretty faces.

Cynthia had trouble telling them apart. Dan couldn't. Sparky, their ever-present cocker puppy, padded along behind them. Like the girls, his hair was also black, and he had his own red bow tied jauntily around his neck. Emily handed the puppy to her mother and it promptly licked a warm swath across her nose.

Insistently, Trish asked, "Is who all right?"

"Nothing, dear," Cynthia said, rushing to the dressing table to repair her make-up. "Is Julie here yet?"

"She helped us with our pajamas," Emily said. "We came to kiss you goodnight."

After hugging and kissing their mother, the two little girls wriggled away from her and grabbed Dan's elbows, tugging his arm until he stopped straightening his tie and bent over to return their hugs.

"Goodnight, you two rug rats."

"Sorry, Mrs. Warren," the sitter said, poking her head into the room.

"No problem, Julie. We'll be home late, if it's okay

with you."

"I'll be fine. Come on, girls. Let's go say goodnight to Grandpa."

Cynthia continued combing her hair until the combined stairway clatter of dog and little girls dissipated, and then glanced apprehensively at Dan.

"Sure about this?"

Grabbing her elbow, he pulled her toward the door. "The only thing I'm sure about, my dear, is we're late."

Trish and Emily rushed into their grandfather's room, unannounced, as their parents hurried out the front door. They found the old man on his knees, gazing at the paper Dan had tossed to the floor. Trish handed him the squirming puppy and it promptly licked a warm swath across his mouth.

"What you doing, Grandpa?"

"Reading the paper, Trishy," he said, petting the dog.

"How do you know I'm not Emily?"

"Cause grandpas know everything."

"We came to say goodnight," Emily said, joining them.

John Warren dropped the paper to the floor, placed the wiggling puppy beside it, and hugged the two little girls.

"Pleasant dreams my sweethearts."

Emily wiped her hand across his craggy face. "Grandpa, are you crying?"

"No, Emily. It's just something in my eye."

Turning away, he rubbed his eyes with his shirt sleeve before turning back and kissing them.

"Sleep well my pretties,"

"Please tell us a bedtime story before we go to sleep," Emily pleaded. "Please?"

With a nod, he shrugged his scrawny shoulders, smiled and said, "Old men like their arms twisted."

Both little girls grabbed his arms, squealed and

said, "Please, please."

"Okay, then. Go to your room and get ready. I'll be along to tell you a short one."

"Oh boy!" they said, rushing out the door. "Please hurry. We'll be waiting."

They didn't bother shutting the door behind them. Once their scurrying footsteps evaporated down the hallway, silence engulfed the dark little room. John pulled himself stiffly to his feet with the bedpost, and for a long moment stood staring at the newspaper he'd retrieved from the floor.

"Jake Thompson, you old gutter-snipe," he said, shaking his head.

Jutting away from his craggy cheeks, and sloping abruptly downward, John's prominent nose dominated his face. This, along with closely-spaced eyes, caused him to resemble a hawk, or maybe a bald eagle. Feathery gray hair heightened this illusion. He was also as tall and slender as his son, the family resemblance instantly noticeable.

Wiping another tear from his nose, he shuffled through clothes in his dresser drawer, searching for a hidden bottle of bourbon. Finding it, he tipped up the container and drank until amber liquid dribbled out his thin lips, down the loose skin on his neck.

"Here's to you, Jake."

After taking another long pull from the bottle, he grabbed an overnight bag from the closet's upper shelf and began filling it with clothes from the dresser. Before shutting the bag, he removed his wife's picture from his nightstand and placed it on top of the clothes. Finally finished, he limped down the hall to his granddaughters' bedroom where he found the babysitter, waiting at the door.

"I'll be downstairs if you need me," she said.

"Thanks, Julie," he said, subconsciously resenting her implication, although knowing she meant well.

Already in their beds, the two little girls waited

anxiously as he sat in the chair. He couldn't help smiling at their rapt anticipation.

"What story do you want to hear tonight?"

"A new one," Emily said.

"Something we haven't heard before," Trish said.

Scratching his head, he thought a moment. "I have a new story. It's about Otter and the Salamander. Would you like to hear it?"

"Yes," both little girls shouted.

Staring dreamily at the ceiling, he leaned back in the chair and began, "Once upon a time, an otter lived in a small pond in the woods. The otter was old, like your grandfather, his children grown. So old was he, in fact, almost all his friends, except his best friend Salamander, had passed away. Mr. Salamander's children had moved him far away to a much smaller pond. Otter missed their chess games and swapping of tales, but Salamander kept in contact. They talked every day on the wildlife telephone. One day, Salamander didn't call."

Trish asked, "What happened?"

"Stop squirming, young lady and I'll tell you," he said with a wink. "Otter worried about his friend. He wanted to call, but had caught his toe in a trap the previous spring. Otter was old and the sore toe didn't heal fast as it might. Feeling sorry for himself because of his loneliness, he somehow blamed everyone else. When he learned his old friend had passed away, he felt very, very sad."

"What did he do?" the twins caroled.

"Like I said, Otter was old, but not that old. He decided to leave the pond for one last trip. Visit the Magic Fountain before he died."

Trish asked, "What's that?"

He raised his hand toward the ceiling. "The Magic Fountain is a place in our minds. Crystal water pours from its mouth, revitalizing body and spirit. Otter had visited it once in his youth. Now, on a whim, he decided to go there, one last time. Packing his otter luggage, he set out on an odyssey."

"Grandpa, what's an odyssey?"

Smiling and gently brushing Emily's long hair back away from her sleepy eyes, he explained. "It's a journey to a place far away, and not easy to reach. But Otter had a good heart and strong desire. He left the pond in quest of the fountain."

"Did he find it?"

After kissing both little girls, he tucked the covers around their necks. "Tell you next time. Just remember," he said, pausing on his way out the door. "It's not always so important we find the Magic Fountain, only that we never stop looking."

With that, he turned off the lights and closed the door behind him. Rock music vibrated the hallway walls as he returned to his room. After a frustrating moment spent rummaging through his closet, he realized he no longer had a heavy coat to wear. After taking one last look at the wrinkled newspaper lying on the bed, he switched off the lights and crept downstairs to the hall closet.

Both avid skiers, Cynthia and Dan, had all the expensive trappings of the sport. John had once tried on his son's goose-down ski jacket.

"Sorry, Dan," he said, slipping the jacket over his bony shoulders.

He drew the hood tightly around his neck. With a stubborn smile and only a momentary backward glance, he entered the snowstorm, plodding the icy sidewalk toward a beckoning glimmer of distant streetlights.

Chapter 2

Snow fell in damp white clumps as John walked out the kitchen door, no idea where he was heading, although intent on getting there. Unexpected spring snow had left streets in the swank Tulsa neighborhood deserted. Two blocks from home, sounds of tires slipping in ice and snow attracted his attention. When he rounded the corner he found a large recreational vehicle stuck on the curb, one rear wheel spinning uselessly. He tapped on the driver's window which was hazy with condensation.

A woman's head appeared and he said, "Need help?"

"Sure do. You have a couple of big, strong sons? Or the number of a good wrecker service?"

He chuckled. "Don't have either, but I can get you off the curb if you'd like."

Taking her foot off the gas, she gave him a slow appraisal. "Don't know what horse you rode in on, but I'll bite."

"Have a tire iron in that bus?" he asked, ignoring her sarcasm.

"Yes I have a tire iron, and no, this isn't a bus. It's a recreational vehicle."

"Maybe that's your problem."

"What's that supposed to mean?"

"It means you should probably be in a National Park instead of a snowed-in Tulsa subdivision. Don't worry. You get me that tire iron and I'll get you off the curb."

Closing the window with an annoyed grumble, she disappeared into the RV, returning shortly with a tire iron. With a skeptical glance, she handed him the tool.

He smiled and pointed his thumb skyward. "Turn on the engine and wait for my signal before giving it a little gas."

She watched as he placed the iron beneath the large rear tire. After working it around a bit, he raised his finger. As she applied the gas, he wiggled the tire iron. Lurching briefly, the long RV slid easily off the curb. Driving it to the center of the snow-packed road, she stopped, opening the window when he held up the tool.

"Don't forget your tire iron."

Winking and smiling again, he waited for her to take the tool and drive away. Instead, she sat there, staring at him, a quizzical expression on her face.

"Thanks. I was just about to panic. Can I give you a ride somewhere?"

"Don't know. Where are you headed?"

Smiling for the first time, she said, "Depends on where I am. I've been driving in circles in this crazy neighborhood for nearly an hour."

"61st Street is just around the corner," he said, pointing.

"Is there a filling station close by? I'm almost out of gas."

"Turn right on 61st. There's a station at the intersection."

The nearby thoroughfare was busy with passing cars, tires crunching through patches of snow. The neighbor's dog began barking, hushing when he recognized John.

"You didn't answer my question about the ride."

"You didn't say where you're going," he said.

"The filling station, if I don't get lost again. Show me the way, and I'll drop you off afterwards."

"Deal," he said, offering his hand as he entered the RV. "My name's John Warren."

"Attie Johnson. Buckle up. Never know when we might wind up in the ditch."

John buckled his seat belt, stealing glances at the handsome woman behind the wheel as he leaned back into the high-backed, comfortable seat. When she turned around and caught him looking, he grinned coyly. Attie Johnson had a youthful look about her, big dark eyes, gray-streaked braided hair and classically high cheekbones. He thought she might be in her fifties, though suspected she could easily be older.

They followed the snow-packed street to a well-lighted filling station. While waiting for the attendant, she switched on an overhead light and removed a map from the side pocket, spreading it out on the console between them.

"I'm on my way to play Indian bingo at Red Rock. Can you show me how to get to the Cimarron Turnpike from here?"

"You bet," he said, taking the map and indicating the route with his finger.

When the tanks were full, she cranked the engine and eased back onto the street, slipping in the icy slush, though never really out of control.

"Better let me off here," he said.

"We came from the other direction."

"Not going home. I'm on my way to Hot Springs."

"Surely you aren't on foot."

"Yes I am. I'll hitch a ride on the Interstate," he said.

Attie abruptly put her foot on the brake, skidding to a halt in the snow. "You in a hurry?" she asked, her dark-eyed stare causing him instant discomfort.

"Not really."

"Neither am I. I could use a cup of hot coffee. Let's park this thing and I'll brew us up a pot."

When she parked across the street in a nearly deserted shopping center parking lot, he made himself comfortable as the aroma of brewing coffee saturated dry air in the RV. When the last sputter of coffee poured through the spout, she placed their cups on the built-in table.

"Now, tell me what a man your age is doing out on a night like this, hitchhiking to Hot Springs."

John chuckled as he sipped his coffee. "It sounds silly, even to me. Guess you might say I'm running away from home."

"You're right. It does sound silly. Why?"

"I really don't want my son to know where I am."

"That's irrational, not childish. Maybe you'd better explain."

He slumped back against the bench seat. "My wife died three years ago, about the time I fell and broke my hip. I moved in with my son and his wife. Now I can see I began acting like an invalid, and they started treating me like one."

"Is that all?"

Slowly shaking his head, he eased back against the couch. "No. Sometimes you just let things happen because it's easier than doing something about it. Know what I mean?"

"Maybe. Tell me anyway."

"After Martha died, I just blanked out awhile. Between Martha's death and my broken hip, I didn't feel like explaining my feelings to anyone. Not that they'd have understood. My son interpreted my reticence as senility."

"You sound cognizant to me," Attie said.

"Thanks. Never felt more aware in my life."

"So what happened?"

"Dan, my son, is an attorney. He had me declared incompetent. It's partially my own fault because I knowingly let him do it. Monday, he's putting me in an old folk's home. If I'm there, that is."

"Just explain to him you're not incompetent. Move back to your own house."

"He sold it and liquidated my assets."

"Have him give them back."

"I don't really care about the house and money. Right now, all I want to do is go to Hot Springs."

Staring straight at him with dark piercing eyes, she said, "To die?"

Shaking his head, he grinned. "Not to die. I want to live, at least as long as I can."

Attie leaned across the table and touched his hand. "It's no fun playing bingo alone. Why don't you take a little detour with me to Red Rock?"

Dan and Cynthia returned home from the party to find the twins in bed, Julie asleep on the couch. Trish and Emily let them sleep, undisturbed, until late the next morning. Unable to keep quiet any longer, they pushed open the bedroom door and entered with an assault of noisy heels against hardwood floor.

"Dad, let's go to the park. You promised we could go Saturday, and it is Saturday."

Dan Warren sat up in bed, licked his salty lips, unhinged glue-encrusted eyelids and ran his hand across dark stubble on his face. His stomach churned and pain reverberated between his temples. Without answering the little girl, he lifted himself out of bed and rushed to the bathroom.

"I don't think Daddy feels well," Cynthia said. "I'll take you to the park after I dress."

"But Daddy promised," Emily pouted.

"Next Saturday," he said, returning from the bathroom. "Now go outside and play until your mother's ready."

Cynthia cast him a dirty look as the two little girls rushed from the room. "I don't feel much better than you, Tarzan. Why can't you take Trish and Emily to the park every once in a while, and let me stay in bed?"

"Because I'm working on a big case. I brought some things home I need to finish," he said, glancing at his watch. "If I don't hurry, I'll miss the ball game."

Cynthia threw her hands in the air as she went to the bathroom. "Heaven help us!"

She dressed and joined him at the breakfast table, finding him sipping coffee as he read the morning paper. Billie, the cook and housekeeper, poured her a cup when she sat down.

"Would you like bacon and eggs, Ms. Warren?"

"Yes, thank you Billie."

"Old Mr. Warren didn't eat this morning," she said, scraping the food from a plate into the disposal."

Dan glanced up from his paper. "Is that unusual?"

"Yes sir," she said. "The old man, I mean Mr. Warren, usually eats like a sled-pulling dog."

"Humph!" he allowed, burying his head into the paper. "I didn't realize he ate that much."

"I know. You wouldn't think a skinny man like that could put away so much food."

"Maybe you should check on him," Cynthia said.

He shook his head. "I'm sure he's fine. You couldn't hurt the old bat with a lead-weighted club."

"That's not a very nice thing to say about your father."

"But true. The old bird will probably outlive us both."

With an abrupt clatter of little heels on the living room's polished wood floor, Trish and Emily, followed by the panting cocker puppy, appeared from around the corner.

"Mommy, Mommy, Grandpa's not in his room."

"Whoa," Dan said, holding up his hand. "Didn't I tell you not to run in the living room? You know it'll scratch the floor."

"Daddy, Grandpa's gone," Emily said.

Again, he buried his head in the paper. "Probably just down the hall."

"Does he move around the house during the day?" Cynthia asked.

Billie shook her head. "He sticks mostly to his room."

"Dan," Cynthia said. "Check on your father." He continued staring stoically at the paper. "Dan!"

His stubborn glare was his only reply. Frowning, she went upstairs, followed closely by Trish, Emily and Sparky. Grumbling, he slapped the unfinished paper against the kitchen table and started after them. When they reached the old man's bedroom, they nudged the door and stood looking at his tidy living quarters.

"Dan, he's not here."

"Where the hell is he?" he said, still grumbling.

Trish and Emily hung on their mother's legs, looking worried. Even the usually frenetic puppy crouched against Cynthia's foot.

"Don't know," she said. "Maybe you should call the police."

"That's ludicrous. He must be somewhere in the house. Let's find him."

Cynthia called Billie and they began methodically searching the large house. Twenty unsuccessful minutes later, they gravitated back to the old man's room.

Genuinely worried, Cynthia frowned and said, "Where could he have gone?"

Something on the bed caught Dan's eye. Seeing the newspaper he'd left on the floor the previous night, he immediately reached for the phone.

"Maybe you're right, Cyn. I think I better call the police."

Chapter 3

When Vince Blakeman arrived, Cynthia was sitting on a couch, twiddling her thumbs as her husband paced ever-widening circles around the living room floor. She kept staring at the detective's tweed sports coat and unmatched tie. Sitting beside her, he removed a notepad from his coat. Probably in his mid-thirties, Blakeman had the honest, yet unremarkable looks of a hard working man, tousled hair, a small moustache, and brown eyes that didn't miss much.

"Sorry, Lieutenant Blakeman," Dan said. "I just don't have any idea where he might have gone."

"Has he ever done this before?"

"No,"

"Yes," Cynthia said, interrupting.

"Ma'am?"

Dan glared at his wife, and then resumed his pacing. "Once, after my mother passed away, he visited a friend in Oklahoma City. He didn't return when expected."

"Where was he?"

"Police found him in a bar," Cynthia said.

Blakeman noted the frown on Dan Warren's face. "A bar?"

"He and his friend got a little intoxicated," Cynthia explained. "The bar's owner called the police."

"Is he an alcoholic?"

"Course not," Dan said. "He was a doctor, for God's sake."

"You mean a medical doctor?"

"Yes, a medical doctor."

"Was he on any prescription medication such as Valium, or anything?"

Dan stopped pacing and glared at the detective. "What are you getting at?"

"He may have had a stroke, an allergic reaction to a drug, or maybe an insulin seizure, if he's diabetic."

"He isn't," Dan said.

Cynthia frowned at her husband, then looked away. "Would you like more coffee?" she said, grabbing Blakeman's empty cup. We can provide you with his medical records, if that will help."

"Big help," he said.

Glaring at her husband again, she left the room with the empty coffee cup.

"Mr. Warren, why don't you sit down and relax. We're never going to get to the bottom of this unless you cooperate."

"My father could freeze on the side of the road while I'm answering questions."

"My men have covered every foot in a ten mile radius around your house. An-old man couldn't have walked any farther than that."

"Maybe he's not on foot," Cynthia said, returning with fresh coffee.

When Dan frowned at her insinuation, Blakeman wrote something on his notepad, pretending not to notice.

"We're checking that possibility. State Police are looking for hitchhikers and questioning motorists they stop."

"Damn it!" Dan said, slapping the wall. "This is so frustrating."

"Maybe he's with a friend somewhere in town,"

Blakeman said, ignoring the outburst. "A list of his friends and acquaintances would help us a bunch"

"Certainly, Detective," Cynthia said. "We'll take care of it right away."

"Good. We're checking hospitals and emergency rooms. Does your father have any illnesses you're aware of?"

"He's healthy as a horse," Dan said.

Again, Vince Blakeman caught Cynthia's worried expression. "Mrs. Warren?"

"He has some heart problems, although nothing serious."

"Any indication of Alzheimer's? At first, it's hard to notice."

"Look here," Dan said. "His mind's like a steel trap."

"I'm not trying to be negative. It isn't beyond the realm of possibility he might be a little forgetful."

"You've told me many times that you think your father sometimes has memory lapses," Cynthia said.

"I wasn't serious," Dan replied, miffed at the suggestion.

"Considering his age, a stroke isn't out of the question."

Scratching through the last note, Blakeman sat back against the couch and sipped his coffee, hoping the young couple would relax.

"We're so worried," Cynthia said. "What else can we do?"

"TV's already picked up the story. You could post a reward. That sometimes helps."

"This is being blown out of proportion," Dan said. "How far could an old man have gone? I don't like all this adverse publicity."

This time, both Cynthia and Blakeman frowned at his insensitive statement.

"You're not running for governor and he is your father, you know?" she said.

After folding his notepad and returning it to his jacket, Blakeman draped the overcoat over his arm and started for the door.

"Thanks for your help. We'll find him in no time. I'll stay in touch until then."

Cynthia walked with him to the front door while her husband continued to frown and pace, not acknowledging the detective's departure. Twin sets of running feet greeted her, Sparky right behind.

"Girls, remember what your father said about running on the living room floor."

Trish asked, "They found Grandpa yet?"

"Not yet. Very soon now."

Emily said, "Will he be all right?"

Cynthia smiled and pointed toward the door. "He'll be fine. Why don't you take Sparky into the back yard?"

The twins disappeared out the door as fast as they had appeared, Sparky's nails scraping against wood as he followed close behind. By now, Dan had stopped pacing. Cynthia found him leaning against the wall, frowning as he stared out the picture window with a blank gaze.

"They'll find him," she said, touching his shoulder.

Giving her a sour look, he walked away without a word.

❧

When sunlight awakened him the following morning, John Warren didn't remember where he was. Cracking the window shade, he squinted out across the parking lot already filled with Saturday morning shoppers. Rising, he bumped his head on a cabinet above the couch. His eyes finally focused on an attractive older woman in an old flannel robe. She was cooking something on a tiny stove, and the strong aroma of brewing coffee revived his memory.

"Morning, John," Attie said, handing him a cup. "Sleep well?"

"Like a ton of bricks," he said, rubbing his back.

She chuckled. "Sorry about that. It was either the couch or the floor."

He reached down and patted the floor. "It couldn't be much worse."

"You'll feel better after breakfast. Bathroom's in back," she said. "When we finish eating, you can shower and shave. I have an extra razor and toothbrush."

"How about an extra change of clothes? Seems I left my suitcase on the sidewalk while I was helping you off the curb."

"We could go back for it."

"No."

"Then you'll have to make do until we can get you some more."

"Look, ah . . ."

"Attie," she said.

"Look, Attie. Maybe this isn't such a good idea."

She stopped stirring the eggs and said, "Going to Red Rock with me, or going home?"

He sipped his coffee before replying. "Even though I already miss my two granddaughters, I'm not going back there."

"You have granddaughters?"

Fishing through his coat pocket, he found a picture and handed it to Attie.

"Wow, identical twins. How old are they?"

"Five going on twenty."

"They're gorgeous. But so young."

He glanced up into her brown eyes. "I look that old?"

"No," she said.

"I was well into my forties when I married."

Grinning, she patted his shoulder. "I didn't mean to pry. Let's eat. Decide what you want to do when we finish."

After breakfast, John closed the door to the little

room in back of the RV. Attie had showered and dressed before him, and her nightgown hung from a hook in the tiny bathroom. When he touched the silken material, a sensual, almost forgotten message surged from his finger to his brain. The secretly shared intimacy embarrassed him and he backed away to finish dressing, trying not to think about his suddenly confused feelings.

Alone, he studied some of Attie's personal objects. Beside her bed a small picture attracted his curiosity—a man and boy. About ten years old, the boy's hair and eyes were dark, his complexion bronze. Like the man in the picture, his nose had the regal curve of a Native American. The man's long black hair and dignified bearing reminded him of powerful chiefs from another century. Posed like father and son, they appeared frozen in another time.

Staring at the picture, he wondered about the two people, although snooping into the personal life of someone he barely knew caused him even further guilt. Trying to forget his voyeurism, he finished dressing and joined Attie. She'd already put everything away and had opened the flower-print curtains to greet the sun. Shielding his eyes from the glare off the melting snow, he found her waiting in the driver's seat, studying a map.

Without looking up to acknowledge his presence, she said, "Feel better?"

"Much better."

"Decide what you're going to do?"

He finished buttoning his shirt sleeves before replying. "Attie, I appreciate the bunk for the night, the breakfast, and all your hospitality. I just don't feel right intruding on you anymore than I already have."

"You have someplace else to go, I'll understand, though I assure you, you aren't intruding. Still thinking about Hot Springs?" When he nodded, she said, "Told you I'd take you there after I play bingo."

"You really don't mind if I tag along?"

"I'm just a lonely old woman. I welcome the company."

"You're not old. I have to have at least twenty years on you. Where did you say you are going?"

"Red Rock to play bingo, then Oklahoma City to gamble on the horses. After that, I'm heading back to Arkansas. We can detour through Hot Springs, if you like."

He scratched his chin, remembering a nearly forgotten memory, and smiled. "I haven't played bingo since I was a boy."

"Won't be any children playing bingo in Red Rock. It's big business. They give away about a quarter of a million dollars a week," she said.

"You mean two hundred and fifty thousand dollars? Are you kidding?"

"It's the wildest thing this side of Vegas. On an Indian reservation and exempt from state taxes."

"Bet that makes our bureaucrats happy."

Attie nodded, agreeing. "They don't like it one little bit. The place is a gold mine. Saturday night there will be people pouring in from six states."

John's eyebrows arched. "I knew there was gambling involved, but I had no idea."

"You're in for a treat," she said. "I've been twice, though never alone."

"You like to gamble?"

Shrugging, she said, "An old woman's vice."

"Attie, stop saying that. You're not old."

Patting the seat beside her, she said, "Neither are you. Now help me navigate. Don't want to get lost again."

"Tulsa is the easiest town in the world to find your way around," he said with a knowing grin. "Streets are all numbered, or else in alphabetical order."

"Someone could have told me that last night."

"Not to worry. You have me to guide you now."

Reaching across the console, she gave his knee a friendly pat. For an instant, he experienced the same warm feeling as when he'd touched her nightgown. After pulling down the visor to block the imposing glare of bright morning sunlight, she started the engine.

"Just get me out of town. Tonight, we'll break the bank in Red Rock."

Grinning complacently, he crossed his arms and leaned back against the seat. As he did, excited anticipation surged through his veins for the first time in several years.

Chapter 4

Cynthia entered the house through the back door, followed closely by the twins and their black cocker. She snatched a canister from the cabinet and placed a kettle of water on the stove before removing her coat. Not waiting for their hot chocolate, Trish and Emily draped their own coats across the kitchen table and rushed into the hall.

"Whoa! Wait just a minute," Cynthia called after them. "Don't leave your jackets on the table. Where are you going in such a hurry?"

"To see if Grandpa is back yet," Trish said.

"Hang your jackets in the closet, and then go see about Grandpa. Hurry back. I'm fixing hot chocolate."

Screeching to a halt, Trish and Emily grabbed the jackets and continued their race from the kitchen. Cynthia grinned and went to the living room, finding Dan sulking by the fireplace.

"We're back from the park," she said, kissing him. "Is there anything new on Grandpa?"

"Nothing," he said, mumbling the word.

Touching his shoulder, she reacted to his frown, drawing back her hand. Staring sullenly out the window, he ignored her question, until she took his hand and squeezed.

"They'll find him. He'll be fine."

Dark crescents underlined his eyes, his face red and puffy. With muted words, he finally spoke. "I haven't had a moment's rest all day. Phone's ringing off the hook. Everyone wants to know what happened."

With her finger, she inscribed gentle arcs across his unshaven face, and said, "That's wonderful."

Wrenching away, he angrily slapped the wall. Startled by his unexpected outburst, she again drew back her hand.

"No, it's humiliating," he said, eyes narrowed. "Thanks to the radio and twelve o'clock news, every redneck this side of Wewoka knows my father wandered off in the middle of the night."

When she reached for his shoulders, he pulled away. "You have nothing to be ashamed of. No one is blaming you."

"Blame me, no. Laugh at me, yes," he said. "How will I feel in court Monday morning with everyone talking behind my back, knowing they're pointing fingers at the son of the senile old man who walked out of the house in the middle of a snow storm? What do you think they'll say at the office?"

She balled a tight, desperate fist. Loosening it with a frustrated frown, she moved closer and ran her fingers through his hair.

"Who cares, and what reflection does it have on you?"

His face grew even redder. Now his voice was shrill. "He's done this to me all my life—grabbing the spotlight and embarrassing me in front of my friends. I can't stand it."

Little voices and running feet, approaching from behind, startled her. She stopped the running twins at the living room door, pivoting around and holding up her palm.

"Girls, your father and I are having a private conversation. Please go to the kitchen and wait for me there."

Trish and Emily exchanged knowing glances, did an about face and exited the room.

"Forget Grandpa. Isn't there a ball game on television?"

"To hell with the ball game!"

Glancing around at the open door, she said, "Get control. This isn't your fault or your father's. There's a logical explanation for what has happened and Detective Blakeman will find out what it is."

When he didn't reply, she frowned and followed the twins into the kitchen, turning around when she reached the door. Having already returned to his previous posture by the fireplace, he stared lethargically out the window. She found Trish and Emily at the kitchen table. They glanced up with troubled little eyes when she entered the room.

"We're worried about Grandpa. Have they found him yet?"

When Cynthia opened her mouth to answer, she realized her lips were quivering, her hands shaking. Pouring a glass of water from the tap, she downed it before speaking.

"Not yet."

Taking the kettle from the stove, she fixed them cups of hot chocolate, and then poured coffee from the pot on the cabinet for herself. Feeling somewhat steadier, she sat at the table.

"Did Grandpa say anything unusual to you last night before you went to bed?"

Trish said, "Like what?"

Cynthia paused and closed her eyes. "I don't know?"

In unison, they said, "He told us a bedtime story."

Suddenly aware of another presence in the room, she turned around. It was Dan, standing at the door, listening to their conversation. Ignoring her look he poured coffee from the pot, and then joined them at the table.

"I may be grasping at straws," Cynthia said, defensively. "Still, it can't hurt to ask."

"What story did Grandpa tell you?" he said, not waiting for her to raise the question.

"Otter and the Salamander."

When Cynthia glanced at Dan, he motioned her to remain silent. "Never heard that one," he said, clutching Trish's hand. "Can you tell it to us?"

"Otter's friend, Mr. Salamander died and Otter went away to find the magic fountain," Trish said.

"Magic fountain?"

"Grandpa said it was far away and not easy to reach. Otter wanted to visit it again before he died," Emily said.

Pushing away her husband's arm and bending closer to the little girl, Cynthia said, "He told you he'd been there?"

"Once when he was young," they said.

Again, Cynthia glanced at Dan. "Has he ever told you this story before?"

"No," Emily said.

"Did he tell you where the magic fountain is located?" Dan asked.

"Yes," Trish said, excitedly.

"Where?" he asked, grabbing the little girl's shoulders.

"In our minds," she said in a high-pitched squeak.

❧

As John and Attie headed out of Tulsa, a southerly breeze rapidly melted snow from the previous night. Patches of ice remained on both sides of the road although they were no longer ominous enough to fool hungry birds or budding blackjack trees. West of Tulsa the countryside became less urban, rolling terrain gently rounded. Like an emerald mackinaw, vegetation had already begun covering weathered hills. It was spring in Oklahoma and John wanted the world to know.

33

"This is wonderful. I can't remember anything so beautiful."

"Yes it's beautiful. I love these hills."

Leaning back and resting his head in his hands, he said, "I'd almost forgotten."

Attie momentarily turned her gaze away from the winding blacktop and glanced quizzically at him. "How could you have forgotten something so lovely?"

Smiling contentedly, he said, "Too much time indoors, worrying about yesterday, I suppose."

When she didn't reply, he studied her golden complexion, radiant in sunlight reflecting through the windshield. Braided hair, dark eyes, turquoise earrings and silver squash blossom necklace framed her sculpted cheeks.

"You're an Indian, aren't you?"

"It's Oklahoma. Aren't we all?"

"Good point. I'm part Cherokee myself, though not enough for head rights."

"Is that a curse or a blessing?"

He chuckled. "You're not from Tulsa, are you?"

"Born in Tahlequah, though I haven't lived there for years."

"Where are you from?"

"I live on a farm in the Ozarks near Eureka Springs, Arkansas."

As if recalling a pleasant memory, his eyes grew dreamy. "Little Switzerland. I haven't visited in twenty years."

"It hasn't changed much."

"Don't suppose it would," he said. "Why did you move to Arkansas?"

"My husband had an art gallery there."

"Had?"

"I sold it when he died."

"I'm sorry, Attie."

She reached across the console, smiled and patted his knee while keeping her eyes on the winding road.

"It's been awhile. Are you from Tulsa?"

"I've lived here all my life, except for eighteen months, or so, during the war."

"Thought so," she said.

"Where in the world did you get this bus?" he asked, thumping the armrest and changing the subject.

"RV. Roland bought it to tour the country. He died before we ever used it and it sat behind the house, gathering dust. One day, out of curiosity much as anything else, I drove it to town and thought, this isn't so hard. Been taking trips in Ol' Nellie ever since," she said, giving the dashboard an affectionate tap.

Basking in their friendly camaraderie, he found himself grinning, and pinched his arm to make sure he was really awake.

"Martha and I traveled some when I retired. I haven't gone two blocks from my son's house in the past three years."

"Well it's high time you did."

"I love to travel. I do have one small problem."

"And what would that be?" she said, eyebrows raised.

"I wasn't really planning to leave when I did, though I've had it on my mind. Haven't needed money for several years and now I don't have a penny to my name."

A smile of relief spread rapidly across her attractive face. "Is that all? I'll grubstake you."

"Can't let you do that."

"Why not? You have an honest face."

Feeling his honest face burning with embarrassment, he pivoted in his seat and glanced out the window at passing scenery. "I don't know."

"Do you have problems borrowing money from a woman?"

"I have a problem borrowing from anyone if I can't pay it back."

"Tell you what. I'll lend you five-hundred dollars.

You break the bank at Red Rock, we'll split fifty-fifty. If not, I write it off as a bad bet."

He smiled at her proposal. "Mighty kind, but you don't have to lend me money."

"I know I don't have to. I want to."

Still staring out the passenger window, John turned around and faced her, a grin on his thin craggy lips.

"Guess if you're so determined, I'll just have to break the bank at Red Rock."

She patted his knee again, smiling. "That's the spirit."

Basking in the warmth of her touch, he reclined against the leather bucket seat, watching rugged northeast Oklahoma scenery pass the window. They left the main highway, proceeding on an old road bordered by rolling pastures, slow pumping oil wells and white-blooming dogwood trees.

"We'll reach Red Rock before long," he said. "It's still only ten in the morning. What will we do until bingo starts?"

"Find an RV camp, park this bus, fix a bite to eat and relax. Games start at five and we can catch a shuttle or walk over from the camp."

"Bus?" he said with a smile.

"You know what I mean. Make yourself useful and look at the map. Tell me where to turn before we wind up in Ponca City.

John consulted the map and gave her directions. Unable to contain his curiosity any longer, he said, "That a picture of Roland and your son in the bedroom?"

Attie's friendly smile faded instantly.

Realizing he'd touched an exposed nerve, he said, "Sorry. Forgive me for getting too personal."

Her frown softening, she said, "I'm glad you decided to come along. My friend Beth had to cancel at the last minute and I detest traveling alone."

Feeling somehow vindicated by her remark, he said, "If you don't mind traveling with a nosy old man, I certainly don't mind traveling with the most attractive woman in northeast Oklahoma."

Attie's neck flushed bright red and she stifled a smile to prevent revealing her satisfaction at his unexpected compliment. Engulfed in the pleasurable warmth of each other's company, they continued in silence along the lonely country road.

Chapter 5

Slow spring rain replaced the brief stint of morning sunshine as John and Attie arrived in Red Rock. Ice melting in the ditches signaled the week-long lingering cold front had finally retreated. Attie departed the main highway and followed a side street into town.

"Better buy you some clothes," she said. "Can't let you break the bank wearing a pair of bedroom slippers."

He glanced at his feet. "An old man can't think of everything," he said.

"Let's hope there's a store here. Don't want to drive to Ponca City."

Mentally counting Red Rock's half-dozen stores, he said, "Shouldn't be hard to find one if there is."

No optimistic approximation. Carved with a dull knife from hilly terrain, the tiny northern Oklahoma town occupied no more than a square mile. Scrub oaks surrounded four blocks of frame houses and a business district dominated by clapboard gas station, and general store made of crumbling brick.

Attie parked in front of the store and said, "Maybe we won't have to drive to Ponca City after all."

Shrill bells signaled their entrance into the store. A throwback to the fifties, groceries and canned goods occupied half the building, sundries and dry goods the rest. A young woman in a bright print dress straightened clothes on a rack as a white-smocked man stacked cereal boxes in front. Smiling warmly, the woman greeted them when they reached the racks of miscellaneous clothing.

In a pleasant country drawl, she said, "You folks need some help?"

Pointing to the trousers and smiling in return, Attie said, "Just browsing."

"My name's Jane. Need me, I'll be in back." Her starched skirt rustled as she returned her attention to the rack of clothes.

"These are nice," Attie said, holding up a pair of dark gray trousers.

Glancing at the tag, John said, "Too big. My waist is thirty-two inches."

Attie wiggled her shoulders and fluttered her eyelashes. "Sorry. I didn't mean to insult you."

Ignoring her levity, he found another pair of dark pants. "Think these might suit me?"

Nodding her approval, she said, "Try them on. And take these with you."

She handed him a pair of khaki pants and he headed for the tiny dressing room in back. As she waited, she browsed the racks of clothes, selecting several sets of socks and underwear. He returned with both pairs of pants draped over his arm.

"Well?"

"Fit like a charm," he said.

She stopped him as he started to hang the khaki pants back on the rack. "Then let's get both. I like the khakis."

Hesitating briefly, he draped the brown pants over his arm and said, "It's your pocketbook."

"I also found some shirts while you were trying on the pants."

Showing him a light blue pinstripe, a white dress

shirt and a Hawaiian print, she measured one against his chest.

"I'm definitely the white shirt type," he said.

"I like the others better. Since it's my pocketbook and not yours, I'll buy the other two instead."

"You're getting carried away."

"Stop it," she said. "Don't spoil my fun."

He made a face as he followed her to the counter in back of the store. They found Jane in an animated conversation with the man in the white smock. Their appearance halted the discussion.

"Have any shoes?" Attie said, pretending not to notice their discourse.

The man's smile became a frozen mask. "You bet. In the corner, by the flashlights."

Casting a worried glance at Attie, John accompanied her to the shoe department.

"You folks from around here?" Jane asked.

"No. Arkansas," Attie said.

"Here for bingo?"

When Attie nodded reluctantly, Jane said, "I knew it. We got buses coming in on weekends all the way from Dallas and Kansas City. Ralph and me even played once or twice ourselves."

Attie didn't answer and the inquisitive young woman began ringing up the purchases on the mechanical cash register. When she finished, she placed the clothes in a large sack.

"Ninety-four dollars," Jane said.

Attie handed her a hundred-dollar-bill.

"Knocked the heck outta that Benji," Jane quipped as she returned Attie's change.

"Money well spent," Attie said.

"Where you folks planning on staying?" Ralph, the salesman in the smock, asked.

Again John stole a quick glance at Attie, who said, "Don't know yet. On our way to Wichita and were considering bingo. So tired, though, don't know if I'm up to it."

John clasped the package to his chest. Grabbing Attie's elbow, he said, "Better be on our way."

Ralph said, "What'd you folks say your names was?"

"Jones," John said, pulling Attie toward the door. "Sam and Prudence Jones."

Once they were back inside the RV, Attie said, "Prudence?"

"Only thing I could think of impulsively," he said with a grin.

"Do I look like Prudence?"

"If you do, she must certainly be an attractive woman."

Accepting his compliment with a muted headshake, she started the engine. "Let's find a place to park this bus."

John consulted the map and directed her to the Indian reservation.

"You think those people recognized me?"

"Don't know. They acted suspicious."

"I noticed," he said.

"When we reach the RV Park, we'll hook up the antenna and watch the news on TV."

Finding the Park just outside the reservation gates, John waited as Attie went into the office to rent their space for the night. Several camping vans and RVs arrived while he waited. He could see the park was already almost full.

"Just in time," she said when she returned. "They only had four spaces left."

"I didn't realize bingo was so popular," he said.

"It is tonight. Final game's worth fifty-thousand dollars."

John directed Attie, standing behind the RV and motioning with his arms, as she backed the precarious vehicle into the tiny spot. Once in place, he attached water and electricity and dumped the holding tanks.

Upon entering the RV, he found Attie making sandwiches.

"The couple at the store upset me so, I forgot to buy groceries. We'll have to eat bologna sandwiches. Hope you don't mind."

"I've endured more than my fair share of bologna in seventy-odd years," he said with a dead-pan smirk.

"Quite the jokester, aren't you? Everything hooked up?"

"We're in business, Madam," he said.

Attie flipped a switch on the wall that produced a whirring rattle. Opening a cabinet, she pulled out a tiny television set and switched it on.

"Maybe we can get the noonday news."

They listened intently. John despaired when he learned his disappearance was the lead news item. Police speculated everything from suicide to kidnapping. A reward was offered and the newscast included an old photograph of him. After identifying Ralph and Jane's suspicious behavior, he paced ever-widening circles around the RV.

"Have to go back to Tulsa," he said when Attie switched off the TV. "I know my son and daughter-in-law are worried sick. Not to mention my granddaughters."

Touching his elbow, Attie said, "You really think returning to Tulsa will solve anything? They'll be more inclined than ever to put you in a rest home."

"Least they'll know I'm safe and not worry about me. Don't know if I can live with the guilt."

"Then you've made up your mind?"

He nodded. "I saw a pay phone outside the park office. Maybe I'll walk down and give them a call. My son can come get me."

He started slowly for the door.

"John, wait until tomorrow. It won't hurt to spend one night on the town before going home."

Seriously considering her gentle proposal, he

hesitated before answering. "I did sort of have my heart set on playing bingo tonight."

She handed him the bologna sandwich, face red and tears streaming from her dark eyes.

"What's the matter?" he asked, confused.

Turning away, Attie wiped her face with her sleeve. Her voice choked with emotion when she said, "I'm a foolish old woman. Though I haven't even known you twenty-four hours, I know I'm going to miss you when you're gone."

Spring sunshine dissolved into chilly evening as Vince pulled his collar up around his neck, waiting impatiently on Dan Warren's front doorstep. After hearing footsteps on the parquet floor, he felt a blast of warm air as Cynthia opened the door and let him in.

"Detective Blakeman, come in," she said, leading him into the foyer. "Let me take your overcoat."

"Thanks, Mrs. Warren."

"Like a cup of coffee?" she asked as she hung his coat in the hall closet.

"Don't mind if I do. Is your husband around?"

With startlingly expressive eyes, she winked and nodded in the direction of the couch in the living room.

"Have a seat. I'll get him, and the coffee."

He waited on the couch, admiring antique furniture and expensive carpets. Hearing a commotion in the hall, he glanced up as twin little girls and black cocker spaniel walked right up to him. Unafraid, they placed the squirming puppy in his lap.

"Are you a policeman?" Trish asked.

"Yep," he said, trying to avoid the puppy's long tongue. "Who are you?"

"Trish. This is Emily and Sparky."

"How do people tell you apart?"

"They don't, except Mama and Grandpa," Emily said

Before he could field another question, Cynthia

returned with the coffee, and her husband. Looking first at the twins, and then apologetically at Vince, she said, "Girls, take Sparky and get ready for bed."

"Oh, Mama, we want to hear about Grandpa," Trish said, lower lip protruding in an unhappy pout.

"If there's any news, I'll tell you tomorrow. Now scoot."

Emily grabbed the wriggling puppy and hurried from the room.

"Do you have news, Detective?" Dan asked.

"Please sit," Vince said.

Dan frowned and leaned against Cynthia's chair. Folding his arms tightly, he revealed his obvious dislike for the tone of the detective's voice.

Vince ignored his frown. "We've checked every hospital within a hundred miles. None has admitted anyone fitting your father's description in the last twenty-four hours." After a pause to sip his coffee, he added, "Unfortunately, most of your father's friends are deceased. We've contacted everyone still alive."

"Look, Detective Blakeman, why are you here if you don't have anything new?"

Cynthia winced and said. "Don't be so nasty. Detective Blakeman is doing all he can."

Vince gave Dan his coldest stare, until he began to fidget.

"You didn't let me finish."

Cynthia also stared piercingly at her husband. Grabbing Vince's nearly empty cup, she said, "Let me warm your coffee and you can finish telling us about Grandpa."

"As I was about to say," he continued when Cynthia returned. "We all felt sure your father left home of his own accord when we found his suitcase down the block. He either caught a ride with someone, or was abducted."

Vince paused for Dan and Cynthia to absorb this tidbit of information, and then said, "The fact he left the suitcase on the sidewalk suggests the latter, but we tend to believe the former.”

“How can you be so sure?” Cynthia asked.

“Your reward offer has borne fruit. There’s an unsubstantiated report of your father, here in Oklahoma.”

“Where?” Dan asked.

Savoring the rapt attention his unexpected announcement had riveted, Vince sipped his coffee before explaining. Raising his voice slightly for what dramatic effect it might elicit, he said, “Someone spotted him in a store in Red Rock. He was buying clothes, and he wasn’t alone.”

Chapter 6

Attie shook John's shoulder until he opened his eyes. When he did, he blinked several times, not immediately remembering where he was. She waited until he sat up and shook the cobwebs from his fuzzy brain before handing him a glass of water. He drank half and smiled, noticing her quizzical gaze.

"Never could take naps in the middle of the day," he said. "Always makes me feel like my head is stuffed with wet cotton."

Attie grinned and retrieved the glass. "Sometimes you remind me, so very much, of Victor."

John rolled his feet to the floor, stood up slowly and stretched his arms toward the ceiling. "I thought your husband's name was Roland."

"Not my husband," she said, chuckling. "A basset hound I once had."

He blinked, his cheek muscles flinched and his lips curled into a smile. Slowly, he raised his chin toward the ceiling and howled.

Patting his cheek playfully, she said, "Exactly like Victor. If you play bingo like you howl, we're in for a big night."

She went to the back of the RV and shut the door behind her. A moment later she opened it a crack and glanced out, grinning. "I'm dressing, Wolf Man. When I finish, you can use the bathroom.”

Just before five, they left the RV and walked the short distance to the bingo building. Fully a dozen chartered buses crowded the lot beside the giant prefab structure. A throng of people milled around outside, chatting and enjoying warm weather. Attie grabbed John’s elbow and stopped him.

“Better give you this,” she said, handing him five one-hundred dollar bills.

Turning away and looking at the ground, he shook his head and said, “Why don’t I just watch you play.”

Staring into his faded eyes, she grabbed his hand, gently unfolded his fingers and placed the bills into his palm.

“Let’s have just one night before you go. Remember?”

Understanding her meaning, he smiled and said, “All right, one night it is.”

They waited in line five minutes before reaching the door, each paying a hundred dollars for special game packages.

“We’re set, High Roller, unless you can play ten games at once, in which case we’ll buy you another game package,” she said.

“One is probably too many.”

He followed her into the large open room crowded with people. When she spotted a gaming window, she grabbed his elbow.

“Let’s buy some scratch cards,” she said, steering him toward the window.

His eyebrows rose as they worked her way through the large open room to the enclosed booth. She handed the cashier ten dollars and the woman behind the counter counted out ten brightly colored cardboard segments into Attie’s hand.

“Your turn, big boy,” she said.

Smiling at the ticket seller, he held up all ten fingers. Attie nodded approval, and he followed her to a less than crowded corner of the building.

"Now what?" he asked, glancing dubiously at his purchase.

"Scratch off the coating. Find out what you won."

He watched as she took a penny from her coin purse and proceeded to scratch away the black coating on each of her ten cards. When she finished, she shook her head and frowned.

"Shoot! I've never won a nickel with these things."

"Then why keep trying?"

"Because it's fun."

John kept a single card from his stack, handing her the rest. "Take some of mine."

Without bothering to thank him for his generosity, she greedily took the cards and scratched off the coating with the same results as before.

"Try yours," she said, tossing the worthless cardboard into a nearby trashcan.

After scratching the coating from his remaining card, his eyes opened wide, and then his mouth.

"What is it? What did you get?" When she reached for the card, he pulled it away. "John, did you win something, or are you just fooling around?"

Turning the card so she could see, he said, "Fifty bucks. Tonight's my lucky night."

Following a spontaneous hug, she led him back to the counter to cash the ticket. "Way your luck is running, you may drive home in a new Cadillac."

"The way my luck usually runs, the back of a cattle truck is more likely," he said.

Grasping his hand, Attie pulled him through the anxious bingo players to a long table with two adjacent empty seats. "You call that bad luck? I'd like to know where I can get a double-dose. Better find a seat. First game starts in fifteen minutes."

From their vantage they could easily see the elevated platform, enclosed by four short walls, in front of the open room. A woman's upper torso was visible behind a crane-neck microphone, and plastic box filled with brightly-colored, numbered balls floating inside the box on a cushion of air. TV monitors resided near the ceiling in every corner of the building.

John asked, "Why the enclosed platform?"

"They don't want to make it easy for a would-be robber," she explained.

Glancing around the room, he noticed numerous security guards located by the doors and near the booth where they'd bought the pull-tabs.

"Guess that's a consideration."

"You bet," she said. "Seventy-five thousand dollars will change hands tonight."

"I can hardly believe it."

"Look around," she said. "There are at least five or six hundred people here tonight. Costs a dollar a game to play the mini-games and at least three-hundred people will play every time. A game lasts less than two minutes, forty games an hour."

"Twelve thousand dollars an hour," he calculated.

She nodded. "And that doesn't count what they make on scratch cards. Most of these people are old hands and play several cards each game. Some play five at a time. I suspect the house take is close to a quarter-million dollars on a good night."

"Amazing!"

Opening their game packages, they spread the contents in front of them. John held up a red marker.

"What's this?"

"It's an ink dauber. If you have the number they call, daub it with a red mark."

"No corn?"

"Except for you, old man," she said, straight-faced.

Ignoring her humor, John said, "Which of these cards do we play first?"

"Blue one," she said.

Puzzled, he held up the blue rectangular game board. "There are five games on this card. Which one do we play?"

"All of them. You can't win by getting a bingo on a single card. You need two winners, and sometimes three or more."

"And you say a game takes less than two minutes?"

Attie leaned back in her chair and smiled knowingly. "That's right. They draw a ball from the box and place it in front of the television camera. If you don't hear the call, you can see it on screen."

Within minutes, the tables began to fill with excited players, eager to start the game. The couple beside John seemed at least ten years older. When he glanced around the packed hall, he suddenly felt young again and smiled at the white-haired, pleasant-looking older woman beside him.

"First time?" she asked.

"How can you tell?"

Casting a nodding glance at his red dauber, still sitting on the table in front of him, she said, "Game's about to start."

Picking up the dauber, he waited as a man with a leather folder crossed the elevated enclosure. After tapping the woman's shoulder, he whispered something into her ear before leaving the stage. With a smile, the woman blew into the chrome microphone, the resultant whistle blasting from wall speakers. Suddenly, the hall grew deathly quiet.

"We're about ready to start the first game, folks," the caller said. "Card is blue and has number thirty-four in the upper right hand corner."

Seeing John's confusion, Attie pulled the blue card from the pile and handed it to him. "Watch the card and I'll watch the monitor."

"Everyone ready?" the woman in the enclosure asked.

"Yes," the crowd roared.

"Okay," she said. "First game is for twenty-five dollars and you need two bingos. When you bingo, please hold your sheet above your head and yell so the spotters can see you."

Like a cheap speaker, her tinny voice echoed from the large room's bare metal walls. John glanced around and noticed several men in suits standing in the aisles between rows of tables.

"If we're all ready, then let's do it," she said, touching a button and picking a ball from a slot in the floating box. "Bee thirteen," she called.

As the caller placed the ball on a rack, its image appeared instantly on the television screen.

"Oh five," she said, continuing at a rapid pace.

Attie reached across with her dauber and made a red mark on John's colored card.

"Pay attention," she said.

"Gee seven."

Blazingly fast, the game proceeded. "Bingo," someone behind them screamed.

One of the spotters grabbed the card and hurried it to a man behind a teller-like window cage. Immediately the second game began.

"Red card number fifteen," the woman announced. "Eye twelve," she called.

John tried to keep up with the pace of the game, but fell hopelessly behind. The nice white-haired woman reached across him and marked four spots on his sheet.

"You got a bingo," she said, elbowing him in the rib cage.

Attie grabbed his arm and nudged him until he stood. "Say it, John. Hurry!"

"Bingo," he yelled.

Attie applauded wildly and hugged him when he sat down. A burly spotter took his card and rushed away to the window cage, returning with twenty-five dollars in cash that he stuffed hurriedly into his shirt pocket, intent on the next game. Try as he might, he couldn't keep up with the pace of the game. Finally, he dropped the dauber, crossed his arms and sat back in the chair, disgusted, as the white-haired woman beside him chirped and shook her head.

Attie never missed a beat, marking her own cards, and then marking his. Still, five more games passed without either of them getting another bingo. After fifty intense minutes, the woman in the enclosure called for a short break. Like a wave crashing to shore in a hurricane, the room's noise level instantly increased.

Attie grabbed his hand and squeezed, her excited smile so infectious it made him grin.

"Oh, John, I hope you're having fun."

When she continued to hold his hand against her breast, a warm flush engulfed his neck and face. The feeling left him happy, though most uncomfortable.

"I don't quite have the hang of it yet. I'm getting there," he said. "How would you like a cold drink or something to eat?"

"I could use an iced tea."

Reluctantly pulling away from her grip, he got out of his chair. Her smile was so warm he could almost feel the heat three feet away. Feeling more than a little foolish, he broke their locked gaze and backed a step from her chair.

"Be right back," he said with a wink. "Unless there's a team of mules I don't know about."

"I'm waiting," she said.

Blowing her a kiss before turning into the crowd, he felt every bit as foolish as he ever had at sixteen.

Chapter 7

When the caller announced the break, everyone had the same idea as John. Almost as one, the crowd rose up from their seats and headed for bathrooms and concessions. Anticipating the rush, he hurried forward, finding himself in a shoulder-to-shoulder crunch, people so close he could barely see his feet for their bodies. Standing in place without moving for five minutes, his neck flushed from the heat. Finally he glanced at the fluorescent lighting, becoming suddenly dizzy. A man beside him grabbed his shoulder.

"You all right, Mac?"

John nodded and smiled weakly. "Yes, thank you. I'm just a bit lightheaded. Must have stood up too fast."

Releasing his arm, the man tapped his shoulder. "Take it easy, old timer."

John thanked him and the man melted into the crowd. Feeling sick at his stomach, he touched his forehead and massaged his right temple that suddenly began pounding like a rusty piston. When the crowd moved forward, he went to the bathroom and sponged his face with a wet paper towel, breathing deeply to quell his erratic heart before attempting to return to the concession stand. Still dizzy and disoriented, he purchased two large iced teas, and then looked around in desperation for their table. With chest aching and head pounding, he proceeded slowly toward the center of the large room.

"Are you all right?" Attie asked when he handed her the tea.

He nodded without answering. The older couple sitting beside them eavesdropped in concern.

"Take one of these," the white-haired man said, handing John a tiny pill.

He gave the pill a cursory glance before swallowing it, chasing it down with a long drink from the iced tea.

"Thanks," he said.

"What did you give him?" Attie asked.

"Nitroglycerin," the man answered.

Attie glared at the older man, and then shifted her gaze to John. "You took that pill without asking what it was."

Avoiding her question, he glanced in the direction of the bathroom.

"I'm still feeling queasy. Mind if I step outside for some air?"

Her expression dissolved into a worried mask. "I'll go you."

"I'm fine now. Please play my cards for me while I'm gone."

Attie grabbed his hand and squeezed, releasing it after a moment. "Are you sure?"

Feeling her concern, he bent down and kissed her forehead, managing a grin as he patted her cheek.

"I'm okay."

Before turning for the door, he stopped to whisper something in the white-haired man's ear.

"Thanks," he said.

After patting the old man's shoulder he hurried to the main door, finding the well-lighted parking lot deserted. Drawing a deep breath, he leaned against the building for support. He wasn't alone, a man in a wheelchair watching from the shadows.

"Feel okay?"

"I have a little trouble once in a while."

"Better see a doctor about that," the man advised.

John smiled. "It's nothing serious. Why aren't you inside playing bingo with everyone else?"

"I get bored after a few games," he said.

John took another deep breath and sat beside him on a concrete retaining wall. "John Warren," he said, offering his hand.

"Name's Scooter Bates. I seen you on TV.

Scooter had a full head of brown hair that belied his age, and an infectious grin. John glanced away into darkness, not knowing what to say.

"It's all right," Scooter said. "Ain't gonna turn you in. Think I know why you skedaddled."

John faced him again. "You do?"

"Shore I do. Kin can drive you up a tree if you let 'em."

"You're right about that. Still, I'm going back tomorrow."

"Run outa money?"

"It's not that. I miss my granddaughters and don't want them worrying about me anymore."

Scooter lowered his chin and gazed at John over his gold-rimmed glasses. "Weren't them made you run away though, was they?"

John didn't immediately answer. "No," he finally said. "I left because I decided I was too young to die, and too old to live with my son any longer, at least without being able to spank him."

Scooter grinned knowingly. "Same here," he said, slapping his right thigh. "Ain't always been like this. I was a policeman in Tulsa. Worked part time as a security guard after I retired. Got shot in a robbery and paralyzed from the waist down."

"Sorry," John said.

Scooter held up a palm and shook his head. "Don't feel sorry for me. Felt sorry enough on my own after it happened. Wife passed away 'bout ten years ago and I was used to seeing for myself. Still, took me a while to adjust."

"I can imagine," John commiserated.

"I moved in with my boy down in Oklahoma City. Things was fine for awhile, but we commenced to get on each other's nerves before long. When I couldn't take it no more, I moved to Dallas to live with Cassie, my daughter. After a spell, we was at each other's throats, too."

"What did you do?"

"Moved out and went back home to Tulsa. Figured I was too old and set in my ways to live with my kids."

"I know the feeling. What are you doing here if you don't like bingo?"

"Sue, my girlfriend, can't get enough of it. I play once in awhile. Mostly I just sit out here and people watch."

"It is a bit crowded in there," John said.

"Can I give you a piece of advice?"

"I'm not too old to listen to advice."

"Don't go back. You love your family and they love you, but you can't live their lives and they sure as hell can't live yours. Best way to make them happy is to be happy yourself."

Slumping forward, John stared at the ground. "My son wants to put me into a rest home. That's not the problem. I just can't bear to put them through the hell of not knowing where I am, or what happened to me."

"Long as you don't turn up dead in a ditch somewhere, they'll always believe you're okay. I know how families of people who disappear act. I was a cop."

"I'm not so sure."

"How old are your granddaughters?"

"Trish and Emily are twins, both five."

"I'll say it again. Don't go back. Trish and Emily will understand. You can contact them when you're settled someplace."

John shook Scooter's hand again. "Don't know

what I'm going to do, but you gave me some grist for the mill. I thank you."

Scooter smiled and raised his thumb. "Hang in there," he said. "I'm pulling for you."

As he reentered the door to the bingo palace, the crowd hummed with excitement, time drawing near for the big money game. Appearing relieved, Attie smiled and hugged him when he returned to the table. One of his cards had won another twenty-five dollar game. He decided to forget tomorrow. Just have fun with Attie until then.

Minutes later, a tap on his shoulder interrupted his concentration. It was Scooter Bates, behind him in the wheelchair, looking worried.

"You gotta get outa here. Quick."

Attie turned around to see who was talking to him.

"Attie, this is Scooter Bates."

"Pleased to meet you," Scooter said. "There are cops all over the parking lot. They's looking for you."

Again worried, Attie asked, "How do you know that?"

"Hell, I know a cop when I see one. Besides, one showed me a picture and asked if I'd seen you. I told him I hadn't."

Attie cast a questioning glance at John and said, "You ready to go back, old man?"

John's frowning face flushed bright red and he slowly shook his head. "In my own time. I won't let them drag me out of here like a common thief. Besides, we have a date for the races in Oklahoma City."

"That's my man," Scooter said, slapping his shoulder. "What you gonna do?"

"I'm taking your wheelchair, if you'll let me," John said.

A big grin enveloped Scooter's face. "Hot damn! Good idea."

John helped Scooter into his vacated seat. After taking his place in the wheelchair, he draped Attie's shawl over his legs.

"Put these on," Scooter said, handing him a pair of dark sunglasses and an old misshapen baseball cap.

John winked, slipped on the glasses and pulled the cap down over his eyes. "Attie will return your wheelchair."

"Take your time. I'll just occupy myself playing your bingo cards."

Putting her hands on his shoulders, she kissed his forehead. "Thanks. We owe you one."

John leaned back in the chair as Attie pushed him up the crowded aisle toward the door. They noticed several uniformed policemen, and men excessively dressed for bingo before reaching it. Despite two nervous stomachs, they made it out the door without as much as a sideways glance from the police. When they reached the parking lot, their luck ran out.

"Ma'am, wait," a man called to Attie.

When she dug her fingernails into John's shoulders, he didn't have to see her face to perceive her anxiety. A blue-suited man stepped in front of the wheelchair, holding up his hand. Attie froze and John held his breath as he eyed them both, head-to-toe. Silently, the man turned his gaze to Attie.

"Seen this person?" he asked, handing her a snapshot.

John fidgeted as Attie studied the photo. "He does look familiar."

"Well?" the man prompted.

"Afraid I haven't. Is there trouble?"

"No trouble, ma'am," he said. "Thanks for your help."

As he hurried away, back toward the building, Attie hugged him, trembling as she did. Reaching the RV Park in five minutes, she stopped in front of the door.

"Sit here a minute. I'll see if anyone is watching."

John waited until she returned and opened the

RV's door. She didn't switch on the lights. After lowering all the curtains, she said, "Grab that contraption and come inside."

She shut the door behind him. When their anxiety subsided, she giggled and gave him a quick kiss.

"Slick as a whistle," she said. "We should have been spies."

"Not out of here yet. Someone's probably guarding the front gate."

"I'm going to return Scooter's wheelchair," she said. "We'll worry about getting out the front gate when I get back."

Relaxing on the couch, he waited thirty nervous minutes. When she returned, she wasn't alone. Scooter was with her and they were both laughing when he opened the door. They continued laughing as John helped Scooter into the RV.

"Scooter won the fifty thousand dollars," Attie said.

"You're kidding! Why that's fantastic," John said. "Congratulations."

"Congratulations to you. It was your card."

"I gave them to you. You won the money and it's rightfully yours."

"Maybe," Scooter said. "But I ain't keeping it."

John shook his head. "Neither am I. Not after what you did for me."

"You don't want it, I'll give it to Attie," Scooter said.

Attie touched his shoulder and said, "You're the sweetest man. I can't take it either."

Scooter's smile disappeared and he glanced at the door. "I feel like I've known you two forever. I don't treat my friends that way. If neither of you ain't gonna take the money, I'm flat gonna give it back to Red Rock."

Attie studied John with a look of concern. "Don't you dare give that money back, Scooter Bates," she said.

"We earned it fair and square."

"You said it, Attie. You earned it. I didn't help you two out cause of money," he said.

John scratched his wispy-thin hair and began to smile. "We're partners. We split it fifty-fifty."

Attie grinned and so did Scooter. John shook Scooter's hand.

"Wish we at least had beer to celebrate with," John said. "Guess we'll have to make do with iced tea."

"No way," Scooter said, reaching into the backpack attached to the wheelchair and pulling out three cans of cold beer.

"Here's to all of us," John said, holding up a bottle. "Now if we could just get out the front gate."

Scooter drained his beer in one long draw, belched loudly and excused himself with a grin. "Easy," he said. "They's an exit behind the building. Man on the gate is Sue's brother-in-law."

❧

An hour later, John sat in the RV's front seat, staring out at passing light posts on Interstate 35. Neither he nor Attie had spoken since leaving the compound. He watched as her shoulders finally relaxed and she slumped in her seat. When she saw him looking, she smiled.

"We made it, old man. Think we did the right thing?"

Shrugging, he said, "Don't know. It'll take someone older and wiser than me to answer that question."

Chapter 8

Against his better judgment, Detective Vince Blakeman waited on a downtown park bench for an unexplained meeting with Cynthia Warren. Still suffering from winter malaise, he studied the cracks in his shoes, occasionally glancing up at lunchtime strollers enjoying the beautiful weather.

His nerves were shot from too much Precinct coffee. Anticipating his meeting with Cynthia, he fussed with his hair, mussed by gusting Tulsa wind. It felt even thinner than the week before, and the attempt did little to bolster his self-confidence. With much the same result, he tried smoothing the wrinkles in his corduroy suit.

Cynthia appeared, hurrying up the walkway in his direction. When she reached him, out of breath, she shook his hand.

"Sorry I'm late, Vince."

He tried to appear stern, expressing displeasure for having waited forty-five minutes. His expression about as menacing as a sleeping hound, the attempt failed, her infectious smile overpowering his pent-up grumpiness.

"No problem, Mrs. Warren," he said, animosity wafting skyward like the pretty lady's beguiling perfume. "Please sit down."

Cynthia dismissed his suggestion with a roll of her big greenish-blue eyes, and synchronous movement of short black hair.

Pointing at the pathway, she said, "Let's walk. Please."

He could only nod and follow after her like an obedient puppy. Wearing stylish high heels, she seemed to tower over him. Her confident good looks and expensive dress made him feel even more uncomfortable.

"Eaten yet?" she asked.

Vince glanced at his belt as a horn from a passing pickup blared in the street next to them. "I was thinking about skipping lunch. Kinda need to get control of my waistline."

Cynthia licked her-glossed lips, as if suddenly having an idea. "A restaurant overlooks the ice arena across the street." When she noticed him briefly touch his wallet, she added, "My treat."

"You don't have to do that, Mrs. Warren."

"Nonsense, this is my first trip downtown all year without the girls. I insist."

She hurried away along the tree-bordered path without waiting for a negative reply, Vince in tow. He followed her across the street and up the escalator to the second floor of the multi-storied shopping complex where restaurants, shops and other commercial establishments surrounded a large skating arena. She led them to a restaurant on the top floor where a glass-enclosed, fern-draped atrium overlooked the ice rink. Her smile earned them a prize table in a dimly lighted corner. Before the waiter could ask, she ordered a champagne cocktail.

"Light draw, please," he said when the waiter asked what he was having.

When their drinks arrived, Cynthia sipped hers and stared at him with hypnotic eyes that seemed to change colors with the prevailing light. Leaning toward him, she grabbed his hand before he could move it away.

"Although I know it seems unusual meeting like this, I wanted to talk to you alone."

Vince twisted his mustache between his fingers, and glanced around to see if anyone was watching.

"No problem," he said, unable, or unwilling to extricate his hand.

Pretending not to notice his discomfort, she smiled and said, "Dan is very sensitive about his father's disappearance. He thinks everyone blames him."

"Sorry, Mrs. Warren. Afraid I don't understand."

"He's acting moody and has sulked around the house since Friday. It's beginning to affect his work."

"And?"

"And I'd like him to put the incident behind him. Forget the investigation as much as possible. I'd appreciate it if, from now on, you'd confer with me about it and not him."

Vince cleared his throat, gently pulling his hand away from her grasp. Before he could reply to her concern, the waiter returned to take their orders. He didn't answer her until the young man had gone.

"Maybe your husband needs professional help, perhaps counseling."

She sat back in her chair, stroking her dark bangs with worried fingers. Finely manicured nails, satiny slick with polish that matched her lips, flashed in dim lighting. Vince also discerned a flash of agitation in her striking eyes.

"Dan would never go for that."

"Nothing to be ashamed of."

"I know," she said, lowering her eyes. "Nothing's really wrong with Dan. His father was a prominent local physician, his mother a well-known socialite. Dan's an only child. I'm afraid he received very little attention when he was young, and still resents it. I think he somehow feels his own neglect may have resulted in Grandpa's disappearance. The guilt is consuming him."

"Look, Mrs. Warren . . ."

"Please, call me Cynthia."

"We're doing all we can to find your father-in-law. We have some positive leads. See if you can get your husband to talk to a shrink. I'll report directly to you until we find Mr. Warren."

"Thanks, Vince."

Again, the waiter interrupted their conversation, bringing Cynthia's salad and Vince's club sandwich. After a few tiny bites, she sat her fork on the table, leaned back in the chair and sipped her drink.

"Tell me about the positive leads you have."

Though he fingered the sandwich with covetous intent, he realized she'd rather talk than eat. Returning it to the plate, he said, "We checked out the Indian bingo tip."

Below them, on the ice rink, a girl dressed in pink, pirouetted, touching the tip of her outstretched toe as she skated on one foot.

"And?"

"A couple was spotted. They eluded my people. The man fit your father-in-law's description."

Cynthia picked at her salad. "He was with someone?"

The girl in pink rested against the railing as a Zamboni polished the ice. Vince's collar had suddenly become unbearably tight. After loosening it with his finger, he took a small bite from the sandwich.

"An attractive older woman, mid-fifties to early sixties. They were playing bingo together."

"Who identified them?"

The detective's stomach growled in disapproval when he pushed the sandwich aside.

"An elderly couple playing beside them at the bingo table. The picture you gave us is several years old. Still, they made a positive identification."

Cynthia leaned back in her chair. "How did you miss them?"

"Mr. Warren borrowed a wheelchair from someone he met playing bingo. His female companion pushed him out the door, past our officers."

She finished her cocktail before replying. "Then he did run away on purpose."

"That's what it looks like."

Again, she touched his hand. "I'm glad we talked in private. This will be our little secret."

She saw something in his eyes. Something he'd left unsaid.

"What's wrong?"

"The old couple that identified your father-in-law told us he had a problem."

She squeezed her nails into his hand. "What problem?"

"They thought he might have had a minor heart attack."

❦

Soft filtered light pouring through yellow RV curtains awoke John the next morning. Sitting up on the short couch, he slowly straightened his long legs and painfully, rotated his sore neck. Attie was already up, wearing her white terry cloth robe and pouring coffee from the pot. Smiling when she noticed him moving around, she brought him a cup.

"Morning, John. I won't ask how you slept."

He replied grumpily, "You don't want to know."

Placing their cups on the coffee table, she stood behind him and began massaging his shoulders.

"Oh!" he moaned. "Don't stop."

Though she continued rubbing, her smile disappeared. "I could hardly sleep last night, worrying about your heart."

"I'm fine. I have a preexisting condition."

"And your medicine was in the bag you left on the street?"

65

Nodding, he said, "I'll take care of it when we reach Oklahoma City."

"How?"

"I'll think of something."

After finishing breakfast in silence, he showered, put on a new shirt and pair of pants. Before resuming the drive to Oklahoma City, they walked around the roadside park to limber up. A flock of Canadian honkers flew in formation above them, winging their way north. A trucker, roaring past on the freeway, honked his horn and waved.

The sun was fully up, temperature in the comfortable mid-sixties by the time they returned to the RV. Feeling rested, they headed south on the freeway, toward Oklahoma City. When they reached the sprawling prairie town, John spotted a pay phone and motioned Attie to pull over.

"Friend of my son is a doctor in town. I'll call and have him phone in a prescription for me."

"Good," she said. "We'll skip the races and go straight to Hot Springs."

"No way. You have your heart set on watching the ponies."

"But the doctor will report you to the police."

"Maybe he will, maybe not."

"If you want to go back . . ."

Clutching her hand, he said, "I can't remember when I've had so much fun. I've already made up my mind. I've no intention of returning to Tulsa."

❧

Attie waited in the RV while he made his call. A receptionist answered on the second ring.

"May I speak with Doctor Watson?"

"Who may I say is calling?"

"John Warren. Doctor John Warren."

A young man's voice replaced tinny elevator music pouring from the receiver. "Doctor Warren! Where are you?"

"Oklahoma City, Tim. Do a favor for me? My heart condition has flared up again."

"You okay?"

"I'm fine. Same old problem. I need you to call in a prescription for me. The medicine you prescribed last summer worked just fine."

"Everyone is looking for you. Tell me where you are and I'll pick you up."

"Unnecessary. I'm not lost."

"But Sir, your family . . ."

"Tim, please. I can't explain now. I'm fine. I'm not going back to Tulsa just yet."

"But . . ."

"Tim, you remember when you finished pre-med and weren't accepted at OU medical school on your first try?"

John waited through a pause before the doctor answered.

"You know I haven't forgotten, Doctor Warren."

"I called in some chits for you," he said, not letting him finish. "Now I need your help."

Doctor Tim Watson paused again. When he finally spoke, he sounded like the boy John remembered playing cowboys and Indians with his own son, in his backyard in Tulsa.

"Sir, if something happens to you, I won't be able to look Dan in the eye."

"You two spent so much time together growing up, I still think of you as my second son. I want you to call and tell him you helped me, but not until tomorrow."

"Doctor Warren . . ."

"Please Tim. Will you do it for me?"

A resigned sigh followed another pause. "All right then. Where are you?" After John told him, Tim said, "There's a pharmacy on the corner. I'll give them a call."

"Thanks, Tim."

"Doctor Warren?"

"Yes?"

"I'm not sure what's going on here. Please take care."

John hung up the phone and returned to the RV. "There's a pharmacy across the street," he said, pointing.

Attie pulled away from the curb without speaking. When they reached the parking lot, she said, "I'm going with you. If the police are waiting inside, I want to be with you."

They entered the drugstore holding hands like apprehensive lovers. When they reached the pharmacy in the rear, they glanced around cautiously for signs of the police. He asked the lady pharmacist, "Have a call-in for John Warren?"

Nodding, she said, "Doctor Watson just called. We'll have it ready in about ten minutes."

Attie frowned and squeezed his hand.

"We'll do some shopping and come back to pick it up," he said.

Attie's nervous expression failed to camouflage her anxiety as they strolled through the sundry portion of the drugstore, even though John acted nonchalant, patting her hand to calm her.

"Tim won't call the police."

"How can you be so sure?"

He kissed her forehead, not thinking about the intimacy until he pulled away, face red and feeling foolish.

"Because I practically raised him. He and Dan were best friends, almost inseparable. When Dan wasn't at Tim's house, Tim was at ours. He's like my second son."

Attie blinked and pretended not to notice the red flush of his neck and forehead. They continued through the store, fingering through magazines and inspecting vaporizers, until ten minutes had passed.

His theory about Tim's loyalty proved correct.

When they returned to the pharmacy, there were no intruding policemen. After paying for the prescription, they left the drugstore with no difficulty.

Attie stopped the RV halfway out of the parking lot. "John, lets go straight to Arkansas."

Shaking his head, he said, "I've trusted people all my life. Tim promised he wouldn't call my son until tomorrow. I believe him. Now," he said, playfully tapping her chin. "We're going to the races."

Chapter 9

Five miles from the pharmacy they found the racetrack, situated in the rolling hills on the City's northeast side. Upon reaching the giant parking lot overlooking the facility, Attie parked the RV. John poured a glass of water and took one of the heart pills.

"Races start at one. Maybe we should get a bite to eat at the track restaurant while we wait."

Looking up from the sink, he gazed out the window at the racetrack's spring greenery. Sparkling with fresh-painted newness, white stables flanked the track that sprawled for acres across gently rolling, treeless prairie.

"Good idea," he said.

Grinning, she snapped her fingers. "I have another fine idea."

As she rummaged through a closet, he watched with interest. Finding what she was looking for, she returned with a cowboy hat and pair of dark glasses.

"I remembered this morning that I didn't throw away all my husband's clothes."

An almost imperceptible grin rearranged craggy lines of his usually stoic face as he took the hat. Attie laughed, watching as he admired himself in the little mirror. Still grinning, he adjusted and readjusted the hat, cocking it jauntily from one side to the other.

Adding dark glasses, he tossed back his head, admiring the pose.

"Now all I need is a big cigar and pair of cowboy boots."

He turned, surprised, when Attie asked, "What size do you wear?"

Twenty minutes later, they followed the curving path down the hill to the track's entrance. John imitated a rich Texas rancher, complete with cowboy hat, hand-tooled boots and leather vest. Attie looked sleek and jaunty, and much younger than her years, in boots, blue jeans and flower-print western shirt worn beneath a mahogany-colored leather vest. A bright red bandanna secured silver-gray hair back away from her face, revealing and highlighting big dark eyes, high Indian cheekbones and flawless bronze complexion.

She hurried along like a pumped-up race-walker, smiling and moving her arms in wide, synchronous arcs. John followed nervously, shoulders tense. Finally, grabbing her hand, he stopped, silently imploring her with faded gray eyes.

"Attie, I feel like a fool."

Smirking and nudging him with her elbow, she said, "Don't be so self-conscious. You look wonderful. Besides, I've always wanted to go out with a good-looking cowboy."

His grin grew wider and he wrapped his arm around her waist. "Maybe you should call me Lonesome John, King of the Geriatric Cowboys."

Ignoring his glib remark, she nudged his ribs gently with her elbow. Her light-hearted attitude bolstered his confidence and dissolved his nervousness. He followed briskly down the hill, energized by her vitality that crackled like lightning amid distant prairie rain.

When they reached the track's entrance, they purchased tickets and pushed through the turnstile. Because of their early arrival, the giant complex stood nearly deserted. John's boots echoed against tile as they followed the empty hallway to the escalator.

Azure sky percolated banks of over-head windows, melding with primary colors to create a conscious feel of warmth. Bright Oklahoma sunshine flooded transparent walls, imparting openness, integration of man and nature, and instant lightness of being. Holding Attie's hand, he watched the escalator's sleek chrome sides reflect light in sinuous waves.

"I was raised on a cattle ranch and had horses all my life. Now I feel guilty because I never taught my son how to ride."

"Stop this guilt talk. I'll bet he learned dozens of things from you."

He grinned. "Probably all my bad habits."

"If he's anything like you, then he's a wonderful man."

When he kissed her forehead, his own face tinted the color of the bandanna in her hair. Looking away self-consciously, he felt her warm smile and dark-eyed gaze.

"Thanks. He has lots of wonderful traits and hasn't exactly turned out badly. I guess I did teach him a few good things."

As they stepped off the escalator to the nearly deserted second floor, they found a uniformed attendant standing beside a bronze statue of a cowboy on a bucking bronco. He was tapping his finger in boredom against cold metal. Attie playfully slapped John's skinny rear before waving at the man.

"Excuse me. Can you point us toward the track restaurant?"

Removing his hat, the large man scratched his thinning hair. "You bet. Right around the corner, ma'am."

Thanking him, they followed the wide hallway filled with bronze and western art, reaching the restaurant.

"Need reservations?" John asked the white-smocked man standing behind a lectern.

"No sir," he said, words reverberating with deep bass tones. "We got plenty of tables. Eat, watch the races and stay long as you like."

"Sounds great."

When John slipped him ten dollars, Attie turned away to keep from laughing.

"Thank you," the man said, beaming.

Motioning a waiter, he said, "Give these good people any table they want."

A middle-aged black man, wearing white shirt, dark pants and bowtie, appeared from behind the bar. "My name is Roy. Where would you good folks like to sit?"

"Please choose for us, Roy. This is my first visit to the track."

Easing lazily into his role as Texas rancher, John slipped Roy ten dollars, ignoring Attie's silly grin and wildly rolling eyes.

"Yes sir," Roy said, taking the money.

He escorted them to a table on the top tier of the three-tiered restaurant overlooking the track.

Attie couldn't help exclaiming, "This is simply gorgeous!"

Three stories of glass towered above the track. Far as they could see, alive with spring colors, muted clamor of prairie grass moved in wind-blown waves on distant surrounding hills.

"Best table in the house," Roy boasted, helping Attie with her chair. "Would you like something to drink?"

Attie said, "Coffee please."

Roy looked at John as he stared introspectively out the window, thumping the table with one long bony finger.

"Bourbon and branch," he finally said, adding an extra swagger to his already contrived southwestern accent.

"Do you prefer a particular brand, or will our house bourbon be okay?"

"I'm partial to Wild Turkey."

Attie smirked. When Roy left to get their drinks, her dark eyes twinkled. Lowering her chin, she moved aside the vase of wildflowers between them and stared across the white-clothed table at him.

"Bourbon and branch?"

Crossing his arms, he leaned back in his chair. "You said I looked like a cowboy. I'm getting into the role."

Attie laughed loudly.

While waiting for Roy to return with their drinks, they studied the menu. Attie chose a simple dinner salad. John ordered steak and baked potato. Later, she shook her head when he pushed the food, mostly uneaten, aside. The restaurant began to fill with fans, eating, drinking and talking loudly.

Attie suggested, "Maybe we should get a form and decide which horses we want to bet on."

John motioned her to keep her seat. "I'll get it, beautiful lady," he said, tipping his hat.

Blushing like a school girl, she glanced around the room to see if anyone had noticed. He winked as he walked away, though she missed it behind his dark glasses. Ten minutes later, he returned with a racing form and nearly a dozen tip sheets. Ten more minutes passed before he glanced up from the crumpled racing form, looking perplexed.

"What's an exacta?"

"You pick the winning horses in the first two races. Santa Fe Roy and Red Velvet are the best bets. What do you think?"

After folding the racing form, he placed it on the table beside him and raised his hand for another drink.

"Think I'll wait and look at the horses."

Dropping her pencil, Attie rested her chin on her

fists, staring at him. Her studious gaze made him nervous.

"What, may I ask, are you looking at, my dear?"

"I know you said you were raised on a cattle ranch."

"So?"

"Cows aren't horses. I'm wondering how you plan to tell a good horse from a bad one just by looking."

Tipping the hat over his left eye, he explained in a swaggering prairie drawl. "Little lady, I've been chased by the fastest and meanest horses in Texas. My instinct for rapid horseflesh is finely honed."

Attie laughed out loud and the noisy restaurant quieted briefly as the diners at the nearby tables turned to look.

"You must be kidding!"

He wasn't kidding, dragging her down to the paddock to see the horses fifteen minutes before the start of the first race. Behind a white-washed fence, they admired the magnificent animals. Using the racing form to shield his eyes as the horses paraded by, he nodded and scratched his chin like a knowing buyer at a livestock auction. When the last horse disappeared into the tunnel leading to the track, he grinned presumptuously.

"When do we place our bet?"

"Now, cowboy. Who are you picking to win?"

"Thunderbird."

Suddenly absorbed, he started, without waiting for her, in the direction of a betting window. Attie shrugged her shoulders and followed.

Calling after him, she said, "Thunderbird? That nag will probably finish last."

He stopped and turned around, wagging his finger at her. "We'll see about that, little lady. Panama Tex is starting to feel mighty lucky."

Chapter 10

"Panama Tex? What happened to Geriatric John?"

"Left him at the turnstile," he said, walking away through the throng of people viewing the horses.

Moving rapidly to keep up with his long-legged stride, Attie said, "Who is Panama Tex picking in the second race? You won't have time to see the horses if you bet the exacta."

He stopped abruptly. "Hmm! Better look at the racing form."

Attie moved out of the crowded hallway and rested her elbows on a tall garbage container residing in an empty corner. When he eased out of the flow of human traffic, she handed him the form. Studying it ten seconds before dropping it to his side, he started again for the betting window.

"Well, Tex?" she said, hurrying after him.

Without stopping, he said, "Prairie Sunset."

Attie shouted after him, "Prairie Sunset? You must be crazy. He's a thirty-to-one long shot. The nag has never won a race."

John didn't answer, nor did he stop until he reached the betting window and pulled out his wallet.

"Ten dollars on Thunderbird to win in the first race and an exacta bet on Thunderbird and Prairie Sunset."

"Twelve dollars," the clerk replied, dryly.

John stared at the woman, confused. "Beg your pardon?"

The woman glanced around nervously. John and Attie were alone in the line, so she smiled and explained. "I need ten dollars on Thunderbird to win, and a two dollar exacta on Thunderbird and Prairie Sunset. That's a total of twelve dollars."

He shook his head. "Not quite, young lady. I want to bet a hundred dollars on the exacta."

Taking the bill, the teller's eyes widened and she handed him a ticket marked with the Thunderbird, Prairie Sunset combination. Attie smiled and shrugged at the clerk as they turned to leave.

Returning to their table overlooking the track, they waited for the first race to begin. Breaking cleanly from the gate, Thunderbird immediately took the lead, maintaining a one length advantage at the first turn. Steadily, he began pulling away from the other nine horses on the backstretch.

John sat straight up in his chair and exhorted, "Come on Thunderbird."

"He'll never hold that pace," Attie said.

John's gaze never wavered from the track. His voice grew louder. "Come on Thunderbird!"

Thunderbird led the other horses into the third turn by three lengths as they reached the final bend and headed down the final stretch. Slamming his fist against the table, he jumped to his feet, yelling above the noise in the crowded restaurant.

"Come on Thunderbird!"

Thunderbird crossed the finish line, winning by six lengths. John rushed around the table and hugged Attie. He lifted her off the floor and did a twirling jig to show his excitement, then returned to his chair as many frowning race watchers wadded up their losing tickets and threw them away. A mussed-haired, tipsy young man, mustard staining his expensive suit, touched John's shoulder on his way back from the bathroom.

"Who you picking in the next race?"

"Take my advice. Go with Prairie Sunset to win."

Wrinkling his nose, the man returned to his seat. "Beginner's luck," they heard him tell his friends at the table.

They returned to the betting window to place their bets on the second race, and to collect their winnings from the first.

"Ten dollars on Prairie Sunset to win," Attie advised the clerk. "Mother always told me to bet on a winner."

"Prairie Sunset is a winner?"

Patting John's cheek, she said, "Panama Tex."

He placed his own bet and followed her back to the table. As the horses paraded in front of the stands, Prairie Sunset bucked like an unruly colt. At the chute, stewards had to load him in, kicking and biting. Attie made a face at the starting bell. Prairie Sunset tripped and almost fell as he shot out of the gate, dropping four lengths behind the other horses as they sprinted toward the first turn.

"Come on," John said, beneath his breath.

All nine horses showed their tails to Prairie Sunset as they rounded the first turn.

John growled, voice growing progressively louder, "Come on, baby. You can do it."

Near the end of the backstretch, the lead horse gave out, and ten horses drew closer in the third turn. Coming from far behind, Prairie Sunset passed the rapidly tiring rabbit, making a move toward the middle of the pack.

Squeezing the racing form into a wrinkled wad, he yelled, "Come on, Prairie Sunset!"

Sensing an upset, spectators in the restaurant tensed. Halfway through the last turn, the favorite made his move from third to first. Prairie Sunset went with him, making his own move from ninth to fifth. When they reached the final stretch, the favored horse went wide and Sunset's jockey kept him hugging the rail. Suddenly, he became blocked by two stretched-out racers running in front of him. John jumped to his feet, pounding the table and screaming. This time so did Attie.

Yelling in unison, they exhorted, "Come on Prairie Sunset!"

Like any script from a hundred hokey racing movies, the two galloping nags parted, fading like bleached stones in hot Oklahoma sun. Prairie Sunset moved smoothly through the gap. Appearing victorious as he sprinted toward the finish line, the favored horse had already opened up a five-length lead.

John screamed, "Come on, baby! You can catch that nag."

Prairie Sunset responded like a runaway train, rapidly closing the distance between himself and the front-runner as they raced the final hundred yards, gait-for-gait. Then, like a race-bred champion, Prairie Sunset stretched his long neck near the finish line, winning by a nose.

John screamed at the top of his lungs, "All right!"

Grabbing Attie around the waist, he did another twirling two-step between the rows of tables. Everyone else in the restaurant frowned and tossed away their tickets.

A surprised cashier counted out nearly five thousand dollars in hundred-dollar bills. When they turned to leave the window, John noticed the same tipsy young man behind him in line.

"Don't worry," he said, patting the man's shoulder. "It was just beginner's luck."

❧

Later, John found the restroom nearly deserted in anticipation of the day's last race. On his way out the door he noticed someone sitting on the floor, obviously distraught, face buried in his hands. Starting to leave, he had second thoughts and returned to speak with the young man.

Trickling blood marked his balled hand, the short sleeve of his red-checkered shirt torn. Concerned, John dampened a paper towel beneath the faucet and knelt beside him, wiping away the blood. He studied the young man's puffy face, and then brushed an unruly shock of orange-red hair from his eyes, finding them just as red.

"What's the matter? Need some help?"

Many large freckles spotted the young man's pale complexion, making him seem more like a boy than a man. When he didn't immediately answer, John stood and started to walk away. The young man responded before he reached the door.

"I'm okay. Thanks for asking."

Unable to mask the tears forming in his eyes, he tried to smile. Thinking him drunk, John walked back into the rest room, kneeled down and held out his hand.

"Let me buy you a cup of coffee. You look like you could use one."

The young man continued staring at the geometric shapes of black and white floor tile. In a coherent voice, he said, "Too bad that's not all I need."

"You in some sort of trouble?"

He forced a smile and said, "I'm fine. Sorry to make a spectacle of myself."

Sitting beside him on the floor, John placed a reassuring hand on his shoulder.

"What's your name?"

"Jack."

"I know it's none of my business, Jack, but if you tell me what's wrong, maybe I can help."

Jack's voice was barely a whisper when he answered, "Just lost five-hundred dollars."

John glanced around the rest room, checking for

thieves, then back at Jack for marks of a scuffle. Looking again at the cut on his hand, he said, "Someone rob you?"

Wiping his hand on his shirt, Jack shook his head. "No, I punched the wall."

John rolled his faded eyes, remembering having once done the same thing himself. Touching the white-tiled wall, his frown became a smile.

Jack's lips also curled into a sullen grin when the old man spoke. "Least walls don't punch back."

"My only consolation," Jack said, again dejected.

"Five-hundred-dollars isn't that much money. This time next week, it won't feel so bad."

Jack closed his eyes, ran his fingers through thick red hair and slowly shook his head. "It was a whole week's wages."

John commiserated, again patting his shoulder. "Sounds tough, but you'll make do. It's a valuable lesson for you."

"You sound like my father."

"A wise man," John said. "Life is hard. Get up, dust yourself off and go home."

John helped him to his feet and led him by the elbow to the washbasin. Turning on the water, he placed a paper towel from the dispenser on the wall into his hand.

"Wash your face," he directed.

When Jack took the towel, John nodded and started for the door. Before he could exit, Jack mumbled something and John asked him to repeat what he had said. When he did, his voice was low and filled with ire.

"You still don't understand, do you?"

"Something you need to tell me?"

Glaring at John as if he were the cause of all his problems, the young man turned slowly away from the mirror.

"My wife is eight months pregnant. That money

was my car payment, house payment and Sally's visit to the doctor. I can't face her," he said, covering his face to hide his tears.

Without hesitation, John said, "Be a man and tell her. We all make mistakes. She'll forgive you."

He opened the door and started away. Halfway back to the restaurant he stopped and turned around, returning to the bathroom. Still standing in front of the washbasin was Jack.

John opened his wallet, handed the young man a thousand dollars and said, "I'm giving you this, but you have to promise me you won't spend a dime of it at the track."

Staring in disbelief, Jack said, loudly, "Don't want your charity."

"I didn't have that money when I got here. I don't need it now and never will."

"What'll I tell Sally?"

"Tell her it's a gift from Panama Tex and Prairie Sunset."

Letting the door close slowly behind him, he reentered the restaurant. Attie said, "Where have you been? You missed the last race."

He smiled and said, "No I didn't. Not this time, anyway."

⁂

Returning slowly up the rolling pathway to the RV, arm-in-arm, they ignored the throng of people vacating the racing facility. Along the way, he explained the incident with the young man in the bathroom.

"You gave him a thousand dollars?"

"He needed it more than we do."

"Aren't you afraid he'll just squander it at the track tomorrow?"

"It's something I'd never have done for my own son. As I was leaving the restroom, I thought about the way I raised Dan. I said to myself, what-the-heck. Maybe I can do a little atoning."

Piloting the RV, Attie exited the parking lot, weaving skillfully through the traffic leaving the track. When they reached Interstate 40, she turned at the Fort Smith, Arkansas exit. Wispy gray now streaked the sky and fingers of red and orange were beginning to massage the western horizon. John leaned back in his chair, closed his eyes and meditated.

Hours later they stopped at an RV park, just off the highway. When Attie retired to her bedroom, he turned out the lights. Undressing, he prepared for another uncomfortable night on the couch. As he lay in the darkness, deep in thought, hard uncomfortable springs goaded his meatless backbone. The bedroom door opened, disturbing his reflection. It was Attie.

"That old couch is mighty lumpy," she said. "I'm replacing it when I get home. Why don't you share my bed tonight?"

Chapter 11

Cynthia sat in bed, watching her pajama-clad husband pace the floor. Deep lines drawn in his face accentuated the red glow of his neck. As he listened to the one-sided conversation on their house phone, his face grew progressively redder. When he finished hearing the caller's lengthy discourse, he waved an arm wildly around his head, as if he were about to strike the table with his fist.

"Dammit, Blakeman, why didn't you call me earlier? I could have driven to Oklahoma City by now and caught the old man myself."

Cynthia leaned forward in bed, straining to hear the reply to her husband's angry question.

When he glared in her direction, her heart skipped a beat.

Finally, he slammed down the receiver. Before he did, he said, "Thanks for nothing, Blakeman!"

Worrisome red-rimmed eyes imparted a demented pall to his otherwise handsome features. As Cynthia waited, a muscle in her cheek twitched spastically. She focused on the dilated blood vessels in her husband's arms, and his own involuntary muscle twitch. Many times she'd seen him angry, although never to the point of violence. The look in his eyes shrank her against the headboard. She waited, albeit subconsciously, for the angry condemnation that never came. Instead, he continued to rant about his father.

"That son-of-a-bitch Tim Watson talked to Dad today and didn't bother calling me. Believe his nerve?" he said, glaring wildly around the room while looking at nothing in particular.

Relieved his ire was momentarily directed at someone other than herself, she said, "Dan! Tim is your best friend."

"With best friends like him, I don't need enemies."

Holding the sheet demurely in front of her body, she released her grip, letting linen material slip through her fingers, hoping the resultant glimpse of bare skin might change her husband's mood from anger to passion. He just turned away, slamming his fist against the wall. Flinching, she got out of bed and put on her robe. Sitting at the dressing table, she stared aimlessly at her image in the mirror.

"Can you tell me where Tim saw your father, or are you too angry to discuss it?" she finally said, interrupting his mumbling soliloquy.

He didn't immediately answer. Pouring a glass of water from the pitcher on the nightstand, he drank slowly, the cool liquid momentarily calming him. When he sat on the edge of the bed, he continued brooding, though at least he'd ceased his incessant pacing.

"Oklahoma City," he said. "Dad called him from a pay phone for a prescription for his heart."

Her hand went to her mouth. After taking a step toward him, she stopped, holding back, lower lip quivering. His eyes revealed his anguish and she went to him, gently caressing his shoulder with her fingers.

"Oh, Dan, I'm so sorry."

For a moment, it seemed his anger had dissolved. It hadn't. Igniting again, he wrenched away from her grasp and bounded to the bedroom door.

"Where are you going?"

"To make a few calls."

"Can't it wait until tomorrow?"

Her words trailed into darkness as he exited the room without answering, slamming the door behind him with a perfunctory thud. Still awake an hour later when he returned and crawled into bed beside her, she closed her eyes, although finding she couldn't sleep.

"Who did you call?"

"I still have some influence in this state," he said.

"That's not what I asked." she said sternly. "Now, explain to me what you just did."

Her outburst seemed to momentarily mollify him, and he sank into the bed.

"Blakeman talked with the television people in Oklahoma City after Tim called Tulsa police. They updated the story on the local newscast and reported he might be in Oklahoma City. Several people confirmed seeing him."

"Are the reports valid?"

"Three separate sightings pin-pointed him at one location—the horse track."

"That's not all, is it?"

Dan's nod confirmed her guess. "One person firmly identified Dad as the man who gave him a large sum of money. The man had second thoughts, and tried to find him after the races to give it back."

"And?"

"He spotted them in the crowd leaving the track. They left the parking lot in a large recreational vehicle. The RV had Arkansas license tags."

"They?"

"Dad and a woman. They were holding hands."

She remained silent, digesting the information. Leaning forward and wrapping her arms around her knees, she rocked slowly back and forth, hoping he'd never learn she already knew about his father's female companion.

Softly she said, "Maybe you should just let him go. Maybe he's doing what he wants."

"He's completely off his rocker. No telling what he may do."

"You don't know that."

"Cyn, he gave away a thousand dollars to a complete stranger. Where'd he get that kind of money? He could be robbing banks for all we know."

"That's ridiculous. You know him better than that."

"Maybe not. I do know I'm not letting him get away with this."

Dan's smoldering anger startled her and she said, "He hasn't done anything wrong."

"How do you know?" he asked, voice rising.

In a near whisper, she said, "Because your father isn't capable of hurting anyone, or doing anything dishonest. You should be ashamed of yourself for even thinking such a thing."

"Well I'm not ashamed," he said, turning away from her ashen glare.

"You still didn't tell me what you were doing in your office this late."

"State Police are setting up roadblocks all along major thoroughfares leading into Arkansas. By tomorrow, we should have him."

"I don't like your tone. He's your father, for heaven's sake. Not a criminal."

Turning away, he stared sullenly at the opposite wall. "He had no right running away in the middle of the night."

"He's not a convict."

He rolled over and switched off the lamp beside his bed without replying to her remark. Cynthia remained sitting in the darkness, rocking and thinking, long after his heavy breathing signaled he was asleep.

❦

Unlike the curtains in the living area of the RV, the ones in Attie's bedroom blocked out almost all light. The morning after the races, something gently nudged

John's shoulder. He turned away on the soft bed, trying to ignore it. When the irritating presence resisted his somnolent protest, he finally opened his eyes. As he adjusted to the muted light, he stared up into Attie Johnson's smiling face.

"Sleeping all day, Romeo?"

Rubbing his eyes, he glanced around the dark room, momentarily confused.

"Attie!"

"Forget about last night already, old man?"

His face softened into a smile, remembering instantly that he hadn't. "I'm old, but not that old."

"Amen to that," she said, kissing his forehead. "Better drag yourself out of bed and get dressed, or I'll have to eat breakfast without you."

She handed him a cup of coffee and left him alone to dress. With his senses feeling pleasurably acute, he sipped the hot coffee and smiled as he got out of bed. After breakfast, and an early morning hand-holding stroll, they continued along the interstate toward Arkansas. When they reached Henryetta, they stopped to fill the RV's huge gasoline tanks.

The truck stop combined several acres of gas pumps and parked semis. One big truck had a smiling camel painted on the trailer that said Humpin' to Please. Many of the drivers milled around inside the cafe and souvenir shop while others slept in their own air-conditioned trucks. Idling engines hummed synchronously as the acrid odor of burning diesel fuel permeated damp Oklahoma air. John waited outside, watching the attendant pump gas while Attie went inside for a fountain drink.

Though appearing young to him, the attendant was probably almost forty. Still, he had the slump-shouldered posture of a much older man. Dressed in faded overalls over a dirty white tee shirt, his floppy welder's cap rested casually on his head. As he pumped gas, he chewed a wad of tobacco that protruded from his cheek like a chipmunk with a mouth full of nuts. Dark tobacco juice dribbled down his chin. Periodically, he'd wipe away the juice with the back of his hand and rake his fingers through greasy hair. When he spat on the cement, some of the juice landed on his own scuffed boot. He didn't seem to notice. His dirty name tag identified him as Gus.

"You folks on your way back to Arkansas?"

John grinned to himself. "You bet, Gus. How did you know?"

"Saw your tag," he said, stating the obvious.

Glancing at the back of the RV, John nodded and said, "Oh, of course."

"You gonna get stopped when you reach the state line," the man drawled.

"For what?"

"State po-lice got a roadblock. Stopping every RV with Arkansas tags."

"Why?" John asked, trying not to appear overly apprehensive.

"Some ol' coot ran away from home. Po-lice think he's in an RV, just like yours, on his way to Arkansas. They got all the main roads blocked."

John glanced around nervously, not knowing what to do. "We're expected in Arkansas," he lied. "I hope this doesn't detain us too long."

"Heck no," the man said with a grin. "Person they're looking for is lots older than you. They'll know it ain't you right away."

Smiling at the flattering remark, he gave the man's shoulder a friendly tap.

"Thanks, Gus. Second nicest compliment I've had all day."

Hurrying inside, he paid for the gas and Attie's soda. To his relief, the stocky woman behind the register took his money without looking up. None of the truckers even glanced his way. After receiving his change, he grabbed Attie's shoulder and rushed her outside to where Gus was still busy, washing the RV's windshield.

Tossing him a half-dollar, he said, "It's all right, Gus. I'm going to wash it later anyway."

The unsightly man waved, watching introspectively as they opened the door to the RV and climbed in.

"You take care of yourself now," he said.

Attie had already started the engine before John buckled his seat belt. Extracting a road map from the storage flap in the passenger-side door, he unfolded it in his lap and began studying it intently.

She said, "What are you doing? I know perfectly well where I'm going. I've driven this road a thousand times."

"We just changed our plans."

Chapter 12

Attie and John departed the interstate that led to Hot Springs by way of Fort Smith. Near the outskirts of Henryetta they detoured south, down the Indian Nations Turnpike to McAlester. Halfway there, the RV's heat gauge pegged the boiling mark.

Attie pulled off the road, onto the broad shoulder of scenic rolling turnpike. She gave the gauge a disgusted glance as a cloud of thick gray steam billowed up from beneath the hood. John reached across the console, pulled the hood latch and exited the vehicle to check on the problem. Attie followed, watching with folded arms as he fiddled with a loose hose.

"Maybe we should call a tow truck," she said.

"How are we going to do that?"

Glancing around, Attie wondered the same thing. In the distance, the highway disappeared into rolling foothills of the Ouachita Mountains. Overhead, a redwing hawk flew high above blackened pine stumps leveled by a forest fire the previous summer. Like a splash of watercolor against turquoise sky, the large predator seemed frozen on canvas.

Off the shoulder of the road, a spring breeze rustled high grass, harmonizing with angry steam hissing from the radiator. Since leaving the interstate at Henryetta, they'd yet to see another car. In frustration, John finally brushed his thin gray hair back away from his wrinkled forehead.

"No phone booths around. Maybe I better try fixing it myself." Lowering his head for a closer look, he said, "Can you bring me the tool box from the RV?"

Attie returned with a small metal box filled with various wrenches and screwdrivers. After fumbling through the tools, he selected a large wooden-handled screwdriver, reached beneath the RV's hood and touched the steaming hot radiator cap. With a startled yelp, he yanked back his hand.

"Dammit that hurt!" he said, sucking his blistered thumb.

"You don't know what you're doing. Wait until someone stops and helps."

Frowning, he left the screwdriver on top of the radiator, returning shortly with a pitcher of water and a towel from the RV.

"Start the motor," he said, sounding almost angry. "Think I see the problem."

"Sure?"

"Attie, I'm not a mechanic but I believe I can fix this contraption if you'll start the engine for me."

Her dark eyes narrowed at his fractious tone. Indignantly, she kicked a rock into the ditch before returning to the RV to start the engine. After pouring half the water from the pitcher onto the steaming radiator, he pried off the radiator cap with the screwdriver using the wet towel as a pot holder. When the cap popped loose, he poured the remainder of the water into the steaming hole and rushed back into the RV for another pitcher.

With radiator filled and cap back in place, he gave the wires and hoses a perfunctory glance before wiping his face with the wet towel. Slamming the hood, he glanced around at Attie. Frowning, she stood directly behind him, arms tightly folded.

"May not know what I'm doing," he said. "But I

think the old bucket will at least get us to Arkansas now." Attie's direful expression didn't change. Seeing her staring at him, he became suddenly sensitive to her injured feelings and took her hand and kissed it.

"Sorry. I can be an old bear sometimes."

When her frown softened into a smile, she said, "I'm not a pouter."

A twinkle glossed his faded eyes. Staring intently down his hawkish nose, he put his arm around her waist, grinned and said, "I am."

For several wistful seconds they gazed in silence at the distant pine-covered hills, holding hands. Appearing ageless and cloaked in vivid green, weathered, low-lying promontories of the Ouachita foothills clashed against clear blue Oklahoma sky. A lilting breeze ruffled Attie's silver-streaked hair and she straightened it with her palm. After squeezing John's hand, she led him back to the RV.

"Radiator cap's worn out," he explained when they were again on their way. "Anti-freeze evaporated through the loose fitting."

"Can we make it to McAlester?"

"No problem. It'll take a couple of days for the water to boil off again. We'll buy anti-freeze and a new radiator cap when we get to town."

Attie kept quiet for a few miles. So did John, looking out the big windshield at rolling hills and swaying pine trees that seemed to grow taller every passing mile. She finally broke his spell.

"You said back there you're not a mechanic. It made me realize I know very little about you. What did you do before you retired?"

Chuckling, he said, "Guess."

"All right. I'll play your silly game." Drumming the steering wheel with her fingers as she thought, she finally said, "We've ascertained you're not a cowboy."

"No, I'm certainly not a cowboy," he said, still chuckling.

"But you are handy with tools," she said, suggestively.

John raised his bushy eyebrows. "That I am, young lady."

"Tell me. I don't want to guess anymore."

"Doctor."

Turning her gaze away from the road, she glanced at him. "A medical doctor? I should have known."

"And what might have led you to that conclusion?"

"You have steady hands."

"Not so steady when you're around."

Attie took her own hand off the wheel and reached across the console to pat his bony knee.

"You always know just the right thing to say, don't you old man?"

Grasping her hand, he held on tightly as she continued down the four-lane divided highway. They traversed the remaining distance to McAlester, listening to Mozart on a radio station that featured classical music.

When they reached the outskirts of town, he pointed to a service station.

"Pull in and I'll buy some anti-freeze and a new radiator cap."

Attie continued without stopping. "If you don't mind, I'd rather find a garage and have a real mechanic take a look. No slight against your ability as a mechanic, mind you."

Her disbelief in his mechanical ability miffed him more than he cared to admit.

"Suit yourself."

He held his tongue until she turned and looked, then winked and grinned to show he wasn't that upset. Fifteen minutes later, she found a garage and wheeled the RV into its graveled lot. After consulting the mechanic, they waited beneath a giant elm growing alongside the metal prefab building.

Weather-worn letters marked the place as Big Al's

Garage. Big Al himself was buried deep beneath the open hood, studying the RV's engine. Mechanical debris, ranging from wheel casings to entire wrecked vehicles, littered the surrounding yard. John leaned back against a rusting engine block and shook his head. Attie glanced at her watch.

"You think this is a waste of time, don't you?"

Allowing the barest glimmer of a knowing smile to betray his feelings, he said, "Mechanics always find something wrong. It's their job."

"Seems like a few doctors I've known."

Dutifully chastised, he winced.

"Touché, my dear."

After squeezing his hand, she said, "John, I'm worried."

"Don't worry. I'm sure it's nothing serious."

"I'm talking about the roadblock, not the RV. Why are they doing this to you? It's almost like you're an escaped criminal instead of a respected, retired doctor."

"My son," he said softly.

"But why go to such lengths?"

"I've known him all his life and I still don't know him very well. He seems to feel the need to control me. For the life of me, I don't understand why."

"Maybe because he felt controlled and constrained by you all his life," she said.

He blinked and thoughtfully studied her face, trying to fully understand her meaning.

"He had more freedom as a child than most grown-ups. I went my way and he went his."

"I'm not a psychiatrist. Maybe he's lashing out at you for that very reason. Maybe, in some subconscious manner, he's trying to be your father."

He let her supposition soak in and slowly dissolve within the framework of his own comprehension. Big Al's appearance interrupted his thoughts with her theory still bothering him.

Big Al was short, his ample belly protruding from oily blue jeans. Spitting on the ground, he wiped his face with the sleeve of his dirty western shirt. Much like Gus, the service station attendant in Henryetta, tobacco trickled down his cheek. Oil had already darkly discolored the graying stubble. Removing the worn-out cap from his head, he raked calloused hands through thin hair that was anomalously brown from repeated applications of cheap men's hair coloring. John glanced at Attie and winked, amused at his apparent vanity.

"Water pump is out and so is the thermostat," he said.

It was Attie's turn to wink. Looking pointedly at John, she nodded.

He simply shrugged.

"Can you fix it?"

"Course I can fix it," Big Al said, gruffly. "This here's a garage, ain't it?"

"I mean can you fix it today?"

"Shore. I'll start on it now and you can come get it a little later."

"How much later?" asked Attie.

Big Al glanced at the broken crystal of his oily watch and said, "Bout two hours oughta do it."

"Fine," she said. "Can we use your phone to call a cab?"

"Ain't no need for that," Al said. "McAlester ain't that big. I'll give you a ride."

By now, it was already far beyond the backside of noon. Sunshine had already begun to wane. Their engine trouble had taken them past lunch without respite.

"I'm hungry," John declared, glancing at Attie.

"So am I," she said. "Is there a good place to eat around here, Mr. Al?"

Big Al grinned, further emphasizing tobacco-puffed cheeks. "Where you folks from, anyway?

This here's the biggest I-talian colony west of the Mississippi. Ever known an I-talian that couldn't cook?" he asked rhetorically.

Attie and John both shook their heads. Five minutes later, they occupied the front seat of Big Al's wrecker, a six-wheeled behemoth with a huge winch on back. He took them into a near-by neighborhood to a restaurant that looked like many of the other white-framed houses. Except for the gravel parking lot that surrounded it and the neon sign in front that said, simply, Mike's.

"Best steaks and pasta in town," Big Al assured them. "And tell Mike you want a glass of Choc."

Attie cleared her throat and said, "Choc?"

Big Al spat tobacco out the window and wiped his mouth. "Choc beer is homemade and used to be illegal."

"Oh," Attie said.

John asked, "Why do they call it Choc beer?"

"Short for Choctaw," he explained. "Indians once made it." John nodded knowingly as he stepped down out of the truck to give Attie a hand. "Just stick around and I'll be back to pick you up when I finish with the water pump and thermostat."

Attie waved as he drove away. John knew what was coming, but attempted to forestall the reprimand by walking gingerly toward the front door of the restaurant. Grabbing his elbow, she wheeled him around, stern resolution replacing the usual smile on her handsome face.

He winked and strolled away before she could accost him with the inevitable I told you so.

Flippantly, he said, "When it comes to a doctor's prognosis on broken cars, take my advice and get a second opinion."

Chapter 13

A blue and white police cruiser screeched to a neck-popping halt in front of Vince Blakeman's condo complex. The detective tapped the dashboard before exiting, thanking the uniformed driver for the ride.

"Sure you won't join us for a beer at Ten Pin Annie's?" the driver asked.

"Like to, Joe, but I got paperwork coming out my butt. Maybe I'll make it next time."

Smiling as if he expected as much, he said, "Yeah, sure. You bowling this year?"

Glancing at his watch, as if the thirty-dollar time piece somehow held the answer to his question, he said, "You know I usually bowl."

"All right, then. See you tomorrow."

Spinning the tires, Joe the patrolman drove away down the elm-lined boulevard as Vince strolled along the sidewalk, across the neatly manicured lawns. With the weather still cool, the complex managers had yet to fill the swimming pool. It looked like a dull gray hole in the ground as he passed by it. Four old men with spindly legs, dressed warmly in sweaters and soft hats, were playing tennis on one of the green-surfaced courts. When he waved, they just grumbled and continued playing.

Communal flower beds sprouted red and yellow

blooms, none of which he recognized. Picking up the evening paper from his front steps, he caught a glimpse of his attractive neighbor, on her knees planting a tomato vine. Brief cut-off blue jeans tightly girded her shapely rear-end. Vince whistled beneath his breath. Although neighbors almost a year, the shy detective had never introduced himself, or even spoken to her. Realizing how close they were, he sucked in his belly, straightening to his full five-feet-nine inch height. When he opened his mouth, his lips began to quiver and no words came forth.

From the name on his neighbor's mailbox, he knew she was Marla MacDonald. From the uniform she wore to work, he also made her as a nurse. Although they'd never spoken, she'd once seen him looking at her and had smiled. He still remembered that smile.

Her yellow bikini top revealed her shapely shoulders and golden tan, blemished only by a crisscross band of ivory. Tanning booth this time of year he deduced. After giving her long legs one more appreciative glance, he slipped into his condo.

"Some day," he said to himself.

Dropping the newspaper into his faded recliner, he went to the kitchen for a beer. Upon returning to the little den, he found the light on his answering machine blinking red. Two people had called, or at least the same person twice. Wiping the dribble of beer from his chin, he rewound the recorder, cutting off a tinny computer voice in mid sentence.

"This is Cynthia Warren," the second message began. "It's about five on Monday. I need to talk with you. I'll be at Michael's Bar for the next hour or so. Please meet me if you can."

He replayed the message and checked the time on his watch. Chugging the beer, he grabbed his jacket and started out the door. At least he'd get another glimpse of beautiful Marla, he thought. Maybe even another smile. He was wrong on both counts. Her front door was ajar, gardening spade abandoned in the dirt.

"One of these days," he said.

Ducking around the corner to the covered parking lot, he fished out his car keys and gave Jezebel, his twelve-year-old Ford, an affectionate pat. Even with 132,000 miles showing, she was still a crème puff with dark blue leather seats and all the options. Cranking the engine, he headed downtown to find out what Cynthia Warren had on her mind.

Situated in one of downtown Tulsa's newer hotels, Michael's gold letters on dark oak paneling tipped him instantly the place was expensive. Unlike Little Annie's Ten Pin Lounge, Michael's was the watering hole of choice for many city attorneys and oil people.

Filtering out into the paneled hallway, the happy hum of relaxed small talk greeted him at the front door. When the hostess arrived, he saw she was prettier than any waitress at Little Annie's. And, her tiny low-cut outfit made mincemeat of the jeans and sweatshirts they wore at Little Annie's.

She asked, "Table or stool at the bar?"

"Meeting someone," he said, glancing around the room as his eyes continued to adjust.

"And their name is?"

"Cynthia Warren."

"This way."

He followed her past an ornate brass and oak bar to an even dimmer spot in back of the smoke-filled room where she yanked a velvet-covered chair from the table, waiting until he sat down.

"Mrs. Warren will be right back. Would you like something to drink?"

"Light draw, please."

Her dark eyes signaled distress. "We only have imported beer, in bottles. Heineken, Moosehead, St. Pauli Girl, and Corona . . ."

"Moosehead," he said, not letting her finish.

Pivoting on her three-inch pair of heels, she disappeared into the smoky nightclub. Michael's was tiered like a Roman amphitheater around the circular bar. Filled to near-capacity with after-work patrons, the club was alive with music and small talk. Some woman across the room giggled uncontrollably, making him wonder what she was drinking.

Finally, a waitress dressed in a red velvet uniform, skimpier than that of the hostess, interrupted his idle reflection. This young lady's blouse revealed lots of cleavage, even standing straight up. The good detective almost choked when she reached across the table and set the distinctive green bottle, and frosty mug in front of him.

"Three-fifty," she said as he unglued his eyes.

Handing her four ragged ones from his wallet, he advised her to keep the change. She must have nailed him as a cheapskate because she wrinkled her nose when she took the dough. Still, he thought, it was worth four bucks, and her obvious disdain, just for the privilege of watching her dark-hosed shapely legs disappear. After whistling beneath his breath, he instantly regretted it.

"Ahem!" a voice behind him said.

It was Cynthia Warren, smiling like a Cheshire cat. Vince jumped up and pulled out a chair for her, thankful she couldn't see how red his face had become.

Instead, she pointed. "This isn't very private. Let's grab that booth."

Several well-placed potted plants partially hid the booth situated even further in the club's dark recesses. Cynthia, wearing a stylishly-short mauve dress, gave him a swell shot of her own shapely legs as she slid across the velvet-covered booth. She noticed him noticing, her big blue eyes reflecting electrical sparks as she acknowledged his silent compliment by flashing an astute smile. Loosening his paisley tie with a jittery forefinger, he scooted in beside her.

"How are you, Vince?"

"Fine, Mrs. Warren."

"Cynthia," she corrected. "I need to talk about Dan."

Before she was able to explain further, their pretty waitress returned and said, "Your usual, Mrs. Warren?"

"Yes, thank you, Kelli."

As Kelli nodded and started back to the bar, Vince reached for his wallet, wondering if he'd brought enough money.

"Don't worry," she said, responding to his distress. "Dan keeps a running tab here. We'll let him pay."

Relieved, he slugged a shot of cold beer straight from the bottle, pouring the remainder into the frosted glass when he noticed her raised eyebrows. Heavy imported beer foamed over the lip, drenching the cocktail napkin. She grinned again as she helped him mop up the spill with her own napkin. As she did, he inhaled an elusive whiff of expensive perfume, and warmth flushed his face and neck.

"Sorry I'm such a klutz," he said.

Averting her amused gaze, she said, "Dan has acted strangely since his father disappeared. It's getting worse."

"Worse?"

"Scooter Bates."

Vince nodded, already knowing the story she was about to tell. "The interview he gave the newspaper was pretty tough."

"Made Dan seem like an unfeeling ogre," Cynthia said. "The man's been on television and every radio talk show on the air. Dan is outraged."

"Bates made some strong statements. Sentiment around town's running toward letting the old man go free."

"Dan will never let that happen."

"Your husband has powerful friends," he said, stating what everyone at the precinct already knew.

Kelli returned with Cynthia's champagne cocktail before she could reply to his comment. Though he tried not to stare, he couldn't keep from gawking at the statuesque waitress when she bent far over the table with the drink. This time, Cynthia pretended not to notice. Instead, she scooted closer, around the circular booth, until her bare knees touched the detective's trousers.

"Are there any new developments in the case? Anything on the horizon that might possibly return us to normality?"

By now, Vince had a buzz from the strong Canuck beer, and couldn't help feeling nervous about discussing the case in a darkened hideaway.

Leaning closer, he said, "Your father-in-law was spotted at a gas station in Henryetta. State Police have checkpoints along all the major roads entering Arkansas. They're showing Mr. Warren's photograph to the locals. That's how they learned he stopped at the gas station."

When she grasped his wrist, he had to steel himself to keep from recoiling. "Did they get the license number?"

"They didn't."

Not liking his answer, she raked her nails across his wrist, and then turned away. The maneuver failed to hide tears forming in her eyes. This time, he handed her his handkerchief, waiting as she dabbed the tears and gently blew her nose.

"Sorry," she said, regaining her composure.

He nudged her champagne cocktail toward her and waited as she sipped it. She didn't speak until she'd downed it all, the syrupy concoction calming her noticeably.

"Do you understand how I feel?"

Vince could only nod.

She leaned so close to him, he could feel her warm breath on his neck. Kelli saved him, checking on their drinks. When Cynthia straightened in her chair, he held up two fingers. Understanding his signal, Kelli started back to the bar without asking.

"I'm amazed by your husband's connections. I've never seen a simple disappearance get this much attention."

"Dan networks more than CNN," she said, smiling at her own joke.

It didn't seem like much of a joke to Vince. "With all the attention, it's likely we could find your father-in-law before the end of the week."

"Think so?"

"Don't know how he can continue to elude us, though it's obvious he doesn't want to be found."

Cynthia lowered her head and Vince shoved the rumpled handkerchief, still lying on the table in front of her, toward her hand. In response, she smiled, showing no tears.

"I know you think we should just let him go. I feel the same way. What can we do?"

Kelli returned with their drinks before he had to answer her question. This time, when he poured the Moosehead, he hit the frosted glass without spilling a drop.

Chapter 14

Relaxed by three champagne cocktails consumed in rapid succession, Cynthia leaned against the velvet booth and slowly deflated. Vince waited, wondering if he should offer a few words of advice, or simply order another drink from Kelli when she returned to check on them. He finally decided to do both.

"You all right, Mrs. Warren?"

"Cynthia. Sorry I'm making such a spectacle of myself."

Breaking away from her stare, he said, "No way."

Closing her eyes, she tilted her head against the cushy chair. Her face looked ghostly white in the dimly lit bar.

"I don't have many friends, except Trish and Emily. Sometimes it seems I go days without talking to anyone else. Before Grandpa disappeared, I seriously considered asking Dan for a divorce."

Disturbed again by her stare, he turned away, glancing at a rumpled cocktail napkin on the floor.

"Mrs. Warren . . ."

"I decided to stick it out," she said, ignoring his discomfort, "Sorry, I just needed someone to talk to and you so understood the other day. Hope I haven't confused professional courtesy with genuine concern."

Cynthia was starting to get sloshed. Having helped

her get that way, Vince thought it imprudent to inform her of that particular fact. He finally managed a reply, realizing how insensitive it sounded before the words were out of his mouth.

"Can't you talk to your mother, or maybe your sister, about this?"

"My parents have both passed away already, and I was an only child." The light in the bar changed slightly. Azure radiated from her eyes. "I'm making you uncomfortable, aren't I?"

Vince could only blink and nod. Cynthia propped her chin in the palms of her hands, leaned across the table toward him. When she spoke, her words came out slurred.

"Mom died when I was twelve. I lost touch with my friends from high school years ago. I'm not close to any of the ladies I do charity work with, or the girls at the tennis club."

He slurred his own words when he replied to her sorrowful admission, causing her to smile and clutch his hand.

"Your husband sounds like a real jerk."

"I've given all I have. All he returns is cold passivity. With his father missing, it's even worse."

"Was he always this way?"

"Oh no. He was the most thoughtful and caring person, until his father disappeared, that is."

"He has a problem. It's definitively him and not you."

"Where does it leave me? I have to do something or Dan will ruin the rest of his father's life, and ours as well."

Her whispered admission faded into dark woodwork as Vince drank his Moosehead. This stuff was good. Suddenly realizing there were beers other than Bud, he held it to his lips, savoring its robust flavor. He finally managed his own tipsy grin. Again, Cynthia rested her chin in the palms of her hands, her elbows on the table, leaning close to him. He decided she was looking at the shadows of his fast-growing beard, or the funny dimples in his cheeks.

"Let me call your husband down to the station tomorrow. Tell him I have some important info. The police shrink bowls on my team and he owes me a favor or two. I'll have him give your husband the once over. Maybe set him straight."

Cynthia sipped the remnants of her drink, a growing smile returning a glow to her cheeks. "I knew you were the right person to talk to about this."

Vince finished the Moosehead, drinking straight from the bottle.

"You know," he said. "This stuff's pretty good."

✦✦✦

Later, he led Cynthia into the parking garage, steering her toward the car with a shaky elbow. Too many champagne cocktails had left her in a state of giggling inebriation. He wasn't much better off. Still, he probably had more experience handling the situation. When they reached her silver Mercedes, he opted to leave it and drive her home himself. Ten blurry blocks from downtown, he decided to stop for coffee first.

Slumped against the door of the Ford, Cynthia sang a bawdy sea ditty that would have made him blush if he hadn't also been drunk. Finding a corner Big Boy, he parked the car. When he opened the passenger door, she tumbled out into his arms, still giggling like a teenager on her first good drunk. Once inside, it took two pots of hot coffee, toast and scrambled eggs, and a short stack of pancakes drizzled with blueberry syrup before she began to regain her Nordic coolness.

Then she said, "I feel like a fool."

"So do I."

Vince felt his face dimpling into a smile, and redden from the neck up. Scarlet replaced the ashen pallor of Cynthia's neck and face, and she managed a grin.

"What will your wife think of all this?"

"Not married," he said.

"Divorced?"

"I never had the pleasure."

"Sorry I'm so nosy. I just feel close to you, now that we are conspiring against my husband. What's your girlfriend's name?"

"Marla," he blurted.

She smiled and said, "I think the coffee has sobered me enough to make it home now. Take me back to my car?"

Seeing the logic in her request, he paid their tab and escorted her from the restaurant. Back in the parking garage, he opened the door of his car for her, noticing as her skirt rode ten inches up on her thighs. She knowingly glanced up just at the right moment to catch him looking, but only smiled and winked.

"Dan and I are having a cocktail party at our house, Saturday at seven. I'd like you to attend. And Vince, be sure to bring Marla."

Before he could beg off, she slid behind the wheel of her own car and drove away into the night, leaving him alone in the dark parking garage.

John and Attie walked hand-in-hand, up a flower-lined sidewalk to Mike's Restaurant. A dark-haired little man in a short apron met them at the door.

"Come on in heah," he said, his words ringing with a strongly accented Okie accent. "Lunch for two?"

The man's smile seemed perfect, except for a quarter-inch gap between his two front teeth, one normal and one gold. A dark bushy mustache capped his large mouth.

"Don't mind if we do," John said.

"I'm Mike," the man said, grabbing two menus from a stand.

Mike led them across the hardwood floor to a table,

near the window, in the rear of the open restaurant. Once they were seated, he handed them each a menu. Amateur photographs of various celebrities covered an entire wall: movie stars, politicians and other luminaries. Engine noise from a distant lawn mower resonated through the open window, along with the piquant odor of early spring and fresh cut grass. John positioned his chair with his back to the window. Mike, still standing beside their table, startled them back to reality.

"You folks from around here?"

"Just passing through," John said, adjusting the reading glasses he'd borrowed from Attie as he scanned the menu.

"What's your special today?"

"Steak and pasta. Just like every day."

"Then that's what I'll have," John said, smiling and returning the menu.

"Dinner salad for me," Attie said. "Steak sounds a bit heavy this early in the day."

"Not the way Norma cooks it, it ain't. It'll melt in your mouth. I guarantee."

"I'll take your word for it," Attie said. "But I'll pass and save the calories."

"Suit yourself, ma'am. Bet you can't resist a bite of the gentleman's, here."

"You're probably right, Mike."

"What would you folks like to drink?"

Attie said, "Coffee please, with cream."

"I'll try your choc beer," John said.

Mike let the pencil and pad drop to his side. "Are you sure about that? Some people don't like the taste. Maybe you'd rather have a domestic beer, or glass of wine."

"I had my heart set on a choc. Big Al told me to ask for it."

"Big Al?"

"Big Al's Garage," Attie said, clarifying John's

statement. We're from out of town and our vehicle broke down. He's fixing it."

"Don't worry about the choc. Just bring me a Coors," John said.

Mike nodded and disappeared into the kitchen, returning in five minutes with Attie's coffee and a frosted Mason jar brimming with a foamy head on golden beer.

"I brought you a choc to try. It's on me. You'll like it if you're a fan of full-bodied beer."

"Thanks," John said. "Appreciate it." He sipped the sparkling beverage and smiled. "It's very good. This could grow on you."

Because of the hour, there were no other customers. Mike and his wife Norma apparently comprised the entire staff of the restaurant. When the meals were ready, both appeared at their table. After serving the food, they seemed reluctant to leave.

Norma was two inches taller than her husband. Fine reddish hair draped her shoulders in a free-style coif that framed her face. Amber freckles speckled her otherwise pallid facial palette, and her brightly-colored peasant dress with balloon sleeves accentuated her big arms. Her pixie nose seemed mismatched with her large body and wide country mouth.

"Mike says you folks are from out of town," she said, imitating Mike's own regional accent.

"Arkansas," Attie said.

"Whereabouts in Arkansas?"

"Eureka Springs. I'm Attie and this is John."

"Proud to meet you folks," Norma said first pumping Attie's hand, and then John's. "I'm Norma."

Mike flashed his patented gold-toothed grin. "My name's on the sign outside, though it's really Norma that runs the place."

Norma wrapped her big arm around Mike's shoulder and squeezed. "Don't matter. I still love the little guy."

Mike ignored the bone-crushing hug and stared at John as if he recognized him, though couldn't quite remember from where.

"You know, you look awful familiar. Just can't place you."

John cleared his throat and bent his head toward the plate of steak and pasta. "Common features."

Before Mike figured it out, Big Al banged through the front door. Tipping his feedlot cap to John and Attie, he hurried past their table, unaware of the open button on the bottom of his shirt that revealed his big hairy belly. His dark eyes flashed a serious message to Mike and Norma, and they followed him into the kitchen.

Attie finished her salad, rocking nervously in her chair as John continued to work on his pasta and steak. He noticed her agitation. Placing his fork on the plate, he joined her in watching the animated conversation going on just inside the kitchen door.

"Looks like we have a problem," he said.

"Maybe we should make a break for it."

He stretched his shoulders until his vertebrae popped. "We're on foot and wouldn't get far."

"Then what will we do?"

"Hope for the best."

Picking up his fork, he continued eating as Attie tapped her toe and kept rocking.

"How can you be so complacent?" she finally asked. "Big Al must have reported us to the police."

"Nothing we can do about it now."

"I know, but it's so frustrating."

"It'll be all right. They can only take me back to Tulsa. They can't eat us."

Attie didn't seem convinced, so he took her hand, patting it, consoling her, and trying to keep redness around her eyes from becoming a flow of tears. After five minutes, the kitchen discussion ceased. Mike, Norma and Big Al stared out from behind the door at them.

John's attention focused on the grating noise of the mower near the window. When the blade struck a rock, it flew from beneath the mower, slamming into the side of the building. John turned to look. When he pivoted back in his chair, he found Mike, Norma and Big Al in front of their table. Their country smiles were gone and he held his breath when Big Al spoke.

"Folks," he said. "We know who you are."

Chapter 15

Waiting for the proverbial other shoe to drop, John and Attie sat frozen in their chairs. Big Al, Norma and Mike stared down at them, almost as if they were viewing criminals through jail cell bars. Finally, Big Al removed his cap and wearily shook his big head.

"Don't know how they tracked you here, but this-here town's swarming with State Po-lice. I heard it on the scanner on the way over here. They got roadblocks on all the main roads. But," he said, drawing out the word. "If we hurry, we can lead you through the neighborhoods, and into the mountains."

John looked first at Attie and then into Big Al's sad cow eyes. "You'd do that for us?"

"If you hurry."

"But why?" Attie asked.

Norma said, "Dearie, ain't you heard?"

Attie shook her head. "Heard what?"

"You two are the biggest celebrities to come down the pike since Bonnie and Clyde. Ever since that talk show on Tulsa television, the whole state's been buzzing about you. Our radio station gives an update every hour on your reported whereabouts. We even know all about the money you gave away to the man in Oklahoma City, and the paralyzed fellow in Red Rock."

Again, John looked at Attie. Mike explained,

"People are calling in and talking. No one wants to see you sent back to Tulsa and put away in an old folk's home. People 'round here don't cotton to that sorta thing."

"Scooter," John said.

Attie grinned. "Good ol' Scooter Bates."

Shuffling nervously in his chair, he grabbed his wallet and looked up with a grin. "Norma, the lunch was lovely. Best steak I've ever eaten. And Mike, I'm going to miss your choc beer."

"Put your money away," Mike said. "It ain't no good 'round here."

"We would like one thing, though," Norma said, rushing away into the kitchen and returning with an instant camera. "I'd like to get your picture for our wall collection."

For the next half hour, John and Attie accommodated their ensuing picture-taking frenzy. Mike and Norma stood behind them while Big Al shot a half roll of film. Mike took more pictures of Big Al with the two celebrities. One roll of film later, they again occupied the front seat of Big Al's wrecker, returning through town to retrieve their RV from his shop. Dark thunder clouds, blowing in from the southwest, cloaked the sun. When they reached the center of town, Big Al pointed to a black and white police car turning a corner just ahead of them.

"Third trooper car we've seen since leaving Mike's." Glancing at his worn watch, he switched on the radio and said, "Let's see what the talk show's saying."

A local disk jockey's twangy voice instantly flooded the cab. "A McAlester man reported seeing the RV of run-away geriatric, John Warren and his as yet, unidentified female companion. Local police called for immediate back-up to assist in the . . ."

"Son-of-a-buck," Big Al said. "Good thing your RV's out of sight. I parked it inside my shop."

Switching off the radio, he replaced it with the

high-pitched squeal of a police scanner. Roadblocks, they learned, were in place on all routes leading in and out of town. In addition, State Police were actively questioning locals to determine their exact location.

"Maybe you shouldn't get involved in this," Attie said, touching the big man's wrist.

Big Al's ruddy neck flushed red. "Already am. Don't you worry about me, little lady. Gonna get you two outa here, but it looks like we'll have to wait till after dark."

Big Al rounded a corner and instantly slammed on the brakes. Blocking their path was a black and white cruiser. Bending into the open windows of a row of backed up cars, checking driver's licenses, were three troopers in Smokey hats.

"Oh-my-God!" Attie said.

"Back up, Big Al," John said. "Go the other way."

Big Al shook his head. "They's a truck blocking me in."

John opened the front door and grabbed Attie's arm. "Slow down and let us out. Meet you around the corner."

Stepping off the running board, he helped her to the curb. Lowering her head, she covered her face with her hand and rushed toward the sidewalk in the opposite direction. After giving Big Al a quick backwards wave, John followed her. Their ruse worked. The truck was high enough off the ground to shield their exit from the troopers' line of sight.

By now, late afternoon shadows and dark clouds completely cloaked the once pale sky. Sprinkles of rain began to fall as John hurried after Attie. He was out of breath when he caught up to her near the end of a narrow alley separating two old brick buildings. Grabbing her arm, he wheeled her around. Her dark eyes went wide as he clutched his heart, his face suddenly ashen.

"John! Are you all right?"

"I'm fine. Just need a second to catch my breath."

She looked back up the alleyway. Silent lightning framed eastern mountains. Grabbing his elbow, she said, "Let's stop this madness and get you to a doctor."

"No," he said, leaning against the brick wall. "I'm okay."

Fishing in his pocket for the bottle of tiny pills, he swallowed two, and then slumped against faded bricks. His cheeks reddened. Attie clutched his arm. Her tears, trickling down his neck, returned him to his senses.

"I'm all right," he said, touching her shoulder, consoling her until she stopped crying.

"What are we going to do?"

"Find Big Al before he leaves us," he said, leading her toward the beckoning opening at the far end of the alley.

When they emerged at the corner of the deserted side street, they found Big Al and his wrecker, waiting patiently. Spotting them in his rearview mirror, he got out of the cab to help them into the truck.

"What happened? I thought they musta caught you."

Nearby, thunder boomed, punctuating John's terse answer. "No lawman alive is slick enough to take Panama Tex."

Big Al's drooping eyelids opened an extra confused millimeter as he cranked the engine without commenting on the nebulous response. When they reached the prefab repair shop, they found Mike and Norma waiting outside in their car. Worry formed dark shadows on Norma's pale face as she waited for them to exit the truck. Mike followed, carrying a large box.

Thunder preceded a rainy downpour, beginning as they opened Big Al's office door. In dusky clutter, two fugitives and three would-be protectors settled in for a long wait, watching rain stream down the single dirty window pane, and beat a hollow timpani on the building's tin roof. John and Attie slumped on a threadbare old couch while Norma helped Big Al start a pot of coffee. Mike opened an ice chest he'd brought along, fishing out a Mason jar of choc beer.

"Couldn't let you get away without some of my special recipe," he said. "Got a week's supply for you in this here foam chest."

John grinned and unscrewed the lid, sipping the golden liquid. "Mike, you're a life-saver. It's just what I needed."

Though Mike beamed, Attie frowned. "I'm frightened. Why are you two so happy?"

Licking foam from the lip of the jar, John said, "We may be fugitives, but we're not guilty of anything. If they catch us and take me back to Tulsa, I'll just leave again. My son doesn't own me."

"Tell him that," Attie said.

He sat the jar on the cluttered coffee table, his knees touching Attie's, and then her hand. Suddenly, pent-up emotion flowed between them like current through an electrical conduit, and she began to cry. Embarrassed, Mike turned away and peeked out the tattered curtains. Finally, the robust aroma of freshly brewed coffee began permeating damp air as Big Al poured from the pot.

"Coffee's ready," he said, walking out into the garage's open bay, leaving them to their own lonely reflections.

"You folks in a heap of trouble," Mike said. "Po-lice have roadblocks on every road out of town."

"We know," John said.

"You'll have to stay till they get tired of waiting and leave," Norma said.

John began nervously pacing the floor. After screwing the top back on the Mason jar, he returned it to the Styrofoam chest. After joining Attie on the lumpy old couch, he said, "Might take a week."

She squeezed his hand. "Or longer."

Mike's bushy mustache twitched. "You folks can

stay with us."

"Absolutely," Norma said.

"We appreciate your hospitality," John said. "Problem is, with all this publicity, someone is bound to recognize us."

Attie leaned forward on the couch. "We could hide in the trunk of Mike's car. Let him take us beyond the outskirts of town. We can hitchhike to Arkansas."

John shook his head. "I can't let them risk it. Besides, how far would we get, trying to cross the mountains on foot, in the middle of the night?"

"We got a car you could borrow," Mike said.

"Everything we own is in the RV," Attie said.

John returned to pacing circles around the room. A well-worn path on the rug indicated that pacing was also one of Big Al's problem-solving aids as he was going at it himself in the concrete bay of his shop. Mike, Norma and Attie fell asleep on the couch. John settled in behind the clutter of Big Al's government-issue desk. Amid the storm's cacophony, and Mike's resonant snorts, he finished the pot of coffee alone.

Two hours later, Big Al returned from the shop, finding Mike, Norma and Attie on the couch and John asleep at the desk. Leaving behind only moon-bright darkness, the storm had finally dissipated. As he started a pot of fresh coffee, the two couples began to stir, awakening one-by-one. As he watched them blink away sleep from their eyes, he scratched his scruffy day-old beard.

After refilling everyone's coffee cup, and making sure they were all alert, he said, "Folks, I believe I got a plan."

Chapter 16

Big Al waited until everyone was sufficiently awake and had finished at least one cup of his strong shop coffee. Mike woke up out-of-sorts, glaring at Big Al as he brushed past him for a second cup.

He asked, "Fixin' to load 'em up in a hot air balloon and fly 'em out of town?"

"Nope," Big Al said. "But it wouldn't be a bad idea. If we had a balloon, that is."

"Tell us your plan," John said, ignoring Mike's sarcasm.

"After dark, we'll hook the RV up to my truck and I'll tow it up into the hills."

Mike smiled cynically and winked at Norma. "That won't work because authorities have a description of the vehicle, and its tag number."

Big Al agreed. "That they do."

"Then how . . ."

Raising his palm to quiet Mike, he folded his hand, leaving a single upraised finger which he crooked, motioning them to follow him into the bay. Attie gasped when he switched on the overhead lights.

"My God, what have you done to Ol' Nellie?"

Big Al didn't have to answer. Gone was its well-preserved white paint job, replaced by bright fluorescent yellow. Lightning streaks emblazoned both sides of the RV, along with several dark blue peace symbols. One slogan said Free Mandela, another, Save the whales.

Mike's gold tooth glinted in the light as he gazed at the RV, his mouth agape. Norma's ruddy complexion flushed bright red. Attie's hands covered her mouth and nose. John simply leaned against the corrugated metal wall, grinning like a fox.

"Always wanted to do one up like that," Big Al said.

"But why? Surely . . ."

John didn't let Attie finish. Instead, he answered for him. "Perfect. It's so obvious; the police will never suspect it. How did you think of it?"

Big Al beamed. "Even a blind hog finds an occasional acorn. Dawned on me the only way to hide something big as your RV is not hide it at all; make it so visible, it becomes invisible. Even put on a California tag from a wrecked car out in the lot. Make it seem even more normal."

"You're a genius," John said, slapping his meaty shoulder.

"Cain't take all the credit," Big Al said. He pointed to a snapshot on the wall—a Volkswagen bus, painted garish yellow, bearing exactly the same slogans as those now found on Attie's RV. "It was my daughter's. She dropped out of college in the sixties and went to live in a California commune with a surfing bum turned hippie."

"Your daughter lives in a commune?" Attie asked.

Big Al smiled. "Not anymore. Practices law in Los Angeles and has three kids. She married the surfing bum, though. Now he's a Dean of one of them fancy west-coast colleges."

"That's a wonderful story, and a great idea. What now?" John asked.

"It might be kind of risky, but Mike and Norma will have to take you two out of town in the trunk of their car. I'll hook Ol' Nellie to the back of my truck and we'll all meet at Four Mile Flats."

Attie crossed the bay and gingerly touched the side of the RV. Yanking it back, she grinned when she saw yellow paint on the tip of her finger.

"Ain't quite dry yet," Big Al said.

Attie looked at Mike and Norma. "Sure you want to do this for us?"

Returned to his former state of cheerfulness by Big Al's strong coffee, Mike said, "Like John says, they can't eat us. When do we leave?"

Big Al glanced at his watch. "Now's good a time as any. We'll stay in contact by CB."

Attie hugged Mike and Norma, and Big Al blushed when she kissed him, square on the mouth.

❧

At exactly a quarter of twelve, the two couples left the garage. Anticipating the extra time needed to reach the rendezvous, they'd given Big Al a fifteen minute head start. Muddy pools of rainwater and clear darkness were all that remained in the wake of the passing storm. The trunk of Mike's old Cadillac provided ample room for Attie and John, though the air grew stale. They could also hear every word of the other couple's conversation, and Mike's occasional flatulent eruptions.

"You two okay back there?"

Attie giggled and John said, "Fine, Mike. It's just a bit stuffy."

"What'd you say?"

"We're fine," John said again, this time almost shouting.

"They're fine," Norma said.

"Yell if you need anything," Mike said.

"Fat chance," John said with a grin.

Attie elbowed him, even though realizing the impossibility of Norma and Mike hearing his rude comment. She grabbed his hand when Mike slammed on the brakes, throwing them into the firewall.

"Oh hell," Mike said.

John clutched Attie's hand. "You all right?"

"I'm okay."

Norma called, "You two all right back there?"

"None the worse for wear," John said.

"Hold it down back there," Mike said. "There's a roadblock up ahead."

In a moment, the car halted. Glass ground against metal, screeching as Mike lowered the window. John held his breath, and Attie's hand, her pent-up anxiety launching her into another giggling fit. Clutching her shoulder, he clamped his hand over her mouth. He needn't have bothered. Neither the policeman, nor Mike and Norma, could hear a thing above the engine's clatter.

After showing them a snapshot through the window, the policeman asked, "You folks seen this man?"

"Not me, officer. You, Honey?"

"Nope," Norma said. "What's the problem?"

"Nothing to worry about," he said, slapping the door of the car. "You folks can move along now."

Mike didn't move along. Instead, he said, "Is he an escaped murderer?"

"Mike," John said, still holding Attie's mouth. "Get the hell out of here."

"No sir, he's just a missing person."

"Seems like quite a fracas for just a missing person. You boys have three cruisers on this street alone. Do you have any big leads?"

"Mike!" John exhorted beneath his breath.

By this time, his hand had become ineffective. Despite Attie's attempt to hold her breath, a full quaking fit wracked her body. John stiffened, closed his eyes and crossed his fingers.

The policeman said, "We know he's on his way to Arkansas, and that he's in town. Got every man on the force working overtime to see he don't make it outa here."

When nervous Norma elbowed Mike's ribs, they heard a whoosh of expelled air. "We'll keep a look out for them," she said. "Let's go Mike."

When the policeman slapped the door again, Mike accelerated away, a little too fast. "Mike, you idiot," Norma said. "Trying to get us caught?"

"Sorry, Honey. I couldn't resist."

No sooner than they were past the roadblock, Attie's laughter subsided. Hugging John and thinking they were safe, she said, "We made it."

They hadn't.

"We got problems, folks," Norma said.

John asked, his voice a near shout, "What's wrong?"

"Cops had Big Al pulled over at the roadblock. He was standing outside the RV, talking with three of them. They didn't look any too happy."

Five minutes later, Mike again stopped the car. The heavy Cadillac door opened and gravel crunched as he walked around to the rear. Even Attie's jocularity had grown silent as the key turned, sounding hollow in the lock. When the large trunk popped open, fresh air and cold darkness greeted them. Having reached the eastern outskirts of town, the blacktop had ended abruptly, replaced by a narrow dirt road extending into the tree-covered mountain range separating eastern Oklahoma and western Arkansas. Norma joined them as Mike helped them from the trunk.

"What now?" Attie asked.

"We wait," John said. "And hope for the best."

When Attie hugged Mike and Norma, the big red-headed woman began to cry.

"I was so frightened," Attie said.

"I about wet my pants," Norma said.

"Not me," Mike said. "I knew they weren't going to search the car."

Norma elbowed her little husband and said, "You didn't know anything. For a minute, I thought you were going to open the trunk for them."

Again, Attie began to titter nervously. John grabbed Mike's hand and gave it a hearty shake. His gesture was somehow not enough, and he embraced Mike and Norma like children.

"You two are the best friends a lost soul could ask for. You were both wonderful at the roadblock. I don't want you to take any more chances. Go back to McAlester. Attie and I will wait for Big Al alone. If he doesn't make it, we'll hitchhike to Arkansas."

"Hell no," Mike said. "I'll drive you there myself before I let that happen."

Norma and Attie were now both in tears. A chorus of crickets and a gentle breeze whistling through pines was all that interrupted the sniffles and nervous chatter of the two couples waiting in the dark. Finally, a distant moan disturbed the silence. John heard it first, and then Attie. It was the throaty drone of a diesel engine.

Attie asked, "Is that Big Al's truck?"

"Sounds like it," Mike said, glancing at his watch. "It's been a long time. Hope he ain't got the police with him."

"He wouldn't do that," Attie said.

"He mighta broke down under their questioning. Better get back in the trunk," Mike said.

John shook his head. "No, Mike. If it's the police, then it's over and I'll go back to Tulsa with them. You can tell them you found us walking beside the road."

"No, John," Attie said, tugging at his hand.

Shaking his head, he leaned back against the fender and folded his arms. "Folks," he said. "Whatever happens from here on out, it's in the hands of fate."

Chapter 17

Grabbing a towel from the rack, Vince girded it around his waist as he stepped from the shower. With the back of his hand, he wiped a circular swath from the steam-fogged mirror, raking critical fingers through thinning hair as he stared at his hazy image. He moaned in disgust. After wriggling the loose skin around his neck one last time, he drained his warm beer waiting on the dressing counter.

He'd begun worrying about Cynthia's party shortly after leaving her in the downtown parking garage. Now he could kick himself for blurting out that Marla was his steady girlfriend. Sleepless hours had convinced him Cynthia's inebriation would preclude her from remembering the invitation. Her call to him at the station the following morning informed him otherwise.

"Vince, you haven't forgotten about Saturday, have you?"

"Saturday?"

"The party, at eight. And Vince, I want to thank you."

"Thank me?"

"For arranging Dan's talk with the police psychologist."

"Oh yeah. Hope it does some good."

"It's already helped me. And Vince, don't forget to

bring Marla. I'm dying to meet her."

She'd hung up the phone before he could contrive an excuse to skip the party, or at least explain why he wouldn't be bringing Marla. Hell, he'd thought, refilling his cup with strong precinct coffee. I'll just ask her. Why not?

Why not? He could think of no valid reason, except the very idea frightened him worse than cornering a serial killer in a dark alley. Still dripping from the shower, he tossed the empty beer can into the trash and trudged into his small kitchen for something to eat.

After breakfast, he picked through his clothes closet, searching for an appropriate outfit to wear. Something to impress Marla while asking her to the party. Even though it was Saturday, jeans seemed too casual for a first meeting. He settled on blue dress pants and his last starched white shirt. Somehow, the selection seemed benignly incongruous with white socks and sneakers.

"Hell," he mumbled. "All she can do is say no."

The thought terrified him.

At eleven, he could think of no further reason to delay confronting her, so he edged toward the door and peeked out the window. There she was, wearing a skimpy purple tank top and abbreviated khaki shorts, stooping in the flower bed, tending her irises. Her outfit framed darkly tanned shoulders and long winsome legs, and tied a knot in his throat as he edged outside.

Standing frozen on the doorstep, his hands trembled and his heart beat reveille against the old rib cage. Oblivious to the creaking door, Marla continued spading dirt around the flowers as he walked up behind her. Blinking, he drew a deep breath and tapped her shoulder. His action resulted in an unexpected reaction.

Eyes wide, she wheeled around, shaken from her concentration by his cautious touch. Like a released spring, she jerked up from her squatting position, catching him full in the crotch with the gardening spade. The ensuing blow doubled him over. Losing his balance, he tripped and tumbled forward. With a dull thud and explosion of soil and blossoms, he landed in her bed of orange and burgundy irises.

Lying motionless on the trampled flowers, he choked on their licorice aroma, wincing as Marla screamed and ran inside, slamming the heavy condo door behind her. Shaken, he eased out of the flower bed. After brushing the dirt from his white shirt, he knocked on her door. When she opened it, he missed the glint of fear in her big brown eyes, seeing only the barrel of a .38 police special staring back at him. Immediately, he raised his hands above his head.

"Please don't shoot me," he said. "I'm your next-door-neighbor."

He waited until she lowered the pistol before dropping his hands. Her handsome face was flushed, an errant strand of dark hair caught between her quivering lips.

"You scared me half to death."

"Sorry. I was just trying to get your attention."

"You ruined my irises," she said. The worried timbre of her voice darkened with anger as her flush of fright subsided.

"It wasn't my intention."

Glaring at him, she spouted out, "You not only ruined my flowers, but my whole weekend. Thank you very much."

With that, lovely Marla slammed the door unceremoniously in his face.

"I'm really very sorry," he said, voice raised so she could hear him through the door.

When Marla didn't answer or return, he began to feel like the queasy loser in a pie-eating contest. Backing away, he beat a hasty retreat to his condo, hurrying to the refrigerator for another beer to calm his shattered nerves. He found the cupboard bare, his last beer consumed before the confrontation.

Fishing desperately through a lower cabinet, he managed to find the bottle of Jack Daniel's left over from New Years Eve. Tipping back his head, he poured bourbon directly into his mouth, a position he held until the strong brown liquid dribbled down his neck.

Cynthia was worried. Dan hadn't spoken to her since his meeting with the police psychologist. That night, he'd eaten alone in his study. When he finally came to bed, icy silence pervaded the room and he ignored her when she crawled in beside him. Rolling over, he turned out the lights without giving her as much as a peck on the cheek. When she touched his face, the tightness she felt caused her to instantly withdraw her hand.

Dan left for work without eating breakfast and didn't return until six. Cynthia greeted him at the door, already dressed for the party.

"Where have you been? Our party starts in two hours."

Without answering, he went to his study, not emerging until a quarter of seven. A less-than-subtle click of the bathroom door lock resounded like a brass clapper in Cynthia's brain. Turning helplessly away from the indifferent door, she went to the kitchen to help Billie with the refreshments. When she returned to the bedroom she found herself locked out, literally and figuratively.

Knocking, lightly at first, and then more forcefully, she finally gave up and returned to the living room to await their guests alone. By seven-thirty they began to arrive, mostly Dan's business associates and various influential clients. By eight, well-dressed party-goers crowded their large living room. Dan made his appearance at eight-fifteen. Until then, the bedroom door remained locked.

Cynthia, extremely upset, tripped on a stool and almost fell after drinking her third glass of champagne. Still, the warming effect of growing anger and too much alcohol replaced her worried flush. They'd hired a string quartet for the party, and dulcet melodies melded with the dissonance of conversation and clink of champagne glasses.

A senior partner's wife clutched her arm, backing her into a corner to spread the latest society gossip. After five minutes of inane conversation, Cynthia realized she hadn't heard a word the woman had said. Begging off, she retreated through the crowded living room to help Billie clean a spill.

Too upset to fret over a fresh cigarette burn on the couch, she asked, "Seen Dan?"

Billie pointed at the French door. "On the patio, getting some air."

"I could use some myself," Cynthia said.

Handing Billie the glass-filled tray, she started through the packed room. Robert Baker, a senior law partner in Dan's firm, and former U.S. Senator, spotted her, waving to get her attention. Dan's mentor, Baker was also one of Cynthia's closest confidantes. Still, she had other things on her mind. Pretending not to notice, she masked her departure behind a large rubber tree plant.

Finding the kitchen empty, she exited into the moon-bright yard through the back door. Night air clear and cool, she clutched her arms around the low-cut party dress. Slipping on slick grass as she rounded the house, she broke a heel. This time an opportune tree branch kept her from falling.

Holding her breath, she assessed the rip in her blouse, trying without much success to regain her composure. When she opened her eyes and unclenched her fists, she removed her shoes and continued around the house. There, light from a flickering cigarette formed shadows on the porch. Suddenly, someone grabbed her from behind and she screamed, but not before one looping arm went around her waist and a hand over her mouth.

"Cynthia, what the hell are you doing out here? I thought you were a prowler."

Dan's voice instantly soothed her frazzled nerves and wildly racing heart. "And I thought you were a rapist."

Releasing her, he blew nervous smoke into the air and turned away. "I'm going back to the party."

Grabbing his arm, she said, "Not until you talk to me."

"What do you want to talk about? That the police shrink thinks I'm off my rocker? I haven't smoked in months. Now this little episode has me started again."

"You're angry about the meeting with the police shrink."

"Damn right I am. Who gave you the right to pull a silly stunt like that?"

Caressing his arm, she let her hand drop slowly to his side. Her touch failed to dissipate his angry glare and she turned away into the darkness.

"I'm worried about you," she said.

"Worried?"

"Yes, worried. You're acting so irrationally lately. I don't even recognize you anymore since your father disappeared."

Light from the streetlamp blurred dark lines of his face. Stepping backwards, he tossed the cigarette to the ground, stamping it out with his shoe.

"So that's what this is all about. Just butt out and let me handle it."

"You are handling it," she said, again touching his arm.

Wrenching away, he backed even deeper into the shrubbery. "You think I don't know about your secret meetings with Columbo? You must think I'm a complete moron."

It was Cynthia's turn to step backwards. "Dan, I . . ."

"Don't Dan me," he said, almost shouting. "I know what game you're playing."

"I'm not playing games."

"The hell you're not. Don't you want to find him?"

"Maybe he doesn't want to come home just yet. Is that so terrible?"

After he backhanded the bushes with such force it made her flinch, she clasped her arms tightly around her chest.

"Yes! Yes it's terrible!"

She watched, tears in her eyes, as his words ended, though his mouth remained open. She caught her breath and wiped her nose.

"Why is this so important to you? Can't you just let go?"

Backing away, he folded his own arms, and his jaw clenched into a tight mass of angry muscle.

"This is an important party, Cyn. Important for my career. Now you've managed to upset me so, I don't know if I can go back in there."

Putting her arms around him, she began rocking him like a baby. Oblivious to her gentle pressure, his neck and shoulders only stiffened, and she could feel his tortured apathy.

"Don't be self destructive. Let's sneak back in the house and lock ourselves in the bedroom," she said. "The guests won't miss us for thirty minutes. I'll make it better. I promise."

He only shook his head, darkness still reflecting from his eyes. "Don't you think the guests would notice their hosts missing for half an hour? Come on, Cyn. Go change clothes. You look like you've been in a catfight."

Pulling away from her, he disappeared around the house. Feeling very much the fool, she leaned against the wall, tilting her head until it touched brick.

Remaining there for five long minutes, she waited for tears to dry and emotions to equilibrate. When they finally did, she returned to the kitchen, slowly opening the door.

"Miz Warren! Are you all right?"

It was Billie, standing in the doorway, holding a fresh tray of champagne.

"I was looking for Dan in the yard and stumbled over the shrubbery. I'm going to my room to clean up and change clothes."

She grabbed a glass of champagne and exited with no further explanation. Halfway down the hall, she drained the glass and turned around, suddenly determined to face Dan and force him to explain his actions. She spotted him across the room talking with Robert Baker. Dan saw her at the same moment.

Angrily rolling his eyes, he started through the crowded room toward her. "My wife tripped in the garden," he explained to a guest in his path.

When he reached her, the party had suddenly gone ghostly quiet, all eyes on the young couple. The incessant ringing of the front doorbell interrupted their studied voyeurism. As one, they turned to see who was demanding entrance to the party at this late hour. Billie squirmed through the mass of people, making her way to the door.

"Hold your horses," she said. "I'm coming."

As Billie threw open the door, she and the guests emitted a communal gasp. It was Detective Vince Blakeman, dressed in navy blue polyester pants and his best plaid sports coat. Tumbling face-first onto the floor, he shattered the half-empty bottle of Jack Daniel's clutched beneath his arm. As everyone watched, their mouths agape, he sprawled in a heap, bourbon seeping onto an expensive rug.

Chapter 18

Cynthia pulled away from Dan and pushed through the crowded room, the shock of seeing Vince, lying drunk in her foyer, more than her already shattered confidence could take. Mixed feelings darkened her face as she stared down at the floor. Behind her, Dan whispered apologies to curious guests, crowding closer for a better look.

When she knelt and pressed her finger against his neck, a mighty snort informed her, without need to feel his pulse, he was only inebriated and not hurt. Robert Baker touched her shoulder and their shared glance told them both all they needed to know. Nudging her aside, he got his shoulder beneath Vince's arm and hoisted him off the floor, dragging him to the kitchen and into a chair. For privacy, Billie shut the door behind them.

"Miz Warren, if you don't mind me saying so, you look like hell. Why don't you go get yourself cleaned up? I'll take care of this gentleman."

"Do as she says, Cyndi," Baker said, leading her to the side door. "Get cleaned up. I'll help Billie."

"There's something I have to do first."

Wrenching free of his grasp, she opened the kitchen door. Baker called after her and she stopped in the doorway.

"I can't leave Dan in there alone, looking like a fool."

She grinned when Baker said, "You can't stop an avalanche."

Sticking her head into the living room, she raised her arms, momentarily muting the noise.

"Folks, I'm fine. Thought I heard a prowler in the back yard. I tripped on a bush and made a mess of my dress." When she laughed at her own little joke, a nervous titter began to circulate through the party. "The prowler was just our neighbor, having some fun of his own. Billie and Robert are cleaning him up before his wife finds out. Please excuse me and enjoy the party while I clean up a bit myself."

Nervous laughter dissolved into relieved applause. On her way out the door, she caught a glimpse of Dan, smiling confidently, again in control of the situation following her slightly stilted explanation. When she returned twenty minutes later wearing a different dress, she found the decibel level even higher than before, as Billie had wisely dispensed extra bottles of champagne.

Robert Baker, after spotting her, sidestepped his own wife and their circle of friends. Easing through the guests, he grasped her hand and squeezed.

"What's this all about?"

Standing on her tiptoes, she gave him a brotherly peck on the lips. "Next time we have two free hours and a nice bottle of chardonnay, I'll explain."

With a wink, she pulled away from his insistent grasp, joining Dan and a throng of admiring guests.

❧

Because of the extra champagne, the party ended later than expected. When it did, Cynthia pushed Billie out the door, ordering her not to return until much later. After heading straight to the bathroom, she brushed her teeth and washed her face. Slipping one of Dan's tee-shirts over her head, she didn't bother with her lacy negligee. She found Dan waiting in bed.

Contrary to her fears, he didn't seem angry. When she crawled in beside him he even attempted a half-hearted smile.

"Cyn, I'm sorry."

Surprised by the unexpected apology, she pulled him closer, cradling him in her arms.

"Don't be sorry. I'm the one who should be sorry."

"No. I have a confession."

Suddenly fearful he was about to tell her something devastating, she pulled away, instantly imagining the admission of an affair, or maybe worse.

"What do you mean a confession?"

Nodding, he said, "I know you'll think I'm a monster when I tell you."

"Tell me what you've done," she said.

As if trying to recall the exact nuance to express the magnitude of his malfeasance, he paused before answering.

"Remember when I told you I had Dad give me his power of attorney?"

"Yes, to protect his assets and administer his affairs. At least until he accepted your mom's death."

"There's more to it than that."

"Like what?"

In a whisper, he said, "I got more than Dad's power of attorney. I had him ruled incompetent and made him my ward. I'm Dad's legal guardian."

Cynthia shook her head, trying to understand the full significance of his admission. "What does that mean?"

"It means I manipulated his situation to gain control of his affairs."

"But that's not so terrible. He couldn't take care of himself."

"That's the point. He could then, and he obviously can now."

"I don't see the problem. Just go back to court and have them dismiss you. Return your Dad's rights."

"Not so simple."

"You're a lawyer. What could be simpler?"

His sullen expression explained before his words had a chance. "I not only sold Dad's house, I also liquidated all his assets."

It was her turn to pause. After letting the ramifications of his story sink in, she said, "Then return the money."

Dan eyes lowered to the satin sheets and he slowly shook his head. "We don't have it anymore. I paid off the house with part of the money. The rest went into a business venture with some of the partners at the firm. There's no cash left."

Staring at him, stunned, she said, "Can't you sell your interest in the business venture?"

"Maybe for ten cents on the dollar. Real estate belly-flopped this past year, you know."

"I can't believe you spent all his money."

Anger, so apparent in his eyes since his father's disappearance, flashed anew. Turning away from her, he glared at the wall.

"I expected a full return on the investment. Besides, Dad has shown no signs until now of coming out of his malaise. And I did intend to take care of him as long as he lived."

"He's not that old, Dan. He might live ten, maybe twenty more years."

"He's an old man," Dan said, angrily. "He doesn't need the money anymore."

"He's your father, not a steer on his way to the slaughterhouse."

He faced her again and his anger bled away, this time replaced by guilt-laced pain.

"What'll I do? What can I do? Everyone will think I stole Dad's money. They're already talking behind my back at the office."

"You're being paranoid. No one thinks anything except you want to see your father returned home, safe and sound."

Like an errant gust of wind, the demented glint, present since his father's disappearance, returned to his eyes. Springing out of bed, he began pacing the bedroom floor, mumbling to himself.

"I've got to do something. I can't afford to let this continue."

Upset and anxious, Cynthia said, "Just call off the dogs. Let your father come home of his own accord. When he does, you can tell him the truth."

Vince awoke in a strange bed, his head throbbing and ears ringing like a recess bell. Two little giggling girls were staring at him.

"You're the policeman looking for Grandpa."

He massaged his throbbing temple and closed his eyes, not immediately recognizing the twins.

"I'm Vince. Who are you?"

"Trish. This is Emily and Sparky."

When she handed the squirming animal to him, he held on tight, grimacing as the black cocker puppy licked wet swaths across his mouth and nose. One of the little girls grabbed the playful puppy and put him on the floor. He ran out of the room, toenails rasping against wood.

"What's your last name, Trish?"

"Warren."

He failed to suppress a low moan at hearing the name. Continuing to massage his aching temples, he said, "I was afraid of that. Where are your mommy and daddy?"

"Still sleeping. Billie fixed breakfast and cleaned up the house from the party."

"Billie?"

"Yes," Emily said. "She helps Mommy."

Before he could ask another question, the two little girls said, "See you later, Vince."

They hurried out the door after the black cocker.

Vince slowly peeled the sheet away from his neck and peeked down at his chest. Realizing he still had on all of his clothes, except for coat and shoes, he felt an ounce, though only an ounce of relief.

It suddenly occurred to him that a large gap occupied much of his memory of the prior day. It wasn't all missing. Seared into his brain, surreal and painful, the humiliating encounter with Marla remained. He began to remember trying to kill the bottle of Jack Daniel's, and vaguely recalled driving alone to the party.

Finding himself fully dressed in one of their bedrooms chilled his neck like a shot of ice water. What had he done and what price would he ultimately have to pay for his actions, he wondered? Easing out of bed and limping into the bathroom, he searched the cabinets for a much-needed aspirin. Upon returning to the bedroom to search for his shoes and sports jacket, he came face-to-face with Billie. She was propped against the open doorway, staring at him as if he were a serial killer. Under her arm she held a silver serving tray.

"Had yourself quite a time last night, didn't you?"

Choosing to ignore her reproachful remark, he dropped to his hands and knees to search beneath the bed for his shoes.

"Wish I could remember it, if I did. How did I end up here?"

"Me and Mr. Baker drug you in here and threw you in bed."

"Is Mr. Warren angry?"

Billie snickered. "Oh he forgot all about you soon as we carted you out of the room. Mrs. Warren just told everyone you were a drunken neighbor."

"He doesn't know I'm here?"

"No, and if I was you, I'd pack my butt on out before he gets up and you refresh his memory about your grand entrance to the party last night."

Again he moaned and rubbed his head. "You wouldn't happen to know where I can find my shoes and coat?"

"Maybe," she said. "What's it worth to you?"

"Look, I'm in no mood for games. Sorry for whatever I did last night, but I could lose my job if I don't get out of here."

Beginning to feel sorry for him, and perceiving correctly she'd ribbed him enough, she poured coffee from a carafe on the nightstand, handing him the cup.

"You just relax. After last night, those two won't be up for at least another hour. Your shoes and coat are in the closet," she said, pointing.

The coffee tasted like manna from heaven. Billie waited patiently until he'd finished it, and then poured him another cup. She watched as he retrieved his sports coat and shoes from the closet. When he finished dressing, he returned the empty cup and hurried from the bedroom, carefully looking both ways before entering the hall.

Billie followed him. At the front door, he crooked his finger, still having some difficulty functioning properly.

"Billie, right?"

With a grin, the big woman nodded.

"Thanks, Billie," he said. "I owe you."

On his way home, he passed a florist, continuing for half a block down the road before slapping the dash and wheeling around in the deserted street. He returned to the almost empty shop where a surprised clerk sold him two dozen roses. With blurry eyes and palsied hand, he scrawled two message cards. With what was left of yesterday's lunch threatening to erupt from his stomach, he could only acknowledge the florist's thanks with a weak grunt as he rushed for the door.

Upon reaching his apartment, he hurried into the bedroom and collapsed on the bed, remaining under the covers for the rest of the weekend, his thoughts plying fitfully between painful reality and troubled dreams.

Chapter 19

Hazy moonlight, filtering through wispy cloud cover, lightened the eastern Oklahoma sky. Leaning against the fender of Mike's Cadillac, John and Attie held hands, listening to the low diesel drone of Big Al's wrecker coming up the hill. Norma waited nearby, arm around her short husband's shoulder. Even in dim light, no one could miss her tears that mingled with many freckles, creating unique patterns on her face. Staring at the pavement with a frustrated frown, Mike curled strands of dark hair between nervous fingers.

Far down the hill, truck lights appeared through the trees, laboring up steep pavement with the yellow RV behind it. When Big Al reached them, hydraulic brakes screeched as he eased two vehicles behind Mike's Cadillac. Holding their collective breath, they watched as he exited the wrecker and joined them beside the white Cadillac.

Seeing he was indeed alone, Mike's frown changed to a grin and he rushed over to shake his hand.

"Al, we thought they had you back there."

"Thought so too," Big Al said. "Head trooper turned out to be my nephew." Chuckling, he scratched his stubbly chin. "Said the RV must be my daughter's—his cousin's—since he remembered seeing one like it years ago."

Norma said, "He believed your story?"

"Believe it, hell! He spouted it out to the other po-lice fore I got a word out of my mouth."

"Then what took you so long," Mike asked, glancing at his watch. "We've been worried sick."

"Drank coffee with the boys and swapped a few lies. Didn't want to appear too anxious, you know." He chuckled again.

Attie smiled. "What's so funny?"

"Them boys were all leaning up against the RV. Hope the paint's dry. If not, their wives are gonna get a big surprise when they see yellow paint streaked all over those nice khaki uniforms."

Norma began to giggle and Attie joined in, the five conspirators howling with moon-mad laughter. When Attie put her arms around the big mechanic's neck, even the Oklahoma darkness failed to hide his blush."

"Thanks, Big Al," she said.

"My pleasure, Attie."

When she let go of him, she hugged Mike and Norma, her laughter turning into tears. "Don't know how we can ever thank you," she said, finally pulling away.

"We're gonna miss you two," Norma said.

"We'll visit again when this whole mess is settled," John said. "It's not the end of the world."

Pregnant silence followed his pronouncement. Finally, Big Al slapped his shoulder and pointed up the hill.

"This here road goes up over the mountains, eventually into Arkansas. Ain't got no name, so all I can tell you is to keep heading east till you hit Arkansas blacktop. Might be kinda dangerous, so be real careful. Sorry to send you this way, but it's probably the only road to Arkansas without a roadblock."

"Thanks, Big Al," John said. "We better go before a stray patrol car decides to take a moonlight drive to the Arkansas border."

"Wouldn't worry about it on a night like this," Big Al said. "Be sure and send us a postcard when you get settled down."

"We'll do more than that," John said.

"Wish I could do more," Big Al said. "A man's got rights. Don't matter how old he is. God bless you, you hear?"

Without speaking another word, the big man turned away and walked back toward his truck. After one last hug and handshake, Mike and Norma followed him. John and Attie watched the wrecker and Mike's Caddie turn around on the narrow road, their taillights disappearing beyond a distant bend. Attie patted the RV's hood, opened its door and went inside. After a last glance at the cloudy sky, John followed her.

With tires slipping in the mud, she pulled away from the curb. Mud splattering up from the road soon covered the windshield and headlights, diminishing their visibility. Attie pumped the washer button until it ran dry as winding dirt road replaced moderately steep Oklahoma blacktop. After ten miles, the slippery byway showed no signs of flattening.

Lost in thought, Attie finally said, "I'll miss them."

"So will I, and if you don't keep your eyes on the road, we may see them again sooner than we'd like."

Attie tapped the brakes at John's concerned tone, involuntarily sending the RV's nose into a lateral slide toward the right-hand ditch.

"Steady, now. Straighten her up, but don't stop," he warned. "You'll stick us for sure."

Riveting Attie's attention and forcing her to plant both hands firmly on the wheel, she regained control as the big RV shimmied first to the right and then the left.

"Looks bad, John."

His attention was concentrated on the narrow strip of muddy road illuminated by dull headlight glow. Reaching across the console, he touched her shoulder.

"Easy, Attie," he said softly. "You're doing just

fine."

For the second time that night rain began to fall, first slowly, and then in ever-increasing waves. Mud, thrown by front wheels, impeded the windshield wipers clacking against window frame, further obstructing their vision. Attie remained silent as she feathered the throttle and gingerly twirled the wheel to stay centered in the road. The RV began to fishtail.

"Almost there," he said. "It's only a hundred feet or so to the crest."

Too engrossed with the muddy road to respond to his subliminal exhortations, she didn't answer. Unable to do anything else, he kept up a constant, encouraging banter. As they neared what appeared the crest of the hill, both held their breath. Unfortunately, it wasn't the crest they'd reached. After flattening briefly, the road continued, ever-more-steeply, into rainy gloom.

By now John's mouth was dry, his throat lumpy. "False alarm," he said.

Attie maintained even pressure on the throttle and a delicate touch on the wheel. Ten frantic minutes passed before the road flattened enough to stop the RV. Switching off the engine, she let go of the wheel and closed her eyes. When she glanced up at John, she found him staring back at her, smiling.

"Mario Andretti's got nothing on you."

Attie leaned across the console and hugged him.

"We made it," she said.

As the RV slowly slid backwards, its metallic groan interrupted their moment of elation. "Not yet," John said. "Start the engine. Hurry!"

Spinning its wheels in the mud for one heart-stopping moment, the vehicle finally regained traction, moving slowly up the narrow road.

Unable to mask his concern, he said, "Still haven't reached the top. Have to keep going."

Attie needed no prompting. Though she tried centering the RV in the road, she could barely see beyond its stubby hood through thick and cloying fog.

"We're losing traction and still going uphill," she said, voice cracking.

"Keep going. Far as you can. I'll walk the rest of the way and get help."

His suggestion, at best, seemed futile. Still, there was little else to do except continue up the slick grade. This they did, slowly, slipping and sliding. Before long, even that became impossible. Despite Attie's attempts, the RV sputtered to a halt and began sliding, slowly at first, back down the mountain road. Desperately, she gunned the engine, spinning wheels, trying to stop their backward momentum. It didn't help and they continued losing traction. When the rear end spun sideways, John slammed his foot against the floorboard as they slipped into the ditch in a sickening lurch.

Canted at an odd angle, the RV rocked once and stopped dead in the ditch. Unlatching his shoulder harness, he stumbled to the door, grabbing his jacket along the way. When he stepped outside the RV, he realized he'd made a mistake. It was dangling and canted at an odd angle, and even in foggy darkness he sensed the big vehicle was near the edge of the narrow mountain road, its left rear wheel two feet lower than its right. Cautiously, he stepped from the ramp, probing for solid ground. Finding none, he stepped down anyway. A stupid mistake, he instantly learned.

Mud in the ditch immediately sucked up his foot. When he yanked upward to free himself, he lost his balance, and his grip on the door, sliding into sticky muck, not stopping until he'd rolled ten feet down the hill. He found himself hopelessly mired in glue-like mud. Lightning flashed and thunder sounded nearby. A steady rain began to fall. Attie heard his surprised cry and rushed to the door of the RV.

"John. Where are you?"

"Down here."

"You okay?"

"Stuck against a rock and it's too slick to crawl back uphill."

"I'm coming."

"No," he shouted. "Then we'll both be stuck. Get a rope from the tool chest. Tie it to the steering wheel and throw me the other end."

Attie hurried to the back of the RV and began searching through the tools, finding the utility tow rope. Following his instructions, she returned to the open door.

"Where are you? I can't see you."

Even through murky fog, dim light from the RV's open door clearly silhouetted Attie's rain-soaked image.

"Directly below you, about ten feet. Give the rope a good toss and stand back."

She threw the rope, landing it just two feet from his grasp. Despite his efforts, he found he couldn't climb the slick incline far enough to reach the dangling lifeline.

Out of breath and nearly exhausted, he called hoarsely, "Any slack on the other end?"

"Just a little. Stay there. Be right back."

Even in his pressing predicament, he had to smile. "I'm going nowhere," he said to himself.

Propped against a big rock, he waited for her to re-tie the rope to the steering wheel. A flash of yellow lighted the foggy western sky, followed by a nearby clap of thunder and an even heavier downpour. Attie shouted from the door.

"Here it comes."

Wet rope dropped from the RV, striking him in the face. Thinking she'd missed, she pulled it back toward her. John made a diving grab and held on to the slippery line.

"Attie, I have it. Let me get a grip."

Barely able to hear his voice above wind and

pounding rain, she reeled in the wet rope. She tossed it again, this time connecting with the hapless John and waiting until his shout and tug signaled he'd tied it around his waist.

Bracing against the door frame, she pulled. John reached the door ten grueling minutes later. Attie grabbed his shoulders, yanking him into the RV. She collapsed on top of him as he flopped in a muddy pile on the floor.

When her labored gasps subsided, she said, "What now?"

"Wait until morning so we can see what we're doing. And hope the police aren't fool enough to search this road on a night like this."

For moments they lay there, coated with thick brown mud. Then Attie began to chuckle, and despite their tense situation, they both were rolling in laughter on the floor.

Chapter 20

Bright sunlight shining in through the RV's un-shaded window awakened John early the next morning. Groggy, and still exhausted, he found himself lying on the floor with Attie sprawled unceremoniously on top of him. Dried mud caked them both. Something pecking on the window instantly attracted his attention. He rubbed his crusty eyes and craned his head up at the window. It was cocked at an absurd angle, and it took a minute for him to remember why.

"Hello," someone said from outside the RV. "Is anyone in there?"

Recalling the muddy accident of the night before, he briefly closed his eyes. Attie was still not awake and someone, possibly the Oklahoma State Police, had found them. Gently pushing her off his chest, he gingerly extricated himself from the wall. When he attempted to stand, he slipped on the canted floor, crashing into a cabinet with a bang.

"John . . ."

"It's all right. I just slipped a little."

Following a moment of confusion, she rubbed her own mud-crusted eyes and glanced around the RV. Again, a man's voice called from outside the window.

"Are you all right in there?"

Glancing first at Attie, John said, "We're fine. Had

an accident last night and slid into the ditch."

"Need some help?"

"We can't get out the door," John said, remembering their predicament.

"Hang on. I'll climb up on the roof and give you a hand."

They waited as the unknown person went to the ladder in back, listening intently as he crawled across the roof, making his way to the side door facing the drop off.

"This could be the end of the road, Attie."

"Not on your life, old man. If it's the police, I'll go back to Tulsa with you."

"And bust me out of the old folk's home?"

"With chisel and crowbar, if I have to."

"Hey in there," the man called. "Give me your hand and I'll lift you out."

Resounding with the same country twang as Mike, Norma and Big Al, the voice on the roof was strangely friendly and reassuring. John and Attie glanced up and saw a big hairy arm reaching into the window. Red flannel instead of khaki, thankfully, draped the arm. John helped Attie to her feet and guided her to the door where the unidentified man pulled her up to the roof as easily as lifting a baby from its crib. When John inched out the door, he caught a glimpse of the man's curly red hair and ruddy face.

"Grab hold," the smiling man said, extending a muscular arm.

With one easy motion, he lifted him out the window, up to the radically canted roof. Dressed in blue jeans and bright flannel shirt, their rescuer looked like an overgrown Huck Finn. Instead of Huck, it was Hulk.

"Name's Hulk," he said, extending his meaty hand in John's direction.

"You don't know how glad we are to see you, Mr. Hulk," John said. He winked at Attie, still precariously clutching the roof's chrome luggage rack. "I'm John Warren and this is Attie Johnson."

"Pleased to make your acquaintance," the man said. "Ain't Mr. Hulk, though, it's just Hulk."

"We thought you were the Oklahoma State Police," Attie said.

"No way," Hulk said. "You're five miles into Arkansas."

After climbing down from the roof of the RV and brushing off as best they could, John and Attie could only stare. Mud streaked Big Al's yellow paint job and the RV's two left wheels were firmly planted in the ditch. Gone was rain and fluffy cumulus clouds, replaced by sunlight and clear blue Arkansas sky. From their vantage at the top of a gently-rounded mountain, they could see fifty miles in every direction. Below the RV, a steep cliff of solid chert plunged several hundred feet, down to a wooded valley, far below.

Behind them, on the hood of a blue Ford pickup, sat an attractive young woman, about the age of the man who'd rescued them. A large camper occupied the truck bed. From the travel decals on its tan corrugated surface, the couple appeared to be on permanent vacation. A large bass boat on a trailer, attached to the rear of the camper, reinforced this observation.

"That's my wife, Lillie Mae," Hulk said, pointing.

John and Attie smiled and waved. "Thanks for helping us out of the RV, Hulk. Now if you could just get us off the ledge."

John expected no positive response to his flippant statement. Hulk, however, glanced at the big RV as if sizing up that very possibility.

He finally said, "I can do it."

"You have a tow truck hidden in the trees somewhere?" John asked, disbelieving.

"No, but I got a tow rope. I'll just jerk you outa that hole."

Without waiting for John to scoff at his offer, he headed to his pickup for the rope. On hands and knees, he attached the line to the towing connection on the RV's frame. Spitting on his oversized palms, he disengaged the boat trailer from back of his camper and attached the other end to his truck.

"One of you is gonna have to get back in and drive it out of the ditch," Hulk said.

John started immediately for the ladder at the back of the RV. Attie stopped him, grabbing his arm.

"No you don't. I brought us this far. If anyone's going to drive Ol' Betsy off that ledge, it's going to be me."

John grinned and raised both hands into the air. "I wouldn't have it any other way."

Hulk helped Attie back into the RV. "Put it in drive and rest your foot on the gas. Don't spin the wheels. You feel it starting to inch outa the ditch when I jerk it, give it a little. Just don't let them back wheels break loose," he said, wagging his finger at her.

Hulk climbed down and hurried to the wheel of his camper. John waved his arm and said, "What can I do?"

"Stay outa the way," he said.

He did just that, moving to the far side of the road. Lillie Mae, Hulk's diminutive wife, joined him. She was small as Hulk was large, her face fresh, and blonde hair in sharp contrast with Hulk's red mane. Brushing curly-blonde hair out of her big blue eyes, she smiled at John and grabbed his elbow, directing him further off the road.

"Hulk gets a goin', that camper's gonna be all over the place," she said with an accent far sharper than her husband's. "Better steer way clear."

"You don't think the RV will turn over, do you?" John asked, suddenly very concerned.

Lillie Mae shook her head. "Ain't no better driver in Arkansas than Hulk. He can't get her outa there, no one can."

"That's good to know, I guess," he said.

As they watched, Attie cranked the RV's engine and Hulk did the same with the camper, backing until he had about ten feet of slack in the rope. Moving forward slowly, he tested the tautness, barely letting the camper's rear tires break loose as the engine strained against the RV's weight.

Every time the camper moved forward, Attie applied gas. As she did, its rear wheels slipped on loose rock and the RV began creeping sideways. It crept toward the drop-off and not the road. John held his breath, seriously contemplating running up to Hulk's truck and aborting the attempt. Again, Lillie Mae grabbed his arm.

"Give him a chance."

Something in her sweet country voice made him do just that. Backing away from the road, he folded his arms and watched. Again, Hulk backed toward the RV. This time, instead of creeping forward, he gunned the engine. Like a giant rubber band, the slack in the rope popped and disappeared, yanking the RV, lifting its front wheels physically off the ground. This time, Hulk reversed the engine, moving only two feet before jamming the gears into forward, again popping slack from the rope.

Back, forward, back, forward; the maneuver became almost a single fluid motion. Getting the feel for what Hulk was trying to do, Attie furiously worked the gas pedal, gunning the engine when Hulk jerked forward, letting off when he went back. The RV jumped and bumped and began to come loose from the embankment. In one last fluid effort, Hulk launched the truck into a series of reverse and forward motions, so fast it seemed the camper was going in both directions at once.

With a crunch of crushing rock and lurching protest of six tons of combined steel, the RV seemed to bend in the middle. Its rear tires popped off the rock a distance of at least three feet, and the massive vehicle pulled free of its fetters, spinning wildly on the gravel, tossing stone and mud for a frenzied moment before coming to a halt on the flat roadbed.

Attie switched off the RV's engine and exited the door, a mile-wide grin on her face. John looked at Lillie Mae in amazement.

"I wouldn't have believed it."

Meeting Hulk halfway out of his camper, Attie shook his hand. He gave her a smiling thumbs-up and continued past her to detach the rope from the RV. After performing the same task on the camper, he grabbed Attie's arm and escorted her to the spot where John and Lillie Mae waited by the side of the road.

Shaking his hand, John said, "I wouldn't have believed it possible if I hadn't seen it with my own eyes."

"Seen it done once. Wasn't sure it would work with that big bus, though."

"Hulk, you're a genius," John said.

"Ain't nobody ever called me that before," Hulk said with a satisfied grin. "Where you folks headed?"

John glanced back down the steep winding road they'd so recently traversed and said, "Hot Springs."

"Well you ain't gonna make it today."

Visibly disturbed, Attie asked, "What's wrong?"

"You got a hole in your gas tank and its leaking purty fast."

Attie's hand went instantly to her mouth, her questioning gaze to John.

"What will we do?"

Hulk answered the question before John, confused as Attie, had a chance to comment.

"We're camped right down the road a bit. You got enough gas to make it in the big bus. When we get there, you folks can relax and I'll fix the tank for you."

"You can do that?" John said, still confused.

"You bet he can," Lillie Mae said. "Hulk's got welding equipment and tools back at camp. Fix you up in no time. You can camp the night with us and head for Hot Springs when you feel like it."

"We're most grateful," Attie said.

"Then let's get it on," Hulk said, raising his thumb skyward again. "If we finish soon enough, we can get in some river fishin' before sundown. You game, Pops?"

"Lead the way," John said.

They followed the young couple, over the crest to a spot near the top of the weathered mountain range. Complete with switchbacks, u-turns and blind chutes, the flattened roadbed, still muddy from the recent rain, traversed an ancient hogback ridge. In places, sheer drop-offs occupied both sides of the narrow road. They felt like nineteenth century ridge runners thrown back in time to a simpler existence.

Old oaks, pine trees and bare rock cuts punctuated the short trip. After ten miles of slow going, Hulk's blinker signaled he intended to make a right turn. For a moment, both John and Attie studied the thick foliage, wondering where and how he intended to turn off the road. After a perfunctory blink of his brake lights, he disappeared into the trees.

When Attie reached the place where his camper had vanished, she found an even narrower road. Scraping muddy yellow paint on both sides of the RV, she negotiated the turn and immediately started downhill on a fairly steep grade. Only gravel, kicked up by Hulk's camper, and the absence of an intersecting road, told them they were on the right path. The narrow trail was like a tunnel through the thick cover of trees, becoming even narrower as they descended the steep road.

"Hope Hulk knows where he's going," John said. "No place to turn around and we sure can't back out of here."

After five minutes, they saw that Hulk did indeed

know where he was going. A clearing suddenly appeared through the trees and the RV's nose leveled. Hulk and Lillie Mae's camper was already parked. With huge waving arms, he directed Attie to a flat parking place beside his truck. When they got out of the RV and looked around, they realized they had somehow stumbled on a little Shangri-La hidden deep in the mountainous backwoods of western Arkansas.

Chapter 21

Shangri-La indeed! Behind them a sheer limestone cliff jutted straight into the stratosphere, a distance of at least two hundred feet. Making a gentle crescent, a solid wall of rock curved around, enclosing a clearing on two sides. Steady sun had replaced the rain, and the day had grown warm and humid. Hollowed back into the mountain, the resultant cave-like indention in the cliff emanated a sudden abundance of refrigerated air, forming a naturally air-conditioned amphitheater.

Down the hill from the camp a bit, a meandering river flowed slowly past. Eons before, the river had gouged out a path through a steep-walled valley. Now, with modulating shades of azure and emerald, the still water contrasted with greens and earth tones of surrounding trees and rock ledges. Together, they sparkled in refracted light of the valley floor. A blue heron, wading in shallow water, didn't seem to notice them.

"Gorgeous, absolutely gorgeous," Attie exclaimed.

"It is that," Hulk said as he crawled beneath the RV with a pan to catch the gas still dripping from the tank. "That'll hold it till we can patch the tear."

John asked, "How in the world did you ever find this place?"

Simultaneously, Hulk and Lillie Mae glanced at

each other. A flush of red swept up his neck, fading abundant freckles on his face. Lillie Mae grinned, stood on her tiptoes and kissed her blushing husband.

"Hulk was looking for a place off the main road to do a little parking," she said.

"Lillie Mae, you didn't have to tell them that," Hulk said, even more flustered.

She laughed and said, "It's true, though."

Hulk wrapped his big arm around her neck and pretended to thump her head. Lillie Mae elbowed him in the stomach and wrenched away. Attie and John watched, disconcerted, as the young couple chased off down the hill toward the river. When Hulk caught Lillie Mae beneath a giant pine, they embraced passionately, like anxious newlyweds. After watching them a moment, John squeezed Attie's hand and kissed her.

Attie said, "Feeling a little frisky, old man?"

"Must be the mountain air," he said, pulling her toward him.

Imitating Lillie Mae, Attie cuffed him playfully across the cheek, turned and ran for the RV. With old legs and teenage heart, he chased after her, huffing when she let him catch her at the door of the RV.

❦

After showering and changing into fresh clothes, John and Attie spent the remainder of the morning exploring rocky crevices and wooded tracts of their newly found mountain hideaway. Hulk rummaged around camp, setting up lawn chairs, tables and a portable generator. Finally, he backed his boat down the slight incline and set it in the river. At noon, Lillie Mae called them from the gentle clearing below.

"I got some sandwiches ready. Let's eat."

They made their way back down the trail, hand-in-hand. When they reached the clearing, they found a portable picnic table. Lillie Mae had already topped it with cold cuts, white bread, salad dressing and a large bowl of potato chips. Hulk signaled them to help themselves. Sitting on boulders overlooking the river, they did just that.

Between bites, John said, "How long have you been married?"

"Five years," Lillie Mae said. "Right out of high school."

Attie asked, "Live around here now?"

"Just up the road, near Conway. Hulk's got a welding shop there."

"Come here every chance we get," he said, smiling at Lillie Mae. "It's kind of our special spot."

"It is a special place, and so peaceful," Attie said.

Hulk and Lillie Mae beamed at the compliment. Throughout the light lunch, they ate while holding hands with each other. Hulk dwarfed Lillie Mae, but exacted her every wish like a faithful servant. It was obvious, almost embarrassingly so, that they were very much in love. Between bites, they would kiss like enamored teenagers, or Lillie Mae would pinch Hulk in an embarrassing spot, causing his big face to turn instantly red. Attie and John pretended not to notice.

"We never caught your last name," John said, interrupting their mutual groping.

"Dancer," Lillie Mae said, proudly.

"How did you come by your nickname? John asked.

"From the cartoon."

"The Incredible Hulk," Lillie Mae said.

Attie grinned. "You're certainly not green."

"But he's big and beefy," Lillie Mae said, trying, but failing, to extend her tiny hands around his huge biceps.

"Any children?" asked John.

Hulk's blush and Lillie Mae's impish grin faded as one. Lillie Mae's pretty features contorted into a grimace. Without answering, she pushed away from the table and hurried to the camper, slamming the door behind her with a resounding thud. John could only sit with his mouth open, mindful of Attie's fingernails digging into the back of his hand. Reacting to the pallid blankness of Hulk's expression, Attie reached across the table and touched the young man's wrist.

"We're sorry. Why don't you go see about her?"

Blinking once, he nodded and got up from the table. When he disappeared into the camper, John glanced at Attie.

"Did I stick my foot in my mouth?"

"Yes, though I'll bet you're not the first."

Slowly unwinding his lanky limbs from beneath the table, he gazed at the camper. "Shall I knock on the door and apologize?"

Attie held up her hand in a halting motion. "Let's just pretend nothing happened. If and when they want to tell us about it, they will."

They went about their business, Attie straightening the RV, John washing mud off its new yellow paint job with a bucket of water from the river. An hour later, Hulk and Lillie Mae exited the camper, both in a much lighter frame of mind than before. Lillie Mae smiled at John as she brushed past him on her way into the RV to help Attie. Hulk sauntered up with a friendly grin on his Huck Finn face, admiring the older man's work with the bucket and sponge.

"Looks a sight better than it did this morning when I pulled you out of the ditch," he said, his lilting Arkansas twang reverberating off canyon walls. "Are you and Attie hippies?"

John failed to catch the ramification of Hulk's question. Then, remembering sixties graffiti on the RV, he realized he was completely serious.

"There were no hippies in the forties." Seeing Hulk's confusion, he added, "A long story goes along with the paint job. I'll tell it to you when we both have a few hours to spare."

Thankfully changing the subject, Hulk said, "Know

anything about engines?"

Remembering his failed prognosis of the RV's overheating problem, he grinned and said, "Not much, but I'm game to look. What's the problem?"

"My truck has a funny noise under the hood."

"Let's check it out," John said, motioning Hulk to follow him. "Maybe we can get a handle on it before dark."

John spent the rest of the afternoon helping Hulk with various tasks around the campsite. Together, they stripped down, cleaned and rebuilt the truck's carburetor, and cut a load of firewood. Lillie Mae and Attie relaxed in lawn chairs, chatting like school girls.

The two couples watched the sun relinquish its command of the heavens to a big yellow moon, and thousands of glittering stars, a river loon's mournful cry punctuating the darkness. Attie and Lillie Mae prepared a spicy hot pot of chili and beans. Back-dropped by a chorus of frogs and crickets, they savored the chili, served up with cornbread, and some of John's large stash of choc beer. In addition to frogs and crickets, they heard an occasional hoot of owl, howl of wolf or snarl of bobcat tracking its luckless prey. No traffic noise, or any human sound, disturbed the tranquility.

Comforting darkness, piquant chili and the pacifying effect of strong beer combined to loosen their tongues. Coaxed by Attie, Lillie Mae and especially Hulk, John told several amusing vignettes from his youth.

Hulk finally asked, "John, were you in the war?"

After hesitating a moment, he said, "Yes, I was."

"Then tell us a war story," Hulk goaded.

Poignant memories flooded John's mind and he smiled sadly, unconsciously grinding his toe against an empty cardboard carton in front of him.

Hulk prompted, "We're you in the Battle of the

Bulge?"

Waves of nostalgia crested his bow and he said, "Wasn't supposed to be, but I was."

"Please," Lillie Mae said. "Tell us."

He did, beginning slowly, and then warming to the tale. "The Bulge was Hitler's last attempt to turn back the advancing Allies. For a month and a half, the Battle lasted, called the 'Bulge' because Germans failed to break through the line, only succeeding in bending it. I was a radio man in the signal corp. One night, an old colonel appeared at the communications tent, needing to relay a message to Patton. Since we were out of direct radio communication with the main force, he decided to deliver it in person and conscripted me to drive the jeep for him.

"The night turned bitterly cold. Snow had fallen for days, piled high on both sides of the road. Continuing night and day, the line of battle had spread out many miles, constantly moving, like an angry sidewinder. When sun came up the following morning, we realized we had somehow crossed the line.

"Germans, besides many other things, were excellent soldiers. We found ourselves caught, along with an advancing column of American infantrymen, in a crossfire ambush. Fresh from the States, our boys were young, mostly teenagers. Barely trained, none had ever seen a German, much less been under fire.

"Finding yourself caught in the middle of a firefight is like walking a railroad track at night. Hearing the loud blast of a whistle behind you, you turn and stare into the lights of the monstrosity, twenty feet away, and bearing down on you—the remains of your best friend already chewed up beneath its wheels.

"When the attack began, the noise was frightening and extreme—beyond imagination for the uninitiated. Along with gunfire and violent explosions, steel, dirt and stone whistled randomly around our heads. Our boys tossed their rifles and ran for cover. German marksmen began dropping them in their tracks. Blood was running in the ditches, staining the snow crimson, when we reached the center of the column. Unarmed, the old colonel jumped from the jeep and ran directly into the path of the retreating GIs."

"Thrusting rifle after rifle back into the hands of those child soldiers, he admonished them to hold their ground. Around us, the battlefield was alive with explosions, hot lead and wounded soldiers screaming for help. A mortar round exploded near the jeep, spraying me with dirt and shrapnel. When I wiped my face, the blood on my hand wasn't my own.

"Any one of a hundred Hun marksmen could have dropped the colonel. None did. Maybe they were awed by his bravery and coolness under fire. With confused soldiers dying all around him, he coursed the length of that bloody road, exhorting them to turn and fight. One-by-one their youth dissolved in a mire of smoke and torn flesh, and they became men in the hot cauldron of battle. Turning around, they fought, hanging on until reinforcements arrived."

John grew silent and Attie squeezed his hand, feeling the intensity of his pain. Finally he chuckled and it drew into a hoarse laugh.

"Know what's funny?" His rapt audience shook their head without answering. "I remember the Colonel as old, but he was probably no more than forty. Forty years younger than I am now, and I still think of him as an old man. I can't remember his name, and I don't suppose you'll ever read about him in any history book, but he was a true American hero."

Suddenly aware of frogs, crickets and distant owls, John realized no one had spoken for an interminable period. When she saw he'd finished the story, Lillie Mae put her arms around his shoulder like a mother comforting a child. Hulk remained silent, torn by his own conflicting emotions.

Having nothing else to say, the young couple

simply said goodnight, leaving John and Attie alone beneath a yellow moon and sparkling stars. He hugged Attie, drawing for a moment on her strength before speaking.

"In all these years, I've never told that story to another soul."

Attie patted his shoulder and said, "Some of us hold painful memories inside till the day we die. It's good you let one of yours go."

Chapter 22

Awakened from an early morning Technicolor dream, John rolled over in bed. Groggily aware of an incessant tap-tap-tapping outside the RV's bedroom window, he opened his eyes enough to see his watch dial. When he cracked the curtain, Hulk's smiling face, his freckled nose pressed against the window pane, stared back at him. It was still dark outside.

Remembering their planned fishing trip, he eased out of bed and slipped on his pants and shoes, still buttoning his shirt as he exited the door. Hulk greeted him with an ingratiating smile and a steaming mug of coffee. With a morose frown, he accepted both.

"When you said fishing, I didn't realize you meant in the middle of the night," he said, sipping the hot coffee.

"Need to be on the river before first light. Don't want to spook the fish," Hulk explained.

Too early for conversation, John simply nodded. After helping Hulk with the gear, he followed him down the winding path to the river. First morning light filtering into the valley, shined through fog wafting up from the river's tranquil surface, turning its algae-covered cobbles a dull gray. Attracted by insects that had fallen into shallow water, schools of minnows sent interfering ripples against the boat's bow. Hulk lifted the ice chest into the boat, along with rods, reels and fishing tackle. After stepping over the gunwale, he gave John a hand.

The electric trolling motor powered the craft silently away from the bank, propelling it toward the center of the river. In the hazy distance, a beaver's burrow dammed the flow of water. This, along with slow current resulting from a meander in the river, had formed a wide, lake-like environment. When sun crested over sheer rock ledges, John stared up, in awe of their physical setting, at the imposing walls enclosing them.

Limestone cliffs, draped in full bloom of early spring greenery, jutted high into a cloudless sky. Their camp seemed the only evidence of human presence in the lush valley. A large bass, breaking the water's surface, returned him to reality, and the much younger man's grinning face.

Hulk said, "It's really something, ain't it?"

"Yes, it's like we're the only humans to have ever visited."

"That we're not. They's arrowheads all along the river and corncobs in the cliff hollows. Indians lived here hundreds of years before Columbus left Spain."

"What about now?"

"This is National Forest land. Except for squirrels and other critters, no one lives here permanently."

Switching off the trolling motor, he let the bass boat drift lazily toward a brush pile near the opposite edge of the river-lake. Grabbing two rods, he handed one to John.

"I caught a six-pounder right over by that pile of brush just last week."

John hoisted the rod once or twice in his hand, getting the feel for the well-balanced implement.

"Feels great," he said. "I haven't fished in years."

"Don't like fishin'?"

"I love to fish. I just never seemed to have the

time."

Hulk grinned and flipped his silver lure into the water near the brush pile.

"There's always time to fish."

John hefted the rod again. Flipping his own lure into the water beside the brush pile, he slowly reeled it back toward him. Polished smoothness of the mechanical reel sent soothing sensations up his arm, directly to his brain. Within minutes, his neck and facial muscles began to relax, as if he were taking a warm bath.

Leaning back in the comfortable seat, he stretched his long legs, propping them idly against the footrest. Totally pacified by the mindless mechanical motion of casting the lure into water and reeling it back, he nearly lost his grip on the rod when a large fish snatched the bait. Grabbing it in both hands, he held on as the fish swam beneath a mass of submerged brush.

"Oh gosh!" he said. "That caught me by surprise."

Before he was able to coordinate brain and hand, the big fish disappeared beneath the brush pile, hopelessly tangling the lure around the submerged tree branch. Without commenting, Hulk grabbed the nylon line and cut it off with a quick swipe of his pocketknife.

"Sorry Hulk."

"Don't worry about it. I've lost so many lures in that brush that if I fished them all out, I could start my own tackle shop."

Reaching into his well-stocked tackle box, he removed another brightly-shining lure and proceeded to attach it to the nylon line on the end of John's rod. On his next cast, John got another bite. This time, he twisted his wrist and deftly set the hook, reeling in the fish like a professional.

"All right!" Hulk said, grinning broadly as he netted the fish and raised it into the boat. "It's a beaut."

"My, my, my," John said as glistening silver fins of a largemouth bass reflected light from early morning sun.

Removing his camera from his flannel shirt, Hulk motioned him to hold up the fish. He snapped a photo.

Pumped up like the winner of the Boston Marathon, John said, "What now?"

Returning the camera to his shirt pocket, Hulk searched his tackle box until he found a hand scale. Hooking it through the fish's mouth, he held it up, weighing it carefully.

"Three pounds, two ounces," he said.

While holding the big fish with both hands, he carefully lowered it back into cool river water and held it until it swam away.

"Catch it again another day. I got a trotline up the river apiece. We'll check it after lunch. Probably catch a mess of catfish for dinner tonight. Maybe just my opinion, but I think they's better eatin' than most any fish around."

"Hey, you won't get any arguments from me."

"Lillie Mae can cook them any way you like, fried, baked, barbecued, you name it. She's the best."

Totally relaxed, John placed his rod back in the boat, put his hands behind his head and reclined against the headrest, satisfied to watch Hulk fish awhile.

"Why is it I forgot how relaxing this is?"

"Have to ask somebody besides me about that," Hulk said, getting a bite.

Failing to set the hook, he grimaced, watching as the fish disappeared beneath clear water. John grinned and said, "Let me show you a trick."

Appearing confused, Hulk said, "Trick?"

Adjusting the young man's large hand with his own, he said, "Hold your rod like this. It'll give you an angle. When a fish takes the lure, your reflexes will respond with an automatic wrist twist which will set the hook for you."

Even though he held the rod as instructed, his

expression mirrored skepticism.

"Trust me," John said. "Kind of like the western grip in tennis."

Hulk blinked without replying. Another bass nibbled the silver lure as it trailed back toward the boat. He twisted his wrist just as John had said, automatically setting the hook. With a mile-wide grin, he reeled the big fish to the side of the boat.

"Unbelievable," he said as John took his picture.

"A little trick my father taught me," John said. "A variation for use with a cane pole," he added with a smile.

He instantly noticed Hulk's cheerful demeanor darken. Although he flipped the lure back into the water, his big shoulder's seemed to slump.

"Something I said?" he asked, leaning forward and placing a comforting hand on the young man's shoulder. "What's the matter?"

"Guess I'm just feeling a little sorry for myself."

"Because of your father?"

"Never had a father. No one to share fishing tricks with. No father at all."

"Hulk . . ."

"No matter. I ain't a kid no more. I can handle it."

John answered in a low voice, almost a whisper. "I said my father taught me that trick. A slight exaggeration, I'm afraid. My uncle raised me. I never had a father either."

Hulk faced John. Nodding, he said, "Least you had an uncle. Catholic nuns raised me in an orphanage."

"Sorry. Seems I have a penchant for sticking my foot in my mouth."

"No problem."

"I have a problem, and I'm almost ashamed to tell you."

He paused as Hulk raised his chin, staring at the older man, waiting for him to finish his statement. When he didn't, he said, "Ashamed?"

"Ashamed because I always intended to share that little trick with my own son some day. After all these years, you're the only person I've ever told."

Hulk remained silent, assessing the obvious regret expressed in the old man's pale gray eyes. Finally, he said, "Ain't nothin' to be ashamed of."

Staring back at him, John's sallow expression softened into a smile.

"You'd have made someone a fine son. I never shared that fishing trick with my real son. I doubt now I ever will. Could you humor me a bit? Let an old man pretend, just for the day, you're my son."

Hulk's boyish grin returned. "One thing I learned at the orphanage is how to pretend. Maybe I'll just pretend I'm on a fishin' trip with my dad."

John patted his cheek affectionately and said, "Maybe I'll be a better father to you than I was my biological child."

"I'm sure you raised him just fine."

"One likes to think so. Being a parent is mighty hard. Someday, you'll find out yourself."

John's reply failed to produce the desired response. Instead, Hulk's dark frown returned. Reeling in his lure he placed his rod in the holder inside the boat, hurriedly cranked the gasoline engine and pointed the hull toward the far bank.

Petrified by his reaction, John gripped the arm rests, mouth agape.

With his voice permeating unexplained bitterness, Hulk said, "That is somethin' that ain't never gonna happen."

Chapter 23

John remained silent on their trip back across the beaver lake. Already high above valley walls, sun heated his head and he regretted having no cap to wear. As if reading his thoughts, Hulk tapped his shoulder and handed him a cap.

"Almost forgot. Arkansas sun will fry your brains if you don't wear one of these."

John glanced at the logo, smiling before plopping it on his head. It said, hottest chicken, coldest beer—Vian, Oklahoma.

Attie and Lillie Mae were both awake and moving around the campsite when Hulk plowed the boat into the rocky shore. Both men grabbed a handful of gear and proceeded up the graveled path to join them. Aroma of bacon and eggs wafted down the slight incline. It was breakfast, cooking outdoors on a portable, three-burner propane stove. John realized what an appetite he'd worked up.

Alive with sounds of birds and squirrels, the valley engulfed his thoughts. After devouring his third homemade biscuit stuffed with strawberry preserves, he realized that like the valley, all his senses were alive, heightened, located just beneath his skin. From smiles on everyone's faces, he could see they felt the same. Later that morning, he helped Hulk drop the RV's gas tank and fill it with water. Once sure there were no remaining fumes, Hulk welded the tear and set the tank in the sun to dry.

"Good as new tomorrow," he said.

After lunch, Attie and Lillie Mae went in search of a highly touted blackberry patch. Hulk and John returned to the river to run the trotline, a passive southern fishing device used to catch bottom-dwelling catfish. After landing three fair-sized fish, they returned to camp. Lillie Mae and Attie's blackberry expedition also proved a success. They were already preparing a pie. A ground squirrel, apparently more hungry than afraid, hustled up to Hulk, snatching a blackberry directly from his palm.

"Take a load off your mind, John. I'm gonna fillet these catfish for dinner tonight."

"I don't mind helping."

"Won't take me long, and I'm gonna take a nap in my new hammock when I finish."

John nodded, glancing at the large net hammock hanging between two pine trees. "You girls need any help?" he asked, turning his attention to Attie and Lillie Mae.

"Nothing you'd know how to do, old man," Attie said with teasing inflection.

"Try me sometime. I might surprise you," he said, pinching her elbow.

Swatting his hand away, she returned to stirring milk and flour. Seeing he was being ignored, he went to the RV to wash up. When he finished, he sprawled on the couch and fell asleep, not waking until five, the pleasant aroma of frying catfish permeating the RV.

He found Hulk laboring beneath the vehicle, reinstalling the gas tank. Busy at the propane stove were Attie and Lillie Mae, frying catfish and hushpuppies in a big stainless steel boiler. He sauntered over and poked one of the pies with his finger.

"Keep your hands off," Attie said sternly.

"Not even one little piece before dinner?"

"You can wait."

"Don't know," he said, grabbing her shoulders and nibbling her neck. "I'm mighty hungry."

Playfully poking his ribs, she said, "After dinner, we'll be so full we won't be able to eat for a week."

"Then we'll have to work it off before we go to sleep."

"Maybe," Attie said. "If you don't pass out before the sun goes down."

"Let's just make a little bet on who passes out first," he said, grinning mischievously.

Smiling at his implication, she pushed him away to finish cutting potatoes into long slender strands. Wandering to the ledge overlooking the lake, he stretched out in a canvas lounge chair and rested his head in his hands, observing peaceful stillness until Lillie Mae's shrill call alerted him dinner was ready.

"Let's eat!"

They ate. Following his second helping of catfish, hushpuppies, green tomatoes and fried potatoes, he realized he wouldn't have room for blackberry pie if he didn't slow down. They cleared away dishes and leftovers after dinner, and then brewed strong coffee on the stove's burner. Relaxing in lawn chairs overlooking the lake, they watched a crimson sun drop behind valley walls as frogs and crickets tuned up in anticipation of their nightly concert.

Just before engulfing darkness, John retrieved the coffee pot from the burner. He'd saved a little room for a small slice of blackberry pie. Hulk lighted a lantern and hung it in a nearby tree. When he returned, they engaged in idle chatter, letting the satisfying meal further digest.

As they gazed across the valley, vaguely illuminated by flickering lantern light, John and Attie held hands. Hulk stretched out on the canvas chaise and Lillie Mae sprawled lazily on top of him. As before, the young couple kissed and nuzzled like love-struck teenagers.

"Quite a meal," John finally allowed, breaking the silence.

"Everything tastes better outdoors," Hulk said.

"Maybe. There's also something about eating food you caught and gathered that makes it even more wonderful. It does something for you."

"Makes you sleepy?" Attie said, referring to their earlier exchange.

"Not a bit. We might even stay up all night."

"Hah!" Attie said, laughing and giving his hand an expectant squeeze.

"You two turned in early last night," John said.

Hulk smiled. Lillie Mae giggled and said, "Didn't go to bed. We went skinny-dipping in the waterfall pool."

"Oh?"

"Up the hill," Lillie Mae said in her voice flavored with deep country inflection.

John and Attie turned their heads in the direction Lillie Mae was looking. Although it was too dark to discern the color of Hulk's neck, John could tell by his expression it was red.

"We're going again tonight. Wanna come with us?"

"Sounds like a grand idea. A swim is just what I need to work off some of this dinner."

Too old to blush, John simply opened his eyes and mouth wide at Attie's acceptance of Lillie Mae's invitation.

"Maybe if I wore a bathing suit," he said.

"Don't be like that," Lillie Mae said. "It's too dark to really see anything, and being naked in a mountain pool is like nothing you'll ever experience again."

With an enthusiastic smile, she sprang to her feet, grabbing Hulk's big hand and pulling him up from the chaise. Hurrying to the camper, she said, "Doff your clothes and wrap yourself in a towel. It's all you need, except maybe a pair of sandals or flip-flops."

Smiling, Attie grabbed John's hand and pulled him to the RV. "Surely you're not going to make me go skinny-dipping alone?"

"Don't you think we're a bit too old for this?"

"You may be. I'm not."

"Hulk, come on," Lillie Mae said, sticking her head out the camper door.

Hulk shook his head, shrugged his big shoulders and followed his diminutive wife into the camper. Whistling a nervous tune, John glanced once at the starless sky before proceeding to the RV.

Ten minutes later, the adventurous quartet, looking like Roman citizens bedecked in their finest togas, made their way up the hill. Despite appearances, they were really American campers, high in the Ouachita Mountains of Arkansas, traversing a steep and rocky trail by flickering lantern light. John realized as much when he stubbed his bony toe on a rock.

"Oh, oh, oh, oh, oh!" he said, holding the injured digit while attempting to hop up the trail on one foot.

"Don't be so melodramatic," Attie said, not bothering to turn around.

Holding the lantern and leading the way up the trail, Hulk said, "Almost there."

Realizing he was getting no sympathy for his stubbed toe, John asked, "How can you tell?"

Hulk stopped along the path, motioning for them to halt.

"Listen."

At first, John heard only the ubiquitous chorus of crickets and frogs. Then, as his senses became more intense in relative darkness, he heard the sound of falling water.

Lillie Mae nudged Hulk forward and said, "It's the waterfall, just over the next rise."

Hulk, Attie and Lillie Mae hastened their pace. So

did John, very nervous, though anxious to get his sore feet away from the trail's sharp rocks. Around the bend, illuminated by lantern and muted light of half moon, he got his first glimpse of the waterfall pool.

Shangri-La indeed! No movie director or scriptwriter could have done justice to the vision they saw. In their wake lay a perfectly circular pool, thirty feet wide, carved out of solid limestone. A concave wall of stone, extending far into darkness, formed the west end of the pool. From somewhere high above them, a steady flow of water poured, creating the fall that gave the pool its name.

Ferns and flowering bromeliads grew from every cavity, carved by time into the ancient monolith. Diverse lichens, growing on rock and near the waterfall, revealed chameleon-like colors and rapidly changing hues resultant from their proximity to, or distance from, the pool. Water overflowed the pool's east flank, dropping straight down to the river below. From their vantage, they could see the entire valley, including their camp. It seemed tiny in the distance.

Without waiting for the others, Lillie Mae whisked off her towel and dived into the water, swimming beneath the surface to the far bank. Attie joined her. Climbing a ledge ten feet above the pool, Hulk dropped his towel and plunged, headfirst, into the water.

"Don't be a sissy," Attie said, submerged to her neck.

"Is it cold?"

"It feels good."

Cautiously sticking his toe into the pool, he pulled it out. "Too cold."

Lillie Mae crawled out of the pool and climbed along a crevice etched into the limestone wall.

"Don't be a baby," she said.

"It's freezing."

"Not cold once you get used to it," Hulk said as he swam laps.

"Maybe not for a polar bear."

Slipping his toe into the water again, he removed it immediately.

"Can't just ease in," Attie said. "Dive in. It's really not cold as you think."

"If it's half as cold as I think, it's too cold," he replied.

Grinning, Lillie Mae said, "Too embarrassed to let us see your bare butt?"

Goaded by her insinuation, he followed Hulk's steep path to the ledge overlooking the pool.

"I've done lots of things during my many years. Skinny-dipping isn't one of them." Letting the towel drop to his ankles, he said, "Guess it's time I made the plunge."

Chapter 24

John yelped when he touched the water. Not from the cold, but elation at having taken a naked plunge into the unknown. With powerful strokes, he swam beneath the water's surface, finally touching solid undulating stone some ten feet below. When he emerged, he yelped again, this time from pure exhilaration.

Swimming to meet him, Attie wrapped her arms around his neck, almost drowning him in the wake of their ensuing kiss. Laughing as he choked, he began treading water, trying not to sink them both. Attie broke away and swam effortlessly to the shallows, and he followed.

With both feet planted firmly on the pool's limestone bottom, he hugged her, succinctly aware of acute sensations her naked body produced against his own. His entire being relaxed and it made him quite lightheaded. Goosebumps on her taut skin produced within him a stimulating awareness he'd never experienced. It was a feeling, he speculated, something similar to walking barefoot across tactile mounds of cold silver coins.

Now, it seemed, he'd never felt as close to another living being. When Attie pushed him playfully away to continue her exploration of the pool, he experienced a momentary sense of loss. Somewhere, beyond cognizance, on the backside of reality, he drew the analogy of a newborn suddenly expelled from its womb. Like an infant, utter exhilaration overwhelmed him, flooding his senses. Emitting another ear-splitting war whoop, he plunged backwards into the water.

As he backstroked across the pool, time lost its meaning. Hours or minutes might have passed as he explored rough limestone encasing the pool. After bathing beneath cascading water, he leaned against the epiphyte-encrusted stone. Night blooming orchids clung to rough limestone walls, flooding warm air with wild perfume. On a ledge above them, night birds warbled a late night melody.

Attie strolled around the pool to the waterfall as John watched, realizing he'd never seen her completely naked. He swam beneath the falls and waited for her to join him. When she did, they embraced beneath pouring water, feeling at once enraptured, enamored and enthralled. Closing his eyes tightly, he immersed himself in chilled hedonist heaven.

Eddies, ripples and whirlpools formed in the water, along with currents of varying temperature, some almost hot. He soon lost track of the others, as well as time. Brought to his senses by a cold stream of water pouring into his crooked nose, he suddenly realized he was alone. When he looked around, he failed to locate Attie, Hulk or Lillie Mae.

"Hey! Where did everybody go?"

"Up here," Hulk called.

As he climbed out of the pool, a cool breeze chilled the backs of his legs and reminded him of his initial apprehension to the water's likely temperature.

"John," Attie called. "Up here. It's wonderful."

When he pulled himself over the limestone wall, he found what she was talking about—Attie, Hulk and Lillie Mae sitting in a perfectly circular miniature of the pool below. Fingers of vapor, rising up from the steamy surface, imparted the appearance of a health club hot tub. Testing the water with his toe, he realized it was hydrothermal, heated by hot mineral water emanating from the very core of the eroded mountain range.

"Come in," Attie said. "What are you waiting for?"

Easing in slowly, he waded through steam and hot water, joining the smiling trio on a submerged ledge. Damp and heavy, and loaded with pungent mineral salts, was the night air. He took a deep, invigorating breath. Grinning ecstatically, he sank to his neck in hot water.

"Wonderful," he said, closing his eyes and savoring the moment. "I had no idea there were hot springs in this part of Arkansas."

"Neither does anyone else," Hulk said. "Lillie Mae and me found it accidentally."

Around the pool, stunted trees grew, their bark coated with brightly colored epiphloeodal growths. Moss draping the limbs caused them to seem like gray old men, and varicolored algae grew above water and under. Lichens, orchids and other air plants thrived in the moist environment created by the hydrothermal basin. Incense of night-blooming orchids mingled with tangy mineral salts as hot water percolated from the subterranean spring. Everything joined to heighten John's aural, tactile and olfactory senses.

"How hot is the water?"

"About a hundred degrees," Lillie Mae said. "Hulk measured it once."

"Perfect," he said.

"More than perfect," Attie said. "It's paradise."

Glancing upward, he asked, "What causes the dancing lights?"

"Some sort of mirage, I guess," Hulk said. "Sometimes it's even brighter than tonight."

Above them, violet, purple and orange lights cavorted like excited electrons in a portable computer's plasma screen, illuminating the pool with an eerie glow.

Of Love and Magic

Since first taking the plunge, John had forgotten his nudity and inherent modesty. When Lillie Mae rose out of the water, he remembered. If hot water hadn't already caused that particular reaction, his ruddy neck would have flushed crimson.

Sitting on the edge of the pool, she seemed unmindful of her own nakedness as she dangled her tiny feet in the water. Although no more than five feet tall, her body was lithe, well-shaped and perfectly proportioned. Through eyes of a former practicing doctor, John noticed. He also noticed something else: a cesarean scar on her abdomen. Attie noticed him noticing and nudged his ribs, returning him to reality. When Hulk dragged his muscular frame out of the water, John grinned and returned the nudge.

As time lost its bearing, they remained in the hot spring-fed pool. Finally, having no idea of the hour, they realized they were rapidly becoming shriveled prunes and left its warm solace. Recovering their towels and sandals, they trekked back down the winding path to their camp.

Having grown accustomed to muted overhead lights, they returned along the hilly path without using the lantern. When they reached the clearing, a rattling thud from a garbage pail behind Hulk's camper startled them. He raised his hand and walked slowly behind the truck to see who, or what, was there.

"Gotcha."

Hulk's retort was followed by an ear-popping screech. He returned carrying a reluctant cat, so flea-bitten and skinny it could barcly muster a whimper. Lillie Mae rushed forward, grabbed the cat and cradled it to her ample bosom. Barely grown, the captured feline had no energy to resist, and closed its eyes, foundering into Lillie Mae's arms, resigned to its fate.

"Poor little thing," Lillie Mae commiserated.

Grabbing her elbow, Attie pulled her toward the

RV and said, "I have milk in the kitchen. It must be starving."

Lillie Mae followed and said, "Hulk, go get that left-over catfish. Poor little thing."

Turning toward their camper, Hulk complied. John followed Attie and Lillie Mae, still clutching the hapless cat, into the RV. Attie poured a bowl of milk and placed it on the floor. John watched as Lillie Mae gently sat the cat in front of the bowl. Hunger overcoming its fright, the ginger brown cat touched the milk delicately with its nose and began lapping it furiously.

Hulk returned with flaky chunks of left-over catfish. When the stray cat finished lapping milk, it devoured the fish. Then, momentarily satisfied, it lay on the floor of the RV, licking its paws and trying to groom the fur matted on its coat.

"We're keeping him," Lillie Mae said.

"Oh, no, we can't."

Tears formed in her big eyes. Kneeling beside the now purring feline, she lifted it to her bosom and repeated, "We're keeping him."

Rocking the cat like an infant, her face became red and puffy. Through anguished tears, she wailed, "Skittles, Skittles, Skittles."

Hulk's freckled face turned red. To Attie and John's trepidation, he also began to cry.

"He ain't Skittles. He just ain't Skittles."

Pointing John toward the refrigerator, Attie said, "Get something to calm them."

He returned with an icy Mason jar of Mike's choc beer. Not bothering with a glass, he handed the jar to Attie. Hulk and Lillie Mae were hugging each other, tears streaking their faces. Attie put the jar under their noses until they'd both drank.

As John helped Attie hasten them to the couch, Lillie Mae kept saying, "Skittles, Skittles, Skittles."

"It's all right," Attie said, trying to soothe the

young couple and find out what their crying was all about.

From the scar on Lillie Mae's abdomen, and the curious way she and Hulk had acted when children were mentioned, John already suspected what the trouble was. When they finally settled against the couch, and their crying dissolved into a gentle flow of tears, he asked the question dwelling on his mind.

"I know it's painful. Can you tell Attie and me about Skittles?"

His question sent the couple into another fit of tears, and earned him a glaring reprimand from Attie. Unmindful of her reproach, he took the Mason jar, holding it, in turn, to their lips, gently forcing more of the cold beer down each of their throats. Cold choc performed its pacifying function.

"Skittles was our baby's cat," Lillie Mae said.

Her words brought a sorrowful grimace to Hulk's face, almost as if she'd plunged a knife into his breast and was twisting the blade.

"Tommy died in his sleep."

Her words ended in a high-pitched wail. Again, John touched choc to her lips, administering the only anesthetic he possessed. In a minute, she hiccupped and blinked twice, tears momentarily abated.

"Died in his sleep and we weren't there to help," she said.

"No, Lillie Mae, no," Hulk blubbered, her admission of their baby's death too painful for him to bear.

After handing the remaining beer to Attie, John returned to the refrigerator for another jar. Sitting beside the weeping giant, he held beer under his red nose until he swallowed some. Once Hulk began to drink, he lapped all the beer in the jar like a thirsty hound.

Lillie Mae cried softly as Hulk recommenced the explanation she had begun. "A stray kitten wandered up to my shop about the time our Tommy was born. We named him Skittles. He loved that baby much as we did. When Tommy died, Skittles ran away and never came back," he said, his face flushing bright red.

Hulk cried some more, and then hugged Lillie Mae again. When Attie's dark eyes also reddened, John gave her a sip of the cold choc.

He said, "When did this happen?"

"Just a year ago, but it seems like forever," Lillie Mae stammered. "Don't know how I've gone on living this long."

"Sudden Infant Death Syndrome," John said.

Neither Hulk nor Lillie Mae answered, though both nodded.

"SIDS," he said, looking at Attie. "Nothing anyone could have done."

Gently taking Lillie Mae's hand, Attie softly said, "Tommy's passing wasn't your fault. Nothing you could have done would have prevented it."

"We miss him so much," Lillie Mae said.

Attie probed further. "Have you thought about trying again?"

Shaking her head sorrowfully, Lillie Mae said, "Couldn't bear to lose another baby."

"What happened was beyond your control," Attie said. "You have to put it behind you."

"It's normal to feel great loss, accompanied by feelings of remorse and guilt," John said. "But it wasn't your fault and there's no reason to believe it will happen again."

"How do you know?" Lillie Mae lashed out. "How could you possibly know how we feel?"

"Because I also lost a son," Attie said softly. Their attention suddenly riveted, Hulk, Lillie Mae and John listened as she continued her story.

"His name was Roland, like his father's. Roland, my husband, ran his car off the road in an ice storm. Though he wasn't critically injured, our son Rollie died in the crash."

John clutched her hand, feeling her pain. Seeing she wasn't finished, he handed her the jar of choc and she drained it before resuming the story.

"Roland and I were heartbroken. He blamed himself because he hadn't made Rollie buckle his seatbelt. Consumed with guilt, he took his own life a year later, to the day."

Hulk, John and Lillie Mae sat mesmerized by Attie's story. By now, her face was puffed and pasty. Barely able to suppress her emotion, she said, "Roland and I were married ten years before we had little Rollie. I was fifty-two when he died—too old to replace his memories with another child. The void he left was filled with years of pain and unanswered anguish."

She put her arms around Lillie Mae and Hulk's shoulders and said, "I was denied the joy of another child. You're not. You can keep Tommy's memory forever but you have to let him go. Forgive yourselves for whatever you think you may have done wrong. You may never get another chance. If you can't do it for yourself, then please, do it for me."

Later, in bedroom darkness, Attie nestled in John's arms. "In ten years, I've never told that story to another living soul," she said.

Remembering the bathroom picture of the dark-haired man with his arm around his son, John hugged her and said, "Attie, I think tonight you freed one of your own painful memories."

Chapter 25

Detective Vince Blakeman's hands and clothes still reeked of refrigerated death even though he'd left the morgue more than an hour before. Reaching home, he hurried up the condo sidewalk without bothering to wave to the old men playing tennis. Bypassing the refrigerator, he used both hands to crank the faucets in the bathroom shower, then stripped and stepped beneath the water, not waiting until it got hot.

He remained beneath the hot spray of water until it turned tepid, and then cold. Feeling a little better, he draped a blue terry cloth towel around his waist and went to the kitchen for a beer. Like a balm for the soul, the first Moosehead stilled his palsied hands. The second relaxed him. The third almost made him forget the mutilated teenaged body in the morgue. The insistent ring of the house phone interrupted his morbid meditation. It was Cynthia Warren.

"Vince, the roses are lovely. They weren't necessary."

Remembering his impulse purchase at the florist, he asked, "Is your husband upset?"

"He wouldn't have noticed if I'd put them under his nose."

"I meant the scene I made at your party."

Cynthia giggled behind her cupped hand on the

receiver. "Considering his intelligence and advanced education, Dan is lucky if he manages to put on matching socks in the morning. He didn't even realize it was you, and not our neighbor."

"I'm very sorry for my actions . . ."

"Vince, I'm not mad. No harm done. If anything, it broke the tension and livened up the party."

"I know, but I'm . . ."

"The flowers are lovely. Now, no more of that."

"Thanks Mrs. Warren."

"Cynthia."

"Thanks Cynthia. Afraid I was having a bad night."

"So was I. Mine didn't end with the party."

"Sorry to hear that."

"I need to talk. Can I come over?"

"You mean to my place?"

"Is it all right?"

"I suppose so, but . . ."

"Great. Give me directions and I'll be there in an hour."

Chapter 26

Vince was waiting, and answered the front door on the first ring of the door chime.

"Come in," he said, motioning toward the living room. "I have an opened bottle of wine. Like a glass?"

"That would be lovely."

Grabbing two clean tumblers from the kitchen cabinet, he filled them and joined Cynthia in the living room. Ignoring the tumbler, decorated with red sailboats and blue jumping porpoises, she sipped the wine, savoring it an extra moment on her tongue.

"Delightful," she said. "I didn't know you were such a connoisseur."

"Someone gave it to me. Now what's the problem?"

"I want to apologize. Dan pulled some strings to have you removed from his father's case."

"No matter."

"I hope it hasn't hurt your career."

Mention of his career caused him to grin. "Don't worry about it."

"After the party, Dan was distraught but talkative. I cajoled him into explaining why he's so intent on returning his father to Oklahoma."

"Oh?"

"He had Granddad ruled incompetent. The rest of the story is very embarrassing to me."

"There's not much I haven't heard."

"Dan liquidated his father's assets. Now he's afraid if he doesn't do something to show Granddad really is incompetent, everyone will think he's an unfeeling ogre."

Vince began slowly massaging his temples. "I've seen this before. Sometimes their own children are old people's worst enemies."

"Dan can't see that. He's just worried about his reputation."

"And if the police return him to Tulsa against his will, well then . . ."

"It'll look as if he were incompetent, or senile, when he ran away from home in the middle of the snowstorm," she said, finishing his sentence.

"I wish there was something I could do. It's likely the old man somehow made it to Arkansas. Your husband won't benefit from his statewide influence bartering over there. Mr. Warren may never come home."

Cynthia's raven hair rippled in the dim light as she slowly shook her head. "How do you know that?"

"We don't, for sure. No one's spotted him in Oklahoma for days. Still, we've traced the RV to a woman named Attie Johnson who lives in Eureka Springs, Arkansas. It seems likely that's where they're headed. Even if we know where he is, it won't be so easy to make him come home if he doesn't want to."

Cynthia slugged her wine and poured another glass without asking.

"Dan's seen the report. He's talked with the District Attorney, trying to get Ms. Johnson charged with kidnapping and extortion. If he's successful, the police will have her house staked out. When they show up in Eureka Springs, she'll be arrested and put in jail. They'll take Granddad into custody and return him to Oklahoma. I don't know what to do."

"I'm sorry. I have no authority in Arkansas. Your

husband works for the biggest law firm in Tulsa. Isn't there someone you know that can pull a few strings for you?"

Cynthia's frown suddenly turned into a smile, and he blushed when she hugged him like a giant Teddy bear.

Chapter 27

After their late night with Hulk, Lillie Mae and the cat, John and Attie slept late the next morning. When they awoke, they found Hulk and Lillie Mae already up and about, the stray cat nestled in her arms. Much more so than the previous night, their demeanors were cheerful. Hulk bounded about the campsite, cleaning this and repairing that. Lillie Mae had breakfast ready, the satisfying aroma of bacon and eggs greeting them when they exited the RV.

"Morning," Lillie Mae said. "Sleep well?"

"Like a top," John said. "And you?"

"Hulk and me didn't get a wink of sleep," she said with her patented impish grin.

"Oh?" Attie said.

"Had some catching up to do," she said, winking.

"And we're keeping the cat. We named him Charlie."

John and Attie exchanged hopeful glances. "Does this mean Attie and I could be godparents someday?"

Hulk's face turned red and Lillie Mae grinned.

After breakfast, they packed the RV and prepared to depart. Hulk filled their repaired tank with gas from a five-gallon container. After packing, Attie glanced at her watch, seeing it was nearly eleven. Hulk and Lillie

Mae waited by the camping table to say good-bye.

"We're going to miss you two," Attie said.

"And we'll miss you," Lillie Mae said, dropping the cat to the ground.

Tears welled in her eyes as she threw her arms around Attie's neck and hugged her. When mutual tears finally ceased, amid many hugs and handshakes, Attie and John turned to the RV.

"We're keeping Charlie," Hulk said.

Lillie Mae added, "Hulk and I talked it over. We took what happened last night as a sign. With a little luck, Charlie will soon have someone to grow up with."

"That's wonderful," Attie said, hugging them again before saying final goodbyes at the RV's door.

After turning the big vehicle around, they drove slowly away, back up the lonely narrow path. John was chuckling to himself.

"What's so funny, old man?"

Crossing his arms and legs, he turned his knees toward the door.

"Nothing," he said.

"You tell me now or I'm going to throw you out of this RV."

"It's just that Charlie, Hulk and Lillie Mae's new cat, is a calico."

"So?"

"So, all calicos are female."

"Why didn't you say something?"

"I didn't want to spoil things for them, and they'll find out soon enough, anyway."

"You're hopeless," Attie said, shaking her head.

⚜

Much later, finding themselves halfway to Hot Springs, they stopped for sandwiches and cold drinks at a roadside stand. Again on their way, Attie slowly and cautiously negotiated switchbacks and u-turns on the narrow road. A decrease in pine trees and an increase in souvenir shops and filling stations signaled their proximity to the old resort community. After one last sweeping turn, John found himself, finally, in Hot Springs, Arkansas.

Attie asked, "Shall we get a hotel room, take a real bath and sleep in an honest-to-goodness bed for a change?"

"Fine idea," he said. "Let's drive through town first. It's been years since I visited this old place."

"It hasn't changed much."

"No it hasn't," he said, chuckling.

Driving slowly, she traversed the narrow street, bordered on both sides by shops, hotels and limestone cliffs. She continued, passing bathhouse row. Caught in the middle of horse racing season, tourists crowded the drab old town, and cars lined both sides of the street. When they reached Hot Springs National Park, near the town's center, he asked her to find a place to park and stop.

Hot Springs bore all the trappings of a seedy old resort town. Lusterless stone buildings, replete with cracked mortar and dirty windows, guarded rolling streets like worn-out gargoyles. Young couples with runny-nosed children, and old people—very old people—crowded monuments and cheesy souvenir shops. Taking Attie's hand, John ignored the masses and led her to a sparkling spring bursting from a fissure in a gray abutting limestone cliff. Placing his hand beneath gushing water, he touched it to his lips, smiling at its taste.

"We made it Attie. It still tastes the same."

"Told you I'd get you here," she said.

"That you did. I never had a doubt."

An old man, dressed in alpine shorts, hat and lederhosen, appeared from the sidewalk. Seeing John drinking from his palms, he smiled and handed him an empty cup. Thanking him, John thrust it beneath the stream of water, drank some more and handed the half-empty cup to Attie. After satisfying her own thirst, she returned it to the gray-haired old man. Time's weight had shriveled his body, and he seemed almost like a little boy in his colorful alpine costume.

When Attie thanked him again, he began speaking in French that neither she nor John could interpret. Smiling and nodding, John shook the man's hand until he realized they didn't understand him. Finally, with a sad smile, he waved and limped away.

Attie said, "Wonder what he's looking for?"

"Maybe the Fountain of Youth."

"Is that why you had me bring you here?"

"I thought I knew. Now I'm not so sure."

They watched as a hawk swooped, almost to the ground, and then floated slowly upward, disappearing into a puffy cloud. Turning away from the spring, he clasped his hands behind his back and gazed around the flowered courtyard. After five long contemplative minutes, he closed his eyes. When he opened them again, he was grinning.

"You know Attie, we live our lives in a garden of mirages and illusions. For years I've dreamed of this place. Here, now, I see it's, in every detail, exactly like it was when last I visited. Somehow it's not the same as what it had become in my imagination."

She patted his hand knowingly. "Let's find a hotel."

"No. It just dawned on me. We already found the real Magic Fountain, last night in the mountains of western Arkansas. Hot Springs is nothing but a sad illusion. Now that I've found what I was looking for, I want to keep going until we reach home."

Chapter 28

So intent was John's countenance upon leaving the fountain, Attie didn't question his decision to go directly to Eureka Springs. Neither spoke until they were heading north, ten miles out of the old Arkansas spa town.

"It'll be dark before we reach Eureka. Sure you don't want to stop along the way? Get a room for the night?"

"If you're tired, let's stop."

"I was worried about you."

Turning with a smile, he reached across the console and touched her hand. "Not to worry. Can't remember when I've had more energy."

Glancing at the dashboard clock, she said, "We should make it home by nine unless we stop for dinner."

"Let's don't stop. I'm not hungry and I'm anxious to finally see where you live."

"You'll like it. My house is a sprawling old wood frame that sits on an Arkansas mountain top." Giggling, she said, "Mountains in Arkansas aren't high, especially the Ozark Mountains. But they are massive, rounded and covered with trees. From the top of my mountain, you can see all the way to the next county. Vital hues of green, mixed with floating swaths of flawless gray, caress endless brilliant blue. It's quite spectacular."

"I can see it," he said. Do you have a back porch?"

"Of course I do, and it reminds me quite a lot of you."

"Me? I don't recall ever being compared to a porch."

Laughing, she said, "It's old and has lots of character. My porch stretches around the entire house, and it's a perfect place to watch golden Arkansas sunsets while sitting in an old swing. Rusted chains suspend it from the ceiling and they harmonize like dueling harps when you rock."

"Wonderful," John said. "You think we'll be there in time to see the sunset?"

She put her foot on the gas. "We'll give it a shot, old man."

Laboring up steep Highway 71, she managed to pass several slower moving, sight-seeing vehicles. When they reached the highest point, south of Canada, on the old highway, she pointed into the distance.

"Eureka's just beyond the horizon, not really that far away, as the crow flies."

"Look there, Attie, it's a rainbow on the horizon. Must be where our pot of gold lies."

"I don't see it."

"There, in the distance," he said.

"Road's too steep. I'll take your word for it."

They neared the final stretch of highway before reaching Eureka Springs, a road sign warning that the next fourteen miles were steep and winding. It was. Spiraling ever upward, the narrow road flattened only briefly, forming a river valley. Having gouged its course between two rounded peaks, the river meandered lazily into the distance, creating a lovely mountain vale in its wake.

Crossing the river, Attie pointed Ol' Betsy up the

steepest mountain they'd yet encountered. Ascending the incline, the engine coughed and labored. Overlooking the river below, their view became even more dramatic as they climbed ever higher. Near the mountain's crest, the winding roadway took a wide loop, affording a spectacular view of the meandering river far below.

"Pull over Attie."

Responding to the urgency in his voice, she wheeled the RV to a scenic turnout by the side of the road.

"You all right?"

"We're not going to make it to your house before dark. Let's stop here and watch the sunset."

In the western sky, the golden orb had already begun its descent. Attie parked and waited until he opened the door. Fresh air, damp with impending rain, flooded the vehicle. Stepping to the ground, he smiled and stretched his arms.

"Attie, I feel as if I've finally come home."

"You have," she said, taking his hand. "We both have."

Together, they walked to the cliff's edge and sat on a large limestone boulder overlooking the valley. Purple martins, leaving daytime roosts in search of insects, swirled high overhead. In the distance, a chorus of tree frogs began their nocturnal serenade. A damp breeze whistling through the pines joined the melody, harmonizing with a company of crickets lilting like a thousand violins.

Tightly squeezing Attie's hand, John said, "It's beautiful."

"Yes it is," she said, gazing at the red radiating sphere burning a luminous swath in fading sky as it descended toward the valley floor.

"Once," he said. "On a spring night in western Oklahoma, I saw a sunset almost as beautiful. Particles of dust from some volcanic eruption in the Pacific filled the sky. Invisible during the day, dispersed particles became fiery streaks of crimson incandescence at dusk."

"A beautiful sunset is something to remember."

"Attie, you remember the races?"

"Of course I do."

"Remember when I told you which horse I was betting on? You said he was the biggest nag on the track and had never won a race."

"And you were too stubborn to listen."

"I bet on his name, Prairie Sunset, because until I met you, that sunset in western Oklahoma was the loveliest vision I'd ever seen."

"You're incurable," she said, nudging his ribs and moving closer. Putting her arm around his waist, she felt a tremble beneath her touch, like a bridge abutment, stressed with age, beginning to tire and collapse.

"John, do you need a heart pill?"

"Already took two," he said, his breathing suddenly coming faster and then in short gasps.

"John!" Not answering, he closed his eyes and shrank back against her. "Get up John. We're just outside town. There's a hospital there."

Neither speaking, nor opening his eyes, he grasped her hand. Squeezing it tightly, his lips began to quiver and he fought to open his eyes.

"Attie," he said in a whisper. "Help me up."

"No!" she said, tears welling up in her red-rimmed eyes."

"Help me Attie," he said, his voice low and becoming increasingly hard to hear.

Encircling his waist, she struggled to lift him. Managing somehow to boost him into a sitting posture, she positioned herself behind him, bracing his frail weight between her legs, against her body, embracing him as death's head danced ever-narrowing circles above them. Finally, it kissed his cheek.

"This can't be happening. Not now. Not so close to home. Let me help you to a doctor."

Still holding her hand, he said, "Don't cry Attie. This has been the happiest week of my life. I never met a kinder, sweeter person than you." His voice was barely a whisper when he squeezed her hand, one last time. "I love you, Attie. You kept your promise and took me to the Magic Fountain. Before I go, I want you to make one more promise."

Clutching his hand in a desperate clasp, Attie nodded sadly as tears streamed down her red and puffy face.

"Bury me on an Arkansas hillside close to you, facing west. I'm home now and I never want to leave again."

Attie hurried up the hill to the RV, using her CB radio to call for help, though she knew in her heart it was probably too late. Then, until the sun had disappeared below the western horizon, and distant thunder heralded a gentle rain, she clutched him to her breast, crying silent tears as she rocked him in her arms.

Chapter 29

They weren't far from Eureka Springs, and an ambulance arrived, its siren drowning out night's other sounds. Two EMTs hurried toward them, one with an oxygen bottle and mask. Both were young and looked concerned. They didn't bother asking what had happened as they began trying to revive John.

"Let's get him up the hill. They'll have better luck in the ER."

Placing John on the stretcher, they carried him to the ambulance. When Attie tried to join him in back, the ambulance driver shook her head.

"Against regulation. Ride up front with me. No time to argue. Every second counts right now. You okay?"

Attie whimpered. "I think it may already be too late."

"Don't give up yet. Don said he still has a slight pulse."

The young driver never introduced herself and Attie didn't bother asking as they raced toward the hospital in Eureka Springs, siren blaring. When they finally pulled into the entrance to the emergency room and wheeled John out, she followed them through the swinging doors. A nurse grabbed her arm.

"Can't go in there, ma'am."

"But he's dying."

"The doctors will take good care of him. Come with me to the waiting room. I'll call you when it's okay to see him."

She followed the nurse up the long hallway to a tiny waiting area. She was the only one there, at least for the moment. An hour passed before a doctor joined her.

"Did you come in with Mr. Warren?"

"Yes, is he . . . ?"

When the man dressed in white smock averted his eyes, just for a moment, Attie knew he wasn't.

"Oh no," she said, shielding her blurry eyes with her hands.

"I'm so sorry. We thought we had him."

There was a commotion behind the swinging doors leading to the hospital's main reception area. Someone was arguing with the receptionist. Not waiting for her to approve their entrance into the emergency area, one man pushed through the door. Many more people followed, one a cameraman, another had a microphone that he shoved in Attie's face.

"Are you Attie Johnson?" Not waiting for her to answer, he asked, "Is John Warren alive or dead?"

Attie just stood there, tears streaming down her cheeks, when three uniformed men bulled their way through the ever-increasing throng of people watching the melee. One of the policemen was someone Attie knew well.

"Attie, I'm sorry. I have to arrest you."

"You've known me all your life, James Simpson. I even helped you get elected."

The clean-cut young man wearing the Sheriff's badge could only shake his head.

"Afraid I got no choice."

"What did I do?"

No one answered her question. Simpson's two subordinates cuffed her, not being very gentle as they forced her hands behind her back, jamming them into handcuffs. Besides TV cameras, still photographers began flashing pictures. She turned away and closed her eyes as one of the deputies yanked the cuffs and pushed her through the crowd, toward the swinging door.

"Ms. Johnson, did you kidnap Mr. Warren?" a reporter asked, her microphone stuck in Attie's face.

The crowd grew even larger as they exited the hospital, flashes firing, noise level high. It looked as though everyone close enough to hear the news had driven into town to witness the spectacle.

"Out of the way; we're coming through," Sheriff Simpson said, leading them to a police car parked on the sidewalk.

After stuffing Attie into the backseat of the police car, they took off, tires squealing. With sirens blaring, they left the crowd behind, taking her to the small jail in downtown Eureka Springs. Sheriff Simpson shook his head, turned and walked away.

"Jimmy, why are you doing this to me?" Attie called after him.

Simpson didn't answer, and the jailers took her to a cell, mercifully releasing her from the cuffs.

"When can I call my attorney?" she asked as a burly jailer with a crew cut shut the door, leaving her alone in the tiny cell.

Her question went unanswered.

❦

Sheriff Simpson returned later that night, sitting with her on the cell's lone bunk.

"Attie, I hope you'll forgive me for all this. Mom's already called and threatened to disown me if I don't release you."

Attie smiled. "You should listen to your mom."

"You're a real celebrity. Every major network and all the cable channels have crews in town."

"What's going to happen to me, Jimmy?"

201

"Not a damn thing. There are no charges against you."

"Then why did you arrest me?"

"We didn't really arrest you as much as we took you into custody."

"But why?"

"You're like the eight ball in a political pool game. My department's caught in the middle."

Sheriff Simpson nodded when Attie asked, "Is John Warren's son behind this?"

"I don't know what really happened, but the law enforcement grapevine says Dan Warren tried to get the Tulsa D.A. to file kidnapping charges against you."

"Oh my!"

"The D.A. supposedly told him no way, and that neither he nor anyone else in his department believed you kidnapped Mr. Warren."

"That's a relief," Attie said.

"Warren's son is politically well connected, and pulling every string he has. I was told from higher-ups, in no uncertain terms, to bring you in. At least make it appear you were being arrested."

"How long will I have to stay here?"

Sheriff Simpson glanced at his watch and grinned. "About thirty more minutes. Wayne's waiting outside and he's mad as hell."

Sheriff Simpson hugged her and then exited the cell, replaced by Wayne Taylor, Attie's family attorney. Dressed in shorts and tee shirt, he looked as if he'd just come from a company picnic. The lawyer joined her on the bunk.

"Attie, I'm so sorry you had to go through all this. They ain't got a damn thing on you, this whole mess nothing but a sham."

"Jimmy said John's son tried to file kidnapping charges against me."

Wayne smiled. "Hell, Attie, I don't think you've ever even gotten a parking ticket."

"Can you get me out of here?"

"Lady, you're sprung. I just need to tell you a few things before you go out there."

"Like what?"

"This town's turned into a three-ring media circus. Everyone's talking about you and Mr. Warren. Half the people think you're an angel, the other half the Devil. You got to really watch yourself these next few days."

When he stood from the bunk, the jailer opened the door, letting him exit.

"The Sheriff will let you go here in a bit," he said.

It was dark when Sheriff Simpson, a huge smile on his face, led her down the hallway.

"You're out of here, and someone's waiting to pick you up."

Attie was surprised and relieved to see Norma, Mike and Big Al, waiting for her.

Following a group hug and a few tears, Norma said, "We came soon as we heard the news."

"Let's get you outta here," Mike said.

When they exited the jail, Attie realized the circus wasn't over. A large crowd had gathered, complete with cameras and reporters. Mike, Norma and Big Al encircled her, Big Al leading the way. It soon became a shoving match, everyone moving closer, wanting to see, talk to, or touch Attie.

"Everybody step back. Give this lady some air," Big Al said.

One large man took offense, pushing Big Al until he tripped and dropped to one knee. The man was completely bald, tattoos covering his muscular arms.

"Who you telling to step back? You may be big, but I'll whip your ass."

Someone else bulled his way through the crowd. It was Hulk, Lillie Mae beside him. Grabbing the tattooed man around the neck, he lifted him bodily off the ground. The man struggled, trying to wrench Hulk's hands loose as he turned progressively redder. Finally, Hulk let him go and he dropped to the ground.

"You wanna whip somebody's ass, maybe you oughta try picking on someone your own size."

Hulk glared at the man on the ground as a woman pushed a man in a wheelchair through the crowd. It was Scooter Bates and his girlfriend Sue.

"If anyone else wants to hassle Ms. Attie, they're going to have to go through me first. And don't let this wheelchair fool you."

Hulk grinned and reached down to shake Scooter's hand. "You're Scooter Bates. I seen you on TV. I'm Hulk and this is my wife Lillie Mae."

"Pleased to meet you. This is Sue," he said, introducing a slightly overweight woman with short brown hair and big smile.

"I'm the one that pushes him to safety when his mouth overloads his rear-end."

Attie hugged them both as they began creating a path through the crowd. Hulk and Big Al brought up the rear, not letting anyone come close to Attie. They reached the parking lot, and Mike and Norma's Cadillac.

"Where to?" Mike asked.

After introducing everyone, she said, "My house, about ten miles from here."

"I'll drive to the end of the road. Get your vehicles and flash your lights twice when you pull up behind so we'll know you're friendlies."

Norma opened the front door, motioning Attie to slide into the front seat. She scooted in next to her, Big Al climbing in the backseat.

"We've been so worried," Norma said, hugging Attie.

"You and John have been the number one news story for the last two days," Mike said. "When we saw they arrested you, we headed this way."

"This whole thing just ain't right," Big Al said.

Norma continued hugging her until she finally stopped crying. "I don't know what I'd have done if you hadn't showed up."

"We're not the only ones," Mike said. "You and John made lots of friends, some in the vehicles behind us. Tell me where to go, and I'll lead the way.

Chapter 30

Scooter's van and Hulk's camper followed Mike's Cadillac out of town, toward the winding road to Attie's house. They realized they weren't alone, television, radio, and many private vehicles following them. Mike pounded on the steering wheel.

"Dammit! Why can't they leave you alone?"

"Pull up in one of those dirt roads that goes up into the hills," Big Al said.

Attie shook her head. "Not a good idea. Most are dead ends."

Someone keyed the CB radio. "This is the Hulkster, over. Can you read me?"

Attie clutched Mike's arm. "It's Hulk. He's in the camper behind us."

Mike grabbed the handset. "I read you, Hulkster. This is Choctaw speaking. Over."

Another screech. "This is Ironsides, over. I'm right behind you Choctaw, and just in front of you, Hulkster. Over."

"These idiots are right on my back bumper. I'll drop back and hold them up. You two get the hell out of here. We'll hook up later. Over."

"Roger that, Hulkster. Sounds like a plan. Over."

"This is Ironsides, boy. Don't let 'em wreck you. These roads are tighter than Dick's hatband. Over."

Attie grabbed the handset from Mike. "This is Attie. You two be careful."

"Over," Mike said, grabbing the handset back from Attie and flooring the gas pedal.

Scooter followed, though his old white van wasn't as fast as Mike's Caddie. They began pulling away from Hulk's camper that had begun swerving from one side of the road to the other.

"I hope they're okay," Attie said, squeezing Norma's hand.

Norma and Big Al were staring out the back window, watching the long procession of vehicles behind them playing bumper cars, all trying without success to pass Hulk's camper. Norma patted Attie's wrist.

"Don't worry, honey. That boy doesn't need any help. He's good."

Big Al had his elbows propped on the back of the seat, watching the skirmish going on behind them.

"Good, hell! I've seen NASCAR drivers that couldn't block any better than he's doing."

Mike glanced in the rearview mirror as a deer bounded out of the ditch and into their path. Slamming on the brakes, he caused the car to swerve violently. It slid to the edge of the ditch before screeching to a halt. Their heads snapped as Scooter, too close to stop, slammed into the rear bumper.

"Sorry," Scooter's voice said, sounding over the CB. "Everyone okay up there? Over."

Attie grabbed the handset. "Mike did a wonderful job of keeping us out of the ditch. We're okay."

"Not quite," Mike said. "We got a flat tire."

"The broken chat they rock the road with is sharp as knifes," Attie said. "Sorry, Mike. I'll buy you a new tire."

"No you won't. It's not your fault."

Big Al slid out of the back seat. "Pop the trunk."

"No time," Mike said. "The mob will be on us in a

minute or so.”

“Don’t matter. We’re stuck here unless we change the tire. Pop the trunk.”

Mike popped the trunk, watching as Big Al began unloading the spare tire and tool kit. Scooter had already joined him, doing his best to assist. Hulk’s camper pulled to a stop behind them, as did the two dozen or so vehicles in pursuit. Within seconds, reporters, cameramen and paparazzi invaded the area, taking pictures and demanding interviews.

“Just stay in the car, honey,” Norma advised. “Don’t talk to those bloodsuckers.”

Attie took Norma’s advice, watching as the insistent crowd began pushing and shoving. When Scooter’s wheelchair got tipped over, and he was dumped onto the ground, she could stand it no longer. Shaking off Norma’s grasp, she unlocked the door and stepped out of the car. Camera flashes immediately began, along with microphones and spotlights in her face. Big Al, finished with the tire, joined her, trying to fend off the throng of curiosity and information seekers.

The area was as bright as daylight, spotlights trained on them from the filming crew vans, someone standing on a ladder, directing traffic with an electronic megaphone. Big Al pushed his way through the crowd.

“Get back. Leave this woman alone. She ain’t hurt nobody and don’t deserve this.”

“It’s all right. Help me up on the hood. I’ll say a few words. See if that does the trick.”

Big Al picked her up, depositing her on the hood of Mike’s black Cadillac. Then he began shouting.

“All right, listen up! Mrs. Johnson’s got something to say. Shut up and listen.”

Lillie Mae and Sue piled into the Cadillac on the passenger’s side, while Hulk, Mike and Scooter joined Big Al, doing their best to form a human shield between themselves and Attie.

For a moment, the crowd grew quiet.

"I'm Attie Johnson. I'll answer your questions, then please, leave us in peace."

"Did you kidnap John Warren?

"Of course not," she said.

"Did he die because you poisoned him?"

"What kind of question is that? I loved him. I'd never do anything to hurt him."

"Do you know there's a warrant for your arrest in Oklahoma?"

"That's a bunch of hooey. I've done nothing wrong and there's no warrant for my arrest anywhere."

"If not, then why did the police have you in handcuffs? What are you guilty of?"

"Nothing, I've already told you."

"Did you spirit Mr. Warren away from Tulsa, and then demand a ransom from his son?"

Suddenly overwhelmed, Attie began to sob. Big Al leaped up on the hood of the car beside her.

"You people got this story all wrong. John ran away from home because his son was going to put him in an old folk's home. Attie picked him up in a snowstorm, on an icy Tulsa street. Kept him from freezing to death. She's a hero and every one of you out there could take a lesson in life from her."

"If you're innocent, will you stand trial in Oklahoma?" someone yelled from the crowd.

It was more than Hulk could take. "Leave her alone. She has more love and compassion in her little finger than any of you ghouls. Go away and let her grieve in peace."

Hulk's words failed to dissipate the crowd, and the insistent story seekers began pushing and shoving. Big Al jumped off the hood and helped Attie down. Norma opened the door and pulled her inside.

"Get in here girl," she said.

"We gotta do something," Lillie Mae said

Big Al shoved his way through the crowd, standing beside Mike, Hulk and Scooter as people began rocking the car. The reporters were egging things on. If they couldn't get an interview, at least they'd be there to cover a near riot.

They wail of sirens sounded in the distance, and headlights of three police cars appeared down the hilly road, the sirens not stopping until they'd driven right up to Mike's Cadillac, scattering the crowd in the process. It was Sheriff Simpson and his men.

"You folks okay?"

Attie stuck her head out the window. "Scared to death, but otherwise unharmed."

"We'll set up a roadblock and detain this posse for you."

"Thanks, Sheriff," Mike said, opening the Caddie's door and sliding in. "The van and camper are with us."

"We'll let them through. Good luck, Attie."

Sheriff Simpson motioned the driver of the police vehicle. He backed up, letting Mike's Cadillac, Scooter's van and Hulk's camper drive past. They were alone again on the dark road, Attie giving directions.

"Better tell Scooter and Hulk to hang close. The turnoff from the blacktop to my house is so well hidden, sometimes I even miss it."

Chapter 31

Hulk barely had time to shut the gate, barring the road to Attie's house, and relock it before a spring rainstorm began drenching the hillside.

"We'll have to run for the porch," Attie said. "I don't have covered parking."

Though barely twenty feet from the driveway to the porch, they were all soaked by the time they got there. They waited, dripping, as she fumbled with her keys. Big Al produced a flashlight.

"Never know when you're gonna need one of these things."

"Thank goodness for a planner," Attie said, rushing inside and opening windows to expel must and warm air.

"You're house is beautiful," Norma said after her eyes had adjusted to the light.

"Native stone and wood. My husband Roland designed and built it."

"Husband?" Mike said.

"My deceased husband."

"Sorry."

"It's okay. He's been gone a long time. We planned on having a large family. Now it's just me in this large house with four empty bedrooms, though tonight, it's perfect for guests."

"We don't want to impose," Sue said.

"Nonsense! You can get your bags when the rain lets up. I was planning to turn the house into a bed and breakfast. You can tell by the ramp outside that it's handicap friendly."

Scooter was grinning when Attie showed he and Sue their room. "You weren't kidding," he said. "This is better than most hotels."

"I even bought guest robes and pajamas. Get out of those wet clothes and try them. I know how tired you all must be. I think I'll stay up awhile."

Already after midnight, no one was in the mood for arguing. When the rain finally slowed to a steady drizzle, they grabbed their bags from their vehicles. Though late, no one wanted to go to bed just yet. They all meandered back to Attie's large den, joining her in front of the stone fireplace.

"I made hot chocolate and coffee. There's also plenty of Choc left over from John's stash."

Rain finally ceased, leaving only a cool breeze blowing through the open windows and flickering the candles Attie had lighted in place of electric bulbs. Norma, Sue and Lillie Mae were all soon hugging Attie, commiserating with her. For the first time that night, Attie allowed herself a good cry.

"We're so sorry, honey," Norma said.

Lillie Mae nodded her agreement. "Same for Hulk and me. Guess we got here a little too late."

"You got here just in time. I don't know what I'd have done if I'd been all alone."

"I miss John already. He was the closest person to a dad I ever had," Hulk said.

"Amen to that," Lillie Mae said.

"Though I only knew him for one night, he was as dear as any friend I have," Scooter said.

"He always knew how to say just the right thing to make you feel good," Mike said.

Big Al broke the tension and everyone laughed

when he added, "Well, he weren't much of an auto mechanic."

Attie's smile didn't last long. Norma noticed. So did Sue and Lillie Mae.

"I know, honey. It hurts for us, too. I can imagine how you feel right about now."

"It's more than that. I feel so helpless."

"There was nothing you could do," Lillie Mae said.

"That's not it."

"What then? Tell us. Maybe we can help."

Attie crossed her arms and legs, shook her head. "I made John a promise. Now I can't keep it."

"What promise?" Hulk asked.

"John wanted to be buried on an Arkansas hillside, near here, his grave facing west. I promised him I would see to it. Now I know it's never going to happen."

"But it's what he wanted. Who . . ."

Mike grabbed Norma's wrist, looked into her eyes and shook his head.

"Maybe John's son will finally come to his senses," Lillie Mae said. "Surely, he can't be so insensitive that he would deny his father's dying wish."

"Who'd have thought he'd have hounded him all the way to Arkansas? He's a different breed of cat," Scooter said.

Attie glanced at the big grandfather clock. "It's late. Please, everyone go to bed. We'll talk more tomorrow."

"You too, honey," Norma said.

Attie shook her head. "I'm going to stay up for a while longer, and I need to be alone. Please."

Feeling the pain in her voice, the little group went to their rooms, leaving her alone on the couch.

✦

The group awoke the following morning to the aroma of bacon and eggs, cooking in the kitchen in Attie's old cast-iron skillet. Unlike the previous night, she had a smile on her face. The sound of popping grease, crackling bacon and the song she was singing

213

reassured everyone she was okay.

"We saw your RV on the side of the road. Give me the keys, Ms. Attie, and me and Mike will drive down and bring it back for you."

"Thanks, Big Al," Attie said, retrieving the keys from a bowl on a kitchen cabinet. "I was wondering what I was going to do about it."

Big Al grinned. "Hope you don't make us leave before we have a bite to eat."

"Wouldn't think of it. I cooked enough for a log rolling. I'll bet there's enough for even you and Hulk."

Lillie Mae elbowed Hulk when he said, "I don't know about that. I'm mighty hungry."

After breakfast, Scooter asked, "Mind if I drive? I didn't get a chance to see much scenery coming in last night."

"Good idea," Norma said. "Me, Sue and Lillie Mae can take the Caddie into town. Pick a few things up for dinner tonight."

"Sounds like everyone's going somewhere except you and me, Hulk."

"Good, I got something to show you a little later. Meanwhile, looks like the storm last night tore up a bunch of trees. I'll clean up the mess for you."

"You know you don't have to do that."

"I don't have to do nothing. I want to. Besides, I need the exercise."

❧

Attie stared out the kitchen window, aimlessly polishing a glass as she watched Hulk dispose of the last tree limb that had fallen the previous night. When he entered the kitchen, her morning smile was gone, replaced again by a sullen expression. He didn't give her a chance to begin reminiscing about John.

"I told you I have something to show you. Want to see?"

"Course I do. What is it?"

"Come on and I'll show you."

214

Attie followed him out to his camper. When he opened the door, the cat bounded out.

Attie smiled. "I was wondering what happened to Charlie."

"Well, Charlie might not have been such a good name."

"Oh?"

Hulk reached into the camper, retrieving two squirming kittens. Charlie's a girl. She brought these two kittens up to camp right after you and John left."

"Then John was right."

"About what?"

Attie smiled again. "He said Charlie was a calico, and that all calicos are females."

"Well Charlie sure is. I hope you don't mind, but we named the two kittens John and Attie because they reminded me and Lillie Mae of you two. I want you to have them."

"But they're . . ."

"They're weaned. Lillie Mae and I can't keep three cats. Please, will you take them to help you remember Lillie Mae and me?"

❧❦

Norma, Lillie Mae and Sue returned from town before noon with several bags of groceries. Mike and Scooter drove in shortly after, followed by Big Al with the psychedelic RV.

"Got there just in time," Big Al said. "A truck already had Ol' Betsy hooked up, ready to tow her away."

"Oh my! How did you stop them?"

"Turned out to be a cousin of mine. He showed me a shortcut here so I wouldn't cause so much attention. Whoever painted that thing up oughta be shot," he said, tongue-in-cheek.

"I kind of like it," she said. "It sort of grows on you."

Everyone piled into the kitchen where Norma and

Lillie Mae were making sandwiches, Sue showing them how to make gazpacho.

"Never thought I'd eat cold soup," Mike said later. "But this is so good I think I'll start serving it at the restaurant."

"Sue don't know how to pick a good man, but she sure knows how to cook," Scooter said.

Attie just grinned and shook her head. "I think she knows how to do both."

"Whatever, you girls aren't cooking tonight. Big Al's not the only one that has Arkansas relatives. My cousin Enzio owns the Limerock Hotel in downtown Eureka Springs. Tonight, we're having a party in John's honor, and me and Norma are footing the tab."

"Bull on that," Big Al said. "I'm chipping in."

"So are we," Lillie Mae said.

Attie was smiling again and Norma noticed.

"You got a plan, don't you?"

Attie nodded. "I'm going to call John's son. Tell him his dad's last wish, and try to convince him to let me bury him here."

"And if he doesn't go for it?"

"At least I'll have tried."

Later that afternoon, as everyone was primping for the celebration, Attie called the Warren's house in Tulsa. Cynthia answered on the third ring.

"May I speak with Dan?"

"Who's calling?"

"Attie Johnson."

"Ms. Johnson, this is Cynthia, Dan's wife and John's daughter-in-law. Are you okay?"

"I'm devastated and I need your husband's help."

"Dan's working late and not home yet. Please, can I help?"

"It's . . . it's about John's last wish."

"Go on."

"Cynthia, can I level with you, woman to woman?"

"Of course you can."

"I only knew your father-in-law for a week, and I know this sounds farfetched, even to me, but I loved him and he loved me."

"I believe you. What can I do?"

"John's last wish was to be buried on an Arkansas hillside, facing west, not far from where I live. I promised him I would see to it. I don't want anything else from you or your husband, and I'll pay for the burial. Do you think your husband will help me?"

"Attie, I . . ."

"I hate to beg. Please, my heart is broken and I don't think I can stand one more stake through it right now."

"Attie, I feel I know you. There's someone I can call that can fix all this. Just take a deep breath and relax. I'll see to it that Grandpa gets his last wish, I promise."

Chapter 32

Cynthia had barely hung up with Attie when she dialed Robert Baker's phone. He answered on the first ring.

"Cyndi, what's up?"

"Robert, sorry to bother you on Saturday."

"I had my calls transferred to the club. Eight over par, I decided to call it a day and head to the clubhouse for a martini."

"You're so nice, you'd say that even if you'd just hit a hole in one."

"Only for you, Cyndi. Now what's so important?"

"First, I want to thank you for intervening with the Arkansas governor."

"My pleasure, although I wish Wild Bill could have reacted before Mrs. Johnson was arrested and publicly humiliated. Sorry about that."

"Nonsense. What you did was wonderful."

"I rue the day Dan finds out I was responsible. He's the smartest lawyer in the firm and I'd hate to see him go somewhere else."

"This story's gotten so blown out of proportion. Half the people think Attie Johnson is a heroine, the other half a murderess."

"It's a real media event. Dan is probably the only person that can rectify the situation."

"Which brings me to the second reason I called you."

"I'm listening."

"I just talked with Attie Johnson. She told me Grandpa's last wish was to be buried on an Arkansas hillside, facing west. I told her I'd help."

Robert Baker paused before replying, and for a moment, she thought they'd been disconnected.

"Cyndi, Ms. Johnson has no legal rights in this matter."

"Dan is dead set on returning Grandpa to Oklahoma and burying him in the family cemetery."

"Next to his wife?"

It was Cynthia's turn to pause and think about her answer.

"Dan's mother was cremated, her ashes scattered across Lake Skiatook where she and Granddad had a weekend home. Dan was against it, but Granddad acquiesced because it was her dying wish."

"Then why is Dan so determined to bury him in Oklahoma?"

"Because he's stubborn, and a control freak. It kills him when he doesn't get his way."

Baker laughed. "The very traits that make him such an effective trial lawyer."

"Yes and an absolute asshole to live with, sometimes."

"Cyndi, my group is waiting for me."

"Robert, I'm so sorry. I was just hoping you could pull some more strings and see that Granddad gets his last wish."

"I can't help you with this one. It's a civil matter. Dan is your father-in-law's next of kin. Mrs. Johnson, I'm afraid, has no legal recourse."

"But I promised her."

"You know I'd do anything for you. This one's out of my hands. No judge on earth is going to overrule Dan's wishes on this."

Cynthia hung up the phone, suddenly aware that Billie was standing behind her.

"What's the matter, Ms. Warren?

"I made a promise I can't keep. Now I feel terrible about it."

"Is this about old Mr. Warren?"

Cynthia nodded. "I just talked with Attie Johnson on the phone. She poured her heart out to me. Granddad's last wish was to be buried in Arkansas."

"Mr. Warren will never go for that. I heard him making funeral arrangements this morning. Someone's picking up the body and bringing it back here. Tomorrow I think."

"This makes me sick. I'm convinced Ms. Johnson loved Granddad. If he'd lived, I'm sure they'd have married. Then Emily and Trish would've had a real grandmother, and not just a memory that someone had told them about."

"That's important to you, isn't it?"

Cynthia nodded again. "I never knew any of my grandparents. I've resented it all my life, and it's not fair to Trish and Emily."

Billie and Cynthia both jumped when someone behind them asked, "What's not fair."

"I spoke with Attie Johnson today," Cynthia said.

"You did what?" Dan said, suddenly animated.

"We had a good long talk."

"Talk? She's a kidnapper. If she ever crosses the state line, I'll have her arrested and doing hard time, I swear to you. Why were you talking with that felon?"

"She's not a kidnapper. Granddad was with her of his own accord."

"Bullshit! She coerced a feeble-minded old man into crossing a state line because she thought she could get some money out of him."

"Your dad was no more feeble-minded than you are. His mind was sharp. You said so yourself."

"Yeah, well things change."

"Attie Johnson didn't come to the house and take Granddad by gunpoint. He ran away from home because you were abusive to him."

"That's about enough, Cynthia. I've never been abusive to anyone in my entire life."

"Oh no? Brutal words can hurt more than a fist in the face."

Dan stood there a moment, mouth agape, when he finally realized Billie had not left Cynthia's side. She stood facing him, arms crossed, glaring.

"Billie, this is none of your business."

"Fine," she said, turning to leave. She stopped before exiting the door. "Call if you need me, Ms. Warren."

"Now explain what this is all about."

"Your dad's last wish was to be buried in Arkansas, on a hillside near Attie. She promised him she'd see to it."

"Oh, so it's Attie now? What else did she promise the old fart?"

"How can you talk about your father like that? Don't you realize how you sound?"

"Stop it! Dad will be buried here, later on this week and that will be the end of it."

"Dan, I made a promise."

"Well you lied, didn't you?"

"You shouldn't have said that."

"What? Call you a liar?"

"You know, there's something I've come so close to telling you on more than one occasion. Well now's the time. I'm divorcing you and taking the girls with me."

"What did you just say?"

"You heard every word. Billie, are you there?"

Billie immediately stuck her head through the cracked door.

"Yes, ma'am?"

"Pack me a bag, and one for Trish and Emily. I won't stay another night under this roof."

"Wait just a minute, Billie. I think you remember who you really work for."

Billie turned, hands on her hips. "I got just two words to say to you, Mr. Warren. You can stick it where the sun don't shine, 'cause I quit."

Trish and Emily, hearing the commotion, rushed into the room. Sensing instantly that an argument was ensuing, they grabbed their mother's legs, frowning at their dad.

"Now don't turn them against me," Dan said, taking a step toward them.

Cynthia raised a clinched fist. "You lay a hand on us and I swear I'll break a lamp over your head."

"What are you talking about? I've never done anything violent in my whole life."

"Physically maybe, but you've mentally bludgeoned me and the girls for the last time. Tomorrow, I'm talking to a lawyer. I never want to see you again."

Dan stood there, mouth open, as Cynthia shoved Billie and the twins out the door, and then slammed it in his face.

Chapter 33

The small group convoyed to Eureka Springs, parking in back of the old Limerock Hotel, and entered through the back entrance. A smiling man that could have been Mike's twin brother met them in the lobby, pumping Attie's hand.

"I'm Enzio. Glad to meet you. You're the most famous person in town, you know?"

"Or infamous, depending on who you're talking to," Attie said. "I've eaten here before. Your food is wonderful. I had no idea you were Mike's cousin."

"Hell, all us I-talians west of the Mississippi are cousins. Mike and me are real cousins, our mothers were sisters."

"I'm glad to meet you, Enzio. Think you can handle this crowd?"

"You bet we can. Follow me."

Enzio led them down a flight of limestone stairs to a warmly lighted basement, complete with a large table clad with white tablecloth, burning candles, jugs of Chianti and antique crystal stemware. A scratchy Billie Holiday melody played softly in the background, the wonderful aroma of good food emanating from the kitchen. They were seated and soon feasting on steak and pasta, almost like Mike's place in McAlester. Norma sat on Attie's right side, Lillie Mae on her left.

After several bottles of wine, Attie stood and spoke.

"When I was a girl, I read every fairytale, fantasy and gothic romance I could lay my hands on. I was sure Prince Charming would someday come riding up on a white charger and whisk me away to a land of make believe. You know, strangely enough, that's exactly what happened."

"Here, here," Scooter said, clinking his wine glass with a fork.

"John wasn't the only knight in shining armor I met. Before this past week, I never knew there were so many wonderful people in the world."

"Here, here," Scooter said again.

"Scooter, you and Sue gave John and me the courage to stand up for what we believed in. Mike, you and Norma gave us shelter, support and love during our darkest hour. Lillie Mae, you and Hulk showed us what it means to love someone with all your heart. Big Al, you were strong when we needed strength, brilliant when we needed a plan, and gentle when we needed someone to hold our hands. God bless you all."

When Attie sat back down, Norma grabbed her arm.

"You've been smiling all day. I'm so happy to see you feeling better.

"Knowing I can keep my promise to John has raised my spirits. Making arrangements today took my mind off everything else."

"Look, honey, even if for some reason it don't work out, it's not your fault. You tried your best. Me and Mike will take you to the funeral in Tulsa, if it comes to that."

Attie shook her head. "I'm not going to Tulsa. If they bury him there, I'll dig him up myself and bring him back here if I have to."

❦

Someone knocked as Vince finished giving directions to Cynthia Warren and hung up the phone.

The kitchen faucet had developed a serious leak and he'd reported the malfunction before work that morning. Thinking the person at the door was Clancy from maintenance, he flung open the door wearing nothing but the blue terrycloth towel. On his porch, smiling at him was Marla, in her hand a bottle of wine with a colorful red bow. Seeing her, he almost went into terminal shock.

"Peace," she said, thrusting the bottle at him. "I want to apologize for what happened the other day."

When he sucked in his gut, he almost lost the towel draped around his waist, managing to grab it with his free hand before embarrassing both of them.

"I also want to thank you for the beautiful red roses. I love flowers and roses are my favorite."

Catching his breath, and hoping she couldn't hear his pounding heart, he moved aside and motioned his favorite leggy brunette inside.

"Please, sit down," he said, his voice an octave too high. "I'll put on some clothes."

He rushed into the bedroom, shutting the door behind him. As he hurriedly rummaged through the closet for something to wear, his heart continued pumping so rapidly, it pushed him toward the brink of hyperventilation. When he pulled too hard on the clothes rod, it collapsed, dumping all his clothes on the closet floor.

Hoping Marla hadn't heard the crash, he yanked a red sports shirt and khaki pants from the pile, and hurriedly put them on. He stopped at the door, his hand on the knob. Rushing back to the bathroom mirror, he dragged a comb through his hair. When he finally made it back to the living room, Marla stood up and extended her hand.

"I'm Marla MacDonald. It was my fault we had such an unpleasant introduction the other day."

"Vincent Blakeman," he said. "The fault was mine, and I'd like to apologize for the whole affair."

Marla said, "No permanent damage done. My irises survived."

"I'm glad."

Realizing he was still holding her hand, he released it abruptly and pointed to the couch. When he plopped down in his old recliner, Marla glanced at the bottle on his kitchen table.

"Hope you like it as much as I've enjoyed the roses you sent."

"I'm not much of a wine person," he said. "But I know I'll enjoy it. Like a glass now?"

"It's white," she said.

"Pardon me?"

"It's not chilled."

Standing, he bumped his shin on the coffee table and felt his face turn red as he retrieved the bottle. He was making room for it in the freezer, between TV dinners, when it dawned on him she may not have intended to stay long enough for the wine to chill.

"This might take awhile. Like a Moosehead until its cold?"

"I love Moosehead. I always keep a few frozen mugs in my freezer for a cold drink after tending garden in the heat."

Having no frozen mugs or any mugs at all, he grabbed two of his best cheap tumblers from the cabinet and placed them, along with two bottles of Moosehead, on the coffee table between them.

Marla said, "I'm a nurse. I work at General. What do you do, Vincent?"

"I'm a detective with the Tulsa Police Department."

"Are you serious?"

"Ten years."

Squirming in her seat, she said, "You won't believe this. My two hobbies are gardening and reading murder mysteries."

"The hell you say."

"I read every new mystery novel when it hits the library, and every mystery magazine and police procedural I can lay my hands on."

Stifling a precinct reply, he said, "Really."

"I even have a police scanner in the bedroom. I've never met a real detective," she said, inching forward on the couch.

Vince filled the tumblers with Moosehead and raised his own in an impromptu toast. "Well, here's to you, Marla."

"And to you, Vincent," she said, tapping his glass. "Were you involved in the Riverside Strangler case?"

"I was there when they arrested him."

Marla fairly squealed. "You were? I don't believe it. Are you working last night's homicide?"

Remembering the gruesome remains of the hapless teenager in the morgue, he lowered his head and nodded.

"It upset you. I can tell."

He could only nod again and hurry to the refrigerator. "Better check the wine. Don't want it exploding on us."

When he returned to the chair, she reached across the coffee table and touched his hand.

"Sorry Vincent. Guess I've read too many cozies. I know it's not like that in the real world."

"You'd think after ten years I'd get used to it."

"I work in the emergency room at General."

"Then you probably see more gunshot wounds than I do."

"Too many, and most are victims of random crime. Surrounded by so much misery every day, it's a wonder I get so involved with fictional mysteries."

"Hey, I think I understand."

Once again leaning forward, she gazed thoughtfully into his eyes. Her own, he saw, were an unnerving violet.

"When we both have lots of time, I'd like to hear all

about the Riverside Strangler. Even though I read newspaper accounts, it would be wonderful to have an actual detective on the case tell me the real story."

He felt his neck and face grow warm. Seeing her nearly empty tumbler, he returned to the refrigerator for two fresh Mooseheads. His stomach gurgled as he filled the tumblers, and he remembered he hadn't had any food all day.

"Have you eaten?"

She shook her head and looked at her watch. "No time. I'm on duty in an hour. Usually I grab a snack when I take a break."

"I have two TV dinners in the fridge. Only take a minute to heat them up in the microwave."

Without thinking about it, she smiled and said, "Sounds great."

Again, he rummaged through the freezer. Remembering the wine, he removed it and placed it on the kitchen counter, trying to remember if he had a corkscrew. He didn't, and began searching cabinets and drawers for something to open it with.

"I have a corkscrew in my condo," she said, sensing his plight.

"No need. I have something."

He searched the drawers of a cabinet by the front door, finally locating his red Swiss army knife. With a clumsy twist, he removed the cork without forcing too many shavings into the wine. In a flash, he put the frozen dinners into the microwave. He didn't bother setting the kitchen table, instead dumping the well-nuked contents onto two plates and serving them on the coffee table. Remembering that he had no wine glasses, he found two over-sized shot glasses, in the cabinet by the sink.

"Not exactly the Ritz".

"It's wonderful. I work such erratic hours, I miss most of my meals. I just won't eat if I can't have something healthy."

Thinking about the chilidogs, tacos and barbecue sandwiches that comprised the bulk of his own meals, he sucked in his gut and sat up straighter in the chair.

"More wine?"

Marla had barely touched what he'd already poured her. She shook her head and said, "I need to stay sober for my shift, even if I'd sometimes rather be inebriated."

Corking the bottle, he pushed it aside. "Then I'll save it for later."

"You're nice. I can't believe I've lived next door to a real detective for the past year and never knew it."

Vince couldn't believe it either. Removing the dirty dishes and putting them in the sink, he wiped the coffee table and plopped back into the chair.

"If you'd like, I could give you a tour of the precinct sometime."

"Love it," she said, glancing again at her watch. "I only have ten more all-nighters before going on days for a month. Maybe I can return the favor and fix dinner for you."

"Sounds wonderful."

Vince couldn't quit smiling at her. Marla didn't seem to notice as she reached across the table to take his hand.

"Now I have to get ready for work."

Reluctantly, he released his grip and walked her to the door, mooning into her big violet eyes. Quite unexpectedly, she kissed him on the cheek before reaching for the door handle.

"Thanks again for the roses," she said.

"Hey, the pleasure's all mine."

Chapter 34

Saying one last prayer, the preacher tossed a handful of dirt into the grave. Stepping forward, Attie followed it with the rose in her palm. Cynthia Warren did likewise, holding Trish and Emily's hands as they gazed down into the hole. Dan Warren stood thirty feet away by a silent sentinel of funeral vehicles, weeping uncontrollably, unable, or unwilling, to approach his father's grave.

The service had turned into a media event, film crews and reporters from all the major networks in attendance, cameras trained and microphones ready. Big Al, Mike and Norma were also there, along with Scooter Bates and girlfriend Sue. Hulk and Lillie Mae were hugging each other, sobbing. The scene turned into a group hug, Mike and Norma, Big Al, Hulk and Lillie Mae all joining in. Attie finally pushed everyone away.

"I'm fine," she said.

One by one, they said their tearful goodbyes, no one left on the Arkansas hillside except Attie, the Warren family and Big Al. He stood there, wanting to say something but unable to do anything except prod a rock with the toe of his shoe. Seeing him, Attie gave him a big hug.

"I hope this isn't the last time we see you, Ms.

Attie."

"Heck no," she said. "Old Betsy needs some maintenance and there's no one I trust more than you, Big Al. I was planning to bring her by in a month or so."

Suddenly beaming, he kissed her forehead and squeezed her hand.

"I hope you're okay, Ms. Attie because I'm feeling about as low as hell right about now."

"Me too, Big Al," she said, hugging him again. "You take care."

Attie waved as he walked down the hill toward the awaiting Cadillac of Mike and Norma. Cynthia was smiling, waiting for her when she turned around.

"Even though we've only just met, I feel I've known you forever."

"Me too," Attie said. "Where will you spend the night?"

"We're heading back to Tulsa. Dan's not very comfortable here."

"I don't know how you talked him into letting me bury John in Arkansas. I'm eternally grateful."

Cynthia grinned. "I had to play every trump card I own, and things are still a little tense with us right now. If it were up to me, we'd stay in town, at least until tomorrow."

Attie grabbed her arm. "Then stay. It will be way past these two darling's bedtime before you make it home."

"Dan has to work tomorrow."

"Nonsense! No one expects him to return to work so soon. I have a large empty house and I don't feel much like spending tonight by myself."

Cynthia stole a glance at her sullen husband, still standing alone, propped against the hood of their silver Mercedes. Hearing the conversation, Trish and Emily tugged at their mother's skirt

"Please Mommy. Can we spend the night with Grandma Attie?"

"You'll have to ask your father. It's okay with me if it's okay with him," she said, relinquishing herself from the heavy burden of decision.

"Daddy," they said, focusing their attention on Dan. "Can we spend the night with Grandma Attie?"

"She's not your grandmother," he said pointedly.

"Mama and Billie say she is. Can we Daddy?"

Attie intervened. "Dan, I know you're upset and I understand the ambivalence you feel toward me. Still, we both loved your father very much. I have some personal items of his at my house. I need to give them to you. He had something he wanted me to tell you."

"Tell me what?"

"Not here, please."

"Dan, it wouldn't hurt to spend the night," Cynthia said.

"Please Daddy," Trish and Emily said.

"Let's pick up Dad's things and then I'll decide," he said.

"Fine," Attie said. "I insist you at least stay for dinner."

Exhausted from grief, he acquiesced with a nod. With a sweep of his head, he motioned them to get in the car.

"Follow close," Attie said. "The road to my house is quite scenic, but also steep and winding."

"Can we ride with Grandma Attie?" they asked, tugging Cynthia's skirt.

She nodded without looking at Dan for his approval. Attie winked at Trish and Emily.

"Get in, girls," she said, pointing to her old green Ford pickup.

Dan frowned at Cynthia as he followed down the narrow dirt road leading away from the secluded hilltop cemetery.

"Why did you let them go with her? You know I don't like that woman."

"I didn't do it for her; I did it for them."

"And what the hell do you mean by that?"

Cynthia swiveled in the big bucket seat and faced him, frowning and arms crossed tightly.

"You grew up with parents and grandparents. I didn't, and I know how much it means to children. You should be happy for them."

"She's a horrible woman."

"Stop it! You don't know anything about her."

"I know what I know."

"You know what I know? You used to be a pretty good judge of character, just like your dad. Well, Grandpa didn't just like and trust Attie, he loved her. That's good enough for me and it ought to be good enough for you."

"Well it's not. When we get to her house, I'm going to get Trish and Emily and go to Tulsa."

"I can't stop you from returning to Tulsa. The girls and I are spending the night here.

"That's not fair. We just buried my dad and I want to go home."

"You do what you have to do. Far as I'm concerned, you can just keep driving, Buster."

"Look, what do you want me to do?"

"Give her a chance, and maybe, just maybe, I'll give you another one."

By the time they reached the house, rain had returned. Attie and the two girls huddled beneath her umbrella as they rushed to the porch. Lightning flashed in the distance, and then thunder sounded. Hurrying back outside with an extra umbrella, Attie found that Dan and Cynthia already had one. She also noticed they weren't exactly huddled together.

"Watch your step," she said. "The porch steps get kind of slippery when it rains."

The back door led into the big rustic kitchen, complete with copper pots and cast iron skillets hanging from hooks.

"Oh, I love this kitchen," Cynthia said.

"Just don't expect I'm a wonderful cook because of it."

"I'll bet you're just saying that."

"I do have a few specialties. I'm going to try one tonight."

"Can I help?"

Attie grinned. "You bet you can. It's always more fun that way. You girls want to help?"

"Yes," they both said at once.

Cynthia's gaze went instantly to her husband when Attie said, "Let me help your dad with the bags first."

After a long pause, Dan said, "We weren't planning to stay overnight, so we didn't bring a bag."

"Then can I make you a drink? Your dad loved Wild Turkey and water."

"Dan usually drinks Scotch," Cynthia said.

"Hey, it's Dad's night. Turkey and water is just what I need, right about now."

Attie led him into the den, showed him an overstuffed leather chair, and then mixed his drink at the wet bar by the big sandstone fireplace. He almost smiled when she handed it to him.

"Let me show you your room," Attie said. "The girls can sleep in the loft. It's just their size."

"Your house is gorgeous," Cynthia said. "It's almost like a bed and breakfast."

"Believe me, I've thought about turning this place into one. It's so big, and gets kind of lonely here sometimes."

❦

Dan was working on his second Wild Turkey when the aroma of southern fried chicken, mashed potatoes and homemade biscuits began wafting from the kitchen, along with occasional delighted squeals from the two little girls. When they finished eating, Cynthia herded the twins upstairs.

"Mind if I tuck them in?" Attie asked.

234

"They'll love it," Cynthia said.

Cynthia and Dan waited in the living room and had started a fire in the stone fireplace, even though it wasn't cold. When Attie returned from the loft, she retrieved a large box from the hall closet.

"These are your father's possessions," she said. "I know why you tried so hard to return your father to Tulsa, even when you learned he was safe and living as he pleased."

For a brief moment, Dan's eyes blazed. Lowering his head, he remained silent.

"Your father knew about the competency action. He told me the first night we met. For what it's worth, he had no intention of ever trying to reclaim the property, and would have given you everything anyway."

Moments of silence, punctuated only by an occasional crackling pop from the fireplace, slipped slowly away.

Attie finally continued. "Your father won a great deal of money at the bingo game in Red Rock, and more at the horse races in Oklahoma City. The money was in cash, and he left it in my RV."

Dan glanced at Cynthia, and then back at Attie. Holding up an appeasing palm, she said, "I just mentioned that fact because it seems to me, since I controlled the funds while John was alive, I should have some control after his death. I visited my own lawyer yesterday and he agreed with me."

"Keep the money," Dan said. "You deserve it."

A smile replaced Attie's grave expression. "You know, you almost looked and sounded like your father when you said that. Maybe there's hope for you yet."

She retrieved something from her roll top desk. "I had my lawyer form a trust in the names of Trish and Emily." Handing the document to Cynthia, she said, "Not that I don't trust you, Dan, but I've named Cynthia executor. When the girls are old enough to go to college, this should provide for their education.”

When she winked, Cynthia allowed herself a momentary grin. Attie returned to the hall closet and came back with the cowboy hat John had worn at the races in Oklahoma City.

“One more thing. Like yourself, your father wasn’t perfect. Not by any stretch of the imagination. But he was a good man. Like many fathers, he let his career come before his family. Though you grew up resenting his lack of attention, you became just like him. Both of you suffered for it. He wanted you to have this,” she said, handing him the hat. “After wearing it awhile, he said he felt somehow free from restraints of the past. He said he hoped you’d try it on for size, shed your three-piece pinstripe, loosen your tie and have a little fun before you’re too old to enjoy it.”

Feeling the soothing effects of the bourbon, Dan allowed himself a slight smile as he accepted the broad-brimmed hat. Placing it on his head, he looked at Cynthia.

“Think I’d look all right dressed in boots, blue jeans and western shirt?”

“You’d look wonderful,” she said.

Tension broken, Attie mixed Dan another drink.

“I’m not much on whiskey or beer but I have a nice bottle of cabernet. Like a glass, Cynthia?”

“That sounds wonderful.”

Distant thunder continued to rumble as Attie handed Cynthia the glass of wine.

“Dan, stay through the weekend. There’s a western store in town and a dancehall up the road. Cynthia and I will teach you how to two-step in no time.”

Chapter 35

Dan awoke the next morning to sounds of laughter coming from the kitchen. Finding a robe and slippers in the chair next to the bed, he plodded down the hall to join them. He found Attie, Cynthia and the girls dressed in jeans, western shirts and cowboy boots. They were all smiling.

"Thought you were going to sleep all day," Cynthia said when she saw him staring at their outfits. "We've already been to town. Don't worry; we got you something to wear, too."

Attie handed him a cup of coffee. "Breakfast won't be ready for twenty minutes. If you'd like to try on your new duds, Cynthia put them in your room."

A covered porch, overlooking a scenic view of the valley far below, encircled Attie's plantation-style house. After changing clothes, Dan found everyone outside on the porch. A hawk, suspended in a thermal updraft, floated high above them in the cloudy sky.

"Dan, isn't it simply gorgeous here? I've never visited this part of Arkansas," Cynthia said.

"Well now that you know what you've missed, you need to return often. You always have a room here."

"Your place is much bigger than it seemed when we got here last night."

"This is the top of Johnson Mountain. It's been in my husband's family for years now, and I could never part with it, though it's kind of lonely here sometimes."

"Husband?" Dan said.

"Deceased. Quite a long time ago, actually. The flat part of the mountain, where the house is, is about forty acres."

"Do you have horses and cows, Grandma?" Trish asked.

"Not anymore. The barns, stalls and pens are still here though. I do have some peacocks that pretty much rule the place."

After breakfast, Dan left the table with barely a word. Cynthia glanced at Attie to see if she'd noticed.

"Sorry about the way he's acting. He's still unsure about you and Grandpa."

"What do you mean, Mama?" Emily asked.

"Nothing you should be concerned about. Why don't you and Trish go look for Grandma Attie's peacocks?"

"Can we?" they asked, looking at Attie for confirmation.

"Go for it," she said. "Just be careful and don't get too close to the edge of the mountain."

The two little girls rushed away from the table, down the steps to the yard below. When they were gone, Cynthia touched Attie's hand.

"I think Dan's somehow blaming you for every shortcoming he and his father ever had."

"He reminds me so much of John, so tall and slender, and with those dreamy eyes and dark, wavy hair. I can see how you fell in love with him."

"I do love him, though I swear he's driving me crazy."

"Hey, he'll lighten up when we get him on the dance floor. Meantime, I want to give you a tour of my little town. They don't call it Eureka Springs for nothing."

They were soon heading down the hilly road from Attie's house. Dan looked considerably more relaxed, dressed in jeans and western shirt. The cowboy hat even rested on the console. Attie sat in the backseat with Trish and Emily, giving directions and describing local landmarks. They soon reached downtown Eureka Springs.

"I've never seen so many motels," Cynthia said.

"It's a tourist town, all right. Just keep following this road, Dan."

The weather mild, he lowered all the windows as they drove slowly through the old Victorian-era town built against rounded Ozark Mountain bluffs.

"It's like a fairy village," Trish said.

"It is," Cynthia said. "All the buildings are built right up against the mountain cut."

"Probably the only place on earth where you can enter three stories, all on the ground floor."

"And so many tourists."

Happy shoppers, dressed in shorts and tee shirts, and laden with shopping bags filled with souvenirs and knick-knacks, crowded the sidewalks and storefronts.

"Eureka's an artist's colony," Attie said. "People come from all over to visit the shops, taste the local fare and listen to the many musicians. It may very well be the most eclectic town in America."

"Just don't get caught smoking pot," Dan said.

"Dan . . ."

Attie chuckled. "He's right. They frown on drug use in Arkansas."

Dan found a parking place, and they walked the limestone sidewalk as it curved up the hill toward the Basin Hotel. A boy dressed in shorts and no shirt guided a skateboard down the middle of the steep street, weaving in and out of cars and pedestrians. After browsing in several shops, Cynthia had her own sacks of tee shirts, postcards and Ozark souvenirs,

Trish and Emily loving every minute of it, Dan frowning and tapping his toes as he waited for Cynthia to try on an Arkansas peasant dress.

Seeing his discomfort, Attie said, "The Limerock Hotel is just up the street. I'm sure we can get a treat for the girls and cold beers for us."

Though Dan didn't acknowledge Attie's comment, he grabbed Cynthia's hand when she returned from the dressing room.

"You look great in it. Pay the man and let's go. There's a cool bar up the street and I need a beer."

"But they have so much neat stuff here."

"You've been here an hour. We can come back later."

Cynthia frowned and paid for her purchases. They were soon back on the sidewalk, heading for the multi-storied Limerock Hotel. Like the name implied, the hotel was constructed of old glass and native rock. The sign on the window said, ESTD 1888. A large cat rested on the front desk.

"Ohhh! Look at the beautiful cat," Emily said, rushing up to the counter.

"His name is Bourbon," the little man behind the counter said. "He's a Maine Coon."

"Is he really a coon?" Trish asked.

"He's all cat. He just has the coloration of a raccoon."

The little man spotted Attie. "Ms. Attie, I'm so glad to see you again."

"Hi, Enzio. These two sweet little girls are Trish and Emily. This is Dan and Cynthia, their lucky parents. Dan is John's son."

Enzio shook their hands. "I'm so sorry about your father. Mike is my cousin and has lots of stories about John and Attie."

Attie shrugged and smiled when Dan glanced at her. "Trish and Emily want something to drink. Dan definitely needs a cold beer."

"Follow me," Enzio said, leading them to a dark bar. "I'll be right back."

He returned with chocolate sodas for Trish and Emily, iced tea for Cynthia, and large draws for Attie and Dan.

"This is really good," Dan said after taking a sip. "What is it?"

"Choc," Enzio said. "I brew it for my special customers. It was your father's favorite."

"How does he know so much about Dad?" he asked once Enzio had left.

"Seems everyone that met John has lots of stories about him. He was that kind of person. It would take six months for me to tell you all of mine."

"Good," Trish said. "I love this place."

"Me too," Emily said.

"Me three," Cynthia added.

They noticed a group of people at another table were pointing and whispering. Perturbed, Dan crossed his arms and stared at one of the men until he turned away, embarrassed.

"Sorry," Enzio said. "I'll boot them if they're bothering you."

Attie shook her head. "Forget it, Enzio."

"What's going on?" Cynthia asked.

"People don't know what to make of me. Hopefully, it'll all blow over when the reporters and TV cameras leave town. Whatever, I'm getting used to it."

Word of Attie's presence spread. When they exited the hotel, a young woman, backed by a film crew, thrust a microphone in her face.

"Are you afraid of being arrested if you return to Oklahoma?"

Attie pushed through the crowd that had begun to gather, the girls following after her. When Cynthia glared at her husband, he just turned his head. When the reporter shoved the microphone under his nose, he swept it aside with the back of his hand.

Realizing their visit to the little tourist town was turning into a circus, they returned to the Mercedes. Dan drove to the main highway.

"Turn here," Attie said. "I'll show you the most scenic route back to the house."

The narrow blacktop followed a ridgeline near the top of the rounded mountain chain, dropping off steeply on both sides. Dan slowed the car when an armadillo lumbered out of the ditch and across the road in front of them. Cynthia was still frowning, her arms crossed tightly, knees pointed toward the door. Attie pretended not to notice. The road finally flattened, pastures on both sides, a tall fence surrounding them.

"Oh, look at those big animals. Stop, Dad!"

When Dan pulled to the side of the road and parked, Attie, Cynthia and the girls got out. Trish and Emily ran up to the fence.

"What are they?" Trish asked.

"They're called bison. Sort of like big wild cows. A local rancher maintains a large herd here."

Cynthia and Attie turned to look when a semi passed on the highway and blew its horn. When they turned back around, they saw Trish and Emily running toward the herd of bison. They'd found a small hole in the fence and had squeezed through.

"Oh my God!" Attie said.

"Trish, Emily! Come back here this second," Cynthia screamed.

Neither girl noticed, both carrying handfuls of grass they were intent on feeding the large animals. Attie managed to scale the fence, jumping to the ground and sprinting, just as the herd noticed Trish and Emily. A female with a calf began pawing the earth and advancing toward them.

Dan was still sitting in the front seat of the car. When he looked up and saw what was happening, he exited, scaling the fence with some difficulty because of his cowboy boots. He landed on the other side just as

Attie caught up with the girls, whisked them off the ground and began running back toward the fence. The female bison snorted and trotted after them.

When Dan's path intersected Attie's, she tried to hand the little girls to him.

"Take them. I'll stop the creature."

"No you won't," he said. "Get them over the fence. Hurry."

With no time to argue, Attie raced toward the fence with the two little girls, both now frightened and crying. Dan faced the female bison advancing toward him, planted his feet and clapped his hands.

"Hah, go back! Hah, you stop right there."

Confused, the bison halted, almost nose-to-nose with Dan. By this time, Attie had pushed the bawling girls back through the hole in the fence and turned to help Dan. Hearing her approach, he shook his head and waved his hand.

"Get over the fence! I know what I'm doing."

Seeing the man wasn't intimidated by her bluster, the female bison turned around, rejoining the herd. Dan started backing up slowly until he reached the fence, and then scaled it like a man possessed. Cynthia and the girls, all crying, and practically in hysterics, grabbed him when he hit the ground.

When everyone finally calmed down, Attie said, "Those animals are anything but tame. That mama bison weighs over a ton. For the life of me, I don't know how you backed her down."

Dan dusted his jeans as Cynthia and the girls looked on with admiring smiles.

"When I was a kid, I once saw Dad face down a bull that had cornered my cousin and me. I just tried to imitate what he did."

⁂

That night, Cynthia and Dan lay in bed in Attie's rustic guestroom.

"Are you asleep, Cyn?"

"No, just thinking."

"About what?"

"Attie. She saved Trish and Emily today at the risk of her own life. I know you saved all of them and I'm so proud of you, but . . ."

"But what?"

"I can't understand why you persist with this crazy vendetta of yours. You didn't tell me you tried to file charges against Attie in Oklahoma."

"Cyn, this hasn't been easy for me."

"Then why make it harder than it needs to be? Attie didn't kidnap your dad. Surely you realize that by now. When are you going to let this whole thing go?"

"I don't know."

"Well I know," she said, sitting up in bed. "Attie's getting a bum rap here. I love you, but I swear, if you don't make amends pretty soon, you and I are going to part ways."

"What do you want me to do I'm not already doing?"

"You're a smart man. You'll think of something."

Chapter 36

Attie was beaming as she served breakfast the next morning.

"Tonight's the night. There's a country and western band playing at the Barn. After yesterday, I know you're a real cowboy. Tonight, Cynthia and I are going to teach you how to two-step."

"What about the girls?" he asked.

"My friend Beth is coming. She has grandkids of her own. Trish and Emily will love her."

"I can't wait," Cynthia said with a grin. "If you can teach Tarzan here to dance, you're a better woman than I am."

"No problem. Two-stepping's easy. You'll be line dancing like pros before the night is done."

After a day of chasing around Attie's ranch, the twins also wanted to go dancing. They changed their minds when Beth, a large woman with big green eyes and a slightly crooked smile, arrived and began showing them how to cook spaghetti. Cynthia, Dan and Attie, decked out in freshly pressed jeans and cowboy shirts, met in the den.

"Let's take my pickup," Attie said. "We don't want anyone thinking we're just Saturday night cowpokes. Beth, do you have everything under control?"

"You know I do. Wish I was going with you, though

I bet the girls and I will have more fun."

"You two listen to Ms. Beth now, you hear?" Cynthia said.

"She's showing us how to make tomato sauce," Emily said.

So excited about their cooking lesson, the twins barely noticed their parents and Attie slipping out the kitchen door. Attie's Ford had a hole in the tailpipe and it started up with a loud bang.

"Sure you don't want to take the Mercedes?" Dan asked.

"We'll make it, I promise."

It was dark when they left the house, visibility limited by patches of low-lying fog caused by humidity left over from the rain. When they reached the parking lot of the large dancehall, aptly named The Barn, they found it overflowing with like-minded people. Attie pulled up to the entrance.

"I'll let you two out here and find a place to park. They have our tickets at the window. Meet you at the front door in a few minutes."

Attie found a parking place across the street and hurried to the front door of The Barn. They were soon inside, along with several hundred other patrons, most already drinking beer and dancing on the large dance floor to the sounds a rocking country and western band, complete with steel guitar.

The tables were little more than park benches with plastic checkerboard tablecloths. Harried waitresses, all young and all wearing boots, tight jeans and jaunty cowboy hats, were taking drink orders as fast as they could move. Attie, Cynthia and Dan staked out a spot at one of the tables and ordered a pitcher of beer.

"The crowd's really getting fired up. Before long, we'll see some of the finest line dancing in three states," Attie said.

"Good, I'll watch. I'm not getting up there," Dan said.

"Why not? Cynthia and I will have you dancing the Cotton-Eyed Joe in no time."

Cynthia laughed. "You'll have to teach me too. I know nothing about country and western dancing."

"It's basic; right, left, kick, dip, or some variation. Come on. I'll show you."

"I'll guard the beer," Dan said.

Cynthia chugged her beer, grabbed Attie's hand and let her pull her to the dance floor. She was a natural, and within minutes, Attie had her dancing like a pro. She was also the best looking woman in the house, quickly becoming the center of attention. Attie left her, grinning wildly as she two-stepped with three cowboys, on the dance floor.

"You better hurry and get out there. There are at least ten horny men vying for your wife's attention."

"I can't. I don't know how to dance."

"Well you better chug that beer and at least give it a try. Looks to me like Cynthia's having the time of her life."

Taking her advice, Dan finished the beer. Attie smiled and winked at him as he headed through the crowded room toward his wife.

Cynthia's would-be suitors reluctantly gave up when the tall cowboy joined her on the dance floor. She shortly had him two-stepping. Attie could see from the giant smiles on their faces that both were enjoying themselves. It was also apparent that the press, tracking their every move for the past several days, had followed them to the dancehall. As Dan and Cynthia danced, a crew began filming them. The Warrens didn't seem to notice.

Their smiles brought a grin to Attie's face. At least until, on her way back from the ladies' room, she bumped into a large man that looked familiar. The tattoos on his arms were her first clue. When he removed his cowboy hat to reveal his totally bald head, she recognized him as the man that had accosted her outside the jailhouse.

"I think you got some apologizing to do," he said.

"Get out of my way."

Instead of complying with her request, he blocked her path when she tried to go around him. Several people brushed past them, unaware of the ensuing altercation.

"I don't think so. I said you owe me an apology."

"Okay, I apologize. Now please, let me pass."

"That ain't good enough. Get down on your hands and knees and beg me."

"You're drunk. Move or I'll call the bouncer."

"Just do it and see what happens," he said, grabbing her shoulder.

"Let go of me," Attie said, wrenching free and then snapping his head back with a hard slap to the face.

By this time, the music had stopped and all eyes were on the two people staring angrily at each other. When the man grabbed her arm again, someone from behind him clutched his shoulder, wheeled him around and delivered a right cross to his chin. It was Dan.

The crowd backed away as the man tumbled backwards, crashing into tables and chairs. He didn't stay there long, bounding up and tackling Dan, sending them both crashing through tables lined with bottles and pitchers of beer. Stouter, though not as tall, the tattooed man wrestled Dan to the dirty dance floor, both exchanging punches, knocking over more tables and chairs, all to the sounds of shattering glass, and country and western music coming from a nearby jukebox that someone had put coins into.

The news crew turned their cameras on the crowd, filming the entire melee as sirens sounded outside the dancehall. Flashing red lights pulsated through the door as several policemen pushed through to quell the brawl. After wading into the fight with working Billy clubs, they subdued Dan and the tattooed man, yanking them off the floor, cuffed and bleeding. They dragged them outside unceremoniously to an awaiting squad car.

The film crew followed them out the door, a reporter breathlessly delivering a blow-by-blow for the ten o'clock news. Half the people in the dancehall, along with Attie and a hysterical Cynthia, also poured into the parking lot, watching as Dan and tattooed man were piled into the back seat of a Eureka Springs police cruiser. They watched as the car tore out of the parking lot to the sound of wailing sirens and scattered gravel.

"Hurry. We have to do something," Attie said.

Chapter 37

Once in the truck, Cynthia said, "Everyone must have followed the police cars and news trucks. I've never seen so much traffic."

After barely moving for minutes, Attie finally wheeled the truck into a church parking lot.

"With this traffic, we can make time faster on foot. It's only about another mile. You up for it?"

"Let's do it," Cynthia said.

Removing their cuffs, the police shoved Dan and the tattooed man into the same cell. When Dan raised his fists. The man held up a placating palm as he rotated his chin with his other hand.

"You pack one hell of a punch. I boxed some in the Army and no one ever hit me that hard."

"Yeah, well it's not as hard as your chin. I think I broke my hand."

The man grinned and extended his hand. "I'm Cal. Sorry about what I did back there. I have an anger management problem and it doesn't mix well with too many cold Buds."

Dan winced when he shook Cal's hand. "I'm Dan."

"You weren't kidding about your hand, were you?"

It was Dan's turn to grin. "I haven't been in a bar fight since college. I broke my hand then, too."

Cal stuck his head up to the tiny window. "Hey, we got a man hurt in here and need a doctor."

No one answered, or came to the cell to see who was causing the disturbance. Dan, still holding his injured hand, sat beside Cal on the cell's single bunk.

"It's okay. I'll live. What do you do, Cal?"

"Looking for a job. Seems no one wants to hire a vet with mental problems."

"I'm sorry. Do you get any help from the military?"

"Hell no. I thing the VA's broke. They don't seem to acknowledge either PTSD, or traumatic head injury."

"Were you in Iraq?"

"I got injured and sent home when our Humvee got a little too close to an exploding roadside bomb. I lost two buddies, and my ears are still ringing."

Dan patted his shoulder. "Thanks Cal. You're a hero to me, and most everyone else in this country."

"You wouldn't know it by the way the Government treats us vets."

Dan grimaced when he reached for his wallet and handed Cal a business card.

"Call me when we get out of here. I'll do what I can to help. And Cal, don't worry about paying. It'll be on me."

The cell door opened as Cal was staring at the card. "Warren, come with me. You're outta here."

"What about Cal?"

"What about him?"

"I'm not going without him. What's his bail?"

"It ain't been set yet."

"Then how am I getting out?"

"Don't worry about it. Just come on."

"I'm staying."

The jailer closed the door behind him, returning with a little man with wispy hair and dressed in a rumpled suit with no tie.

"I'm Wayne Taylor, Attie Johnson's attorney. I saw the whole thing on TV and headed this way. Let's go before the Sheriff changes his mind."

"I'm not going anywhere unless they also release Cal."

Hearing the resolve in his voice, Taylor shook his head and backed out of the cell, returning with Sheriff Simpson.

"You're about a hard head, Warren. Anytime someone gives you a get out of jail free pass, you should take it and not ask questions."

Dressed in a sharply pressed uniform, the clean-cut young Sheriff looked about the same age as Cal.

"Were you in the service, Sheriff?"

"Army, MP. What's that got to do with anything?"

"Cal here was also in the Army. He's kind of down on his luck right now and needs a helping hand."

The Sheriff glanced at Cal, and then back at Dan, as if pondering what to do.

"I can't help every down-on-his-luck ex-G.I. I come across. I wouldn't have time to do anything else."

"I'm not asking you to help every ex-G.I. I'm asking you to help this ex-G.I."

"But he's the one that started the fight."

"We kissed and made up."

Sheriff Simpson frowned and shook his head. "Okay, both of you get the hell out of here before I change my mind."

Cal smiled and followed Dan and Attorney Taylor toward the front door of the jail.

"Thanks Wayne," Dan said.

"Hey, I had a little help getting you out. You're the silver tongued devil that talked your buddy out of there. They hadn't booked you yet so there's no paperwork. Oh, and your night's not quite over just yet."

Dan found out what he meant when they opened the jailhouse door, exiting to a crowd already worked into mob frenzy, and a half dozen or so TV cameras. It was apparent he wasn't going anywhere without making a statement first. Climbing up on a limestone boulder, with some difficulty, he raised his hand. When his eyes adjusted to the lights, he saw Cynthia and Attie, watching from across the street.

"First of all, I want to apologize for my actions tonight. I've done lots of foolish things in my life and this is one of them. Secondly, I want to say how much I love Eureka Springs. This town is gorgeous, the people friendly and wonderful. I've lived in Tulsa all my life, and never knew such an interesting place existed so close to home."

"Mr. Warren, is it true you tried to have Attie Johnson charged with kidnapping?" a reporter shouted from the crowd.

The throng of onlookers began to murmur when he said, "Yes I am. A foolish mistake the Tulsa D.A. refused to let me make."

"Why the change of heart?"

"Because in the last few days since my dad's funeral, I've come to realize Attie Johnson is one of the best human beings I've ever met."

"Even if she kidnapped your father?"

"No one was ever kidnapped. That was only a delusional fantasy I'd convinced myself of, even in the face of reason. I was stupid and bullheaded, and let my emotions get in the way of logic."

"Mr. Warren, over here," another reporter called. "Are you going to publically apologize to Mrs. Johnson?"

Everyone laughed when he said, "I think I just did."

"Mr. Warren, is it true the only reason you're getting out of jail so fast is because Oklahoma governor Tank Rogers called Arkansas governor Wild Bill Barnett and threatened to whip his ass if he didn't let you go?"

Dan grinned again. "Though I haven't a clue, if it ever happens, it's one fight I'd pay big money to watch."

When the crowd stopped roaring with laughter, a reporter asked, "Is there anything else you'd like to say?"

"For anyone that didn't already hear me, I apologize with all my heart and soul to Attie Johnson, my father John, and my wife Cynthia. I did my dead-level best to screw up the last days of Dad's life." Looking toward the sky, he shouted, "Dad, I'm sorry. Please forgive me."

Dan's words brought roaring applause and shouts of approval. When the level of sound died down, another reporter spoke.

"Anything else you have on your chest you want to unload?"

"You bet I do. I want to thank every senior citizen in this country. I can't believe I treated my own father so poorly, yet I realize I'm simply a product of this throw-away society we've created. Barring devastating illness or getting hit by a bus, we're all going to grow old someday. I only hope our children treat us better than we've treated our own parents."

"Mr. Warren . . ."

Dan held up a hand, "One more thing. Cal, get up here with me." Only Cal saw the grimace on his face when he helped him up on the boulder. "Tell the people your name."

"I'm Calvin Reardon."

"Cal's the man I got in a fight with tonight. He's a veteran of the U.S. Army, and served during the Persian Gulf War. He was released from duty when a roadside bomb blew him, his two buddies and their Humvee off the road. Cal survived. Unfortunately, his two comrades didn't. Tell them what you do now, Cal."

"I'm unemployed."

"Are you on disability?"

"No."

"Were you injured in the blast?"

Cal paused. "Yes."

"Tell us how."

Cal paused again. "Sometimes I feel like my head's about to explode. I have trouble remembering things; things I should know, but don't. Daily, I get so frustrated, I just want to lay down and die. And the anger. It just keeps coming back, over and over."

"Any help from the VA?"

Cal shook his head. "No."

"Have you asked?"

Cal nodded. "They say there's nothing wrong with me."

Dan shook Cal's hand and said, Thanks for your service, Mr. Reardon."

Cal wiped away tears as he jumped down from the boulder, acknowledging with a wave the long round of applause from the rapt audience.

When the throng quieted, Dan said, "I'm not a doctor but any fool can see Cal is the victim of a traumatic brain injury. He not only needs, he deserves our help. It's time we did better by our elder citizens and our veterans, the two very groups that protect us from birth and allow us to enjoy the freedom we have in this country. I don't know if I got hit in the head tonight, or what. I do know that now I see the light, and I hope someday everyone else will."

He jumped from the boulder, the crowd applauding and issuing roars of verbal approval. Beth, after watching the unfolding events on television, had brought Trish and Emily to town. They, along with Cynthia and Attie, ran across the road, hugging their smiling and waving husband and father.

The phone was ringing when they finally walked into Attie's house. It was Robert Baker.

"Ms. Johnson, can you put Dan on the line?"

"You bet. It's for you," she said, handing him the phone.

"Dan, I don't know what you've been drinking there in Arkansas, but you put on one of the best shows tonight I've seen in a quite a while."

"I'm so sorry I embarrassed the firm."

"Embarrass hell! If you were running for President, I'd be the first to vote for you."

"Thanks, Robert."

"You owe me more than that. I spent the better part of an hour refereeing the governors of Arkansas and Oklahoma. Your comment about a fistfight wasn't far from the truth. If and when you run for public office, I want to be your campaign manager. I haven't heard a better stump speech in years."

"Well, I'm not planning on it anytime soon."

"Never say never. My old seat's coming open next election, and the name Senator Warren sort of rolls off the tongue."

"Anything else?"

"Let me talk to Cynthia."

Dan handed the phone to his wife, and then hugged Attie and the two little girls.

"Thanks again, Robert," Cynthia said.

"Be safe, and give my regards to Ms. Johnson. She must be quite a woman. And Cynthia, I'm so proud of you."

Chapter 38

Everyone was exhausted and rain had again begun falling. With the help of warm milk and the gentle patter on the roof, sleep finally caught up with the twins.

"Will you tell us a story, Grandmother?"

"I'll come up when you're in bed," Attie said, smiling. "I have a special one for you."

"Oh boy!" they said, rushing up the steep stairway to the loft.

While Cynthia readied the twins, Dan rested in the overstuffed armchair in the living room. Attie sat on the couch across from him.

"I saw a lot of your father in you tonight. I loved him. Thank you for believing me."

"You're the one that needs thanking. I was ready to toss him away like yesterday's garbage. I was a fool. I'm sorry. You two taught me a lesson I don't ever want to forget."

They were both smiling when Cynthia returned from the twin's bedroom.

"They're waiting for you," she said. "Hope you don't mind."

"I've been waiting for them all my life," Attie said, starting up the stairs.

She found two little girls already in one old

four-poster bed, squirming and giggling beneath the colorful patchwork quilt. They quieted when she entered the room.

"We're ready for the story," they chimed.

Attie sat on the edge of the bed, stroking Trish's long dark hair before beginning.

"Last time you saw your Grandpa, he began a story about Otter and Salamander. Would you like to hear how it ends?"

"Oh yes! Tell us," they said.

"Otter was very old," Attie began. "But he had a good heart and strong desire. When he heard about his old friend the salamander, he decided to take a journey to a place he hadn't visited since his youth. Do you know where his journey took him?"

"The Magic Fountain," said two little girls.

"That's right. He packed his otter luggage and sat out to find the Magic Fountain. But everything didn't go as planned."

"What happened?"

"Evil Zoo Keeper wanted Otter for his zoo. Unlike regular zoos, this one was different. Evil Zoo Keeper kept his animals in dark dungeons, away from sunlight and friendship."

"Did he catch him," asked Emily.

"You're getting ahead. Otter was old, but also very smart. Along the way he met a lion, and Connie Otter. Connie was also lonely. A hunter's bullet had crippled Lion, yet he was fierce and brave. At the risk of his life, he held off Evil Zoo Keeper, allowing Connie and Otter to escape.

"But Evil Zoo Keeper wouldn't be denied. He tracked them to a grizzly's lair. Bear was old and cranky but liked Otter and not what Evil Zoo Keeper was doing. Along with Benny and Bertha Chipmunk, he helped Otter and Connie escape Evil Zoo Keeper again. Free at last, Otter found the Magic Fountain, high in the mountains of his very own imagination. There, he and

Connie met Elephant and Rabbit, who guarded the fountain."

"What happened?"

"Crystal clear water poured from the fountain, revitalizing their bodies and spirits. Otter and Connie fell in love and lived happily ever after."

"Tell us more."

"Another time, child," she said, kissing them, tucking them in and turning out the lights. "No more tonight."

Epilogue

It was raining once again as Attie sprawled on the front porch, playing ball and jacks with Trish and Emily, watching Cynthia and Dan finish packing the Mercedes for their return trip to Tulsa.

"Don't forget your visit next month," Emily said from the car window as they prepared to drive away.

"And don't you forget about spending a few weeks with me next summer."

"We won't, Grandma."

As Attie watched the silver Mercedes disappear down the hill, two kittens came running around the corner of the porch, skidding between her ankles. With a sad smile, she picked up the kittens, pressed them to her breast and glanced up at the sky, dark with rain. It didn't stay that way.

A hawk with a beak that reminded her of John's nose, swooped almost to the ground, and then floated upward, parting the clouds to reveal the sun for the first time in a week.

Squirming from her grasp, the two kittens, one black, the other gray, ran back around the house to chase the peacocks. Both were filled with life.

END

Eric Wilder's Bio

Born a mile or so from mysterious Black Bayou in northwest Louisiana, Eric now lives and writes, along with wife Marilyn, four dogs and three cats, in Edmond, Oklahoma. If you liked Prairie Sunset – Of Love and Magic, please check out some of Eric's other books at EricWilder.Com.

9 780979 116544